I0565575

The Way of Lucherium

Christopher J. Rziha

En Route Books and Media, LLC

Saint Louis, MO

⊛ *ENROUTE*
Make the time

En Route Books and Media, LLC
5705 Rhodes Avenue
St. Louis, MO 63109

Contact us at
contactus@enroutebooksandmedia.com

Cover and Map Credit: Charles Rziha
Copyright 2025 Christopher J. Rziha

ISBN-13: 979-8-88870-326-7
Library of Congress Control Number: 2025931316

All rights reserved. No part of this book may be reproduced, stored in a retrieval system, or transmitted in any form, or by any means, electronic, mechanical, photocopying, or otherwise, without the prior written permission of the author.

Table of Contents

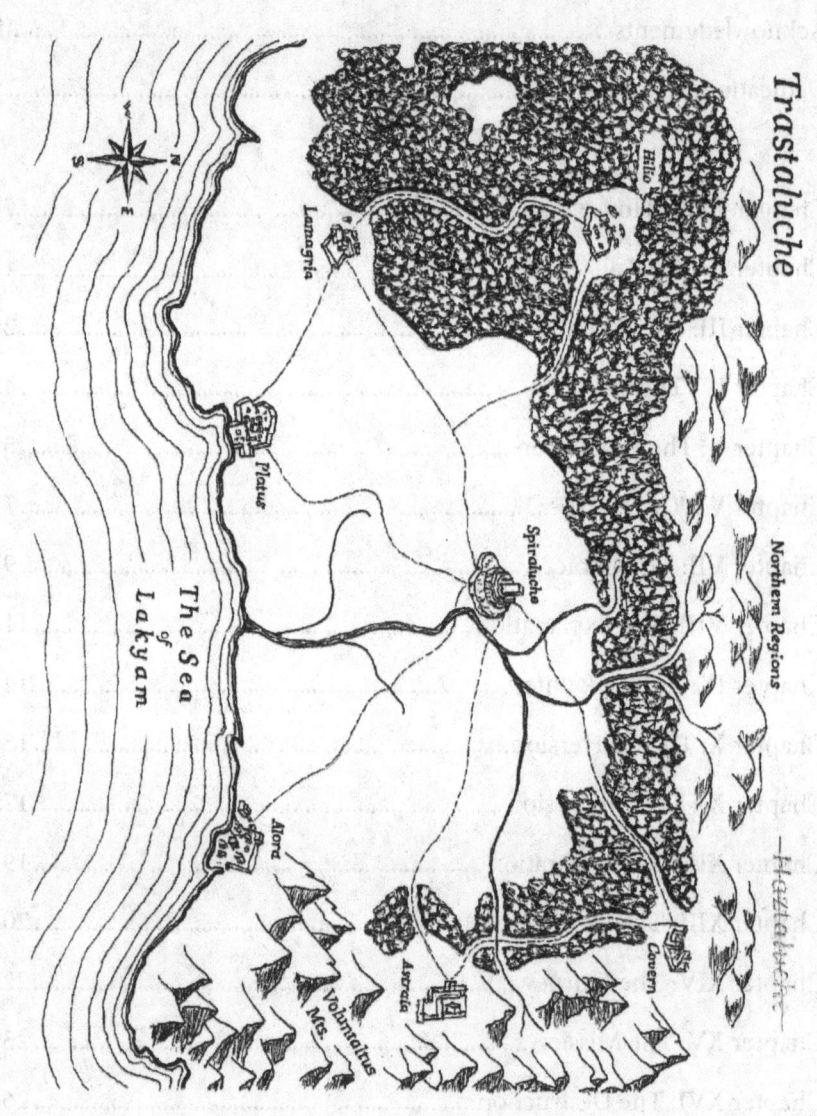

Acknowledgments

I wish to extend my most sincere thanks to all who have helped in the creation, revision, and promotion of this book, including (but not limited to): Joshua Hren, Cole Lehman, James Merrick, Steve Mirarchi, Edward Mulholland, Matthew Myjak, Suchi Myjak, Joseph Rziha, Michael Rziha, Thomas Rziha, Jordan Vanderpool, Richard White, and Joe Wurtz. In addition, I wish to offer special notes of gratitude to: Charles Rziha, for his generous contributions to map and cover design; Jeanne Rziha (or Mom), for proofreading the text and spending countless hours discussing it with me; John Rziha (or Dad), for his continued guidance in the realms of theology and publication; and my wife, Kayla, for being my first reader and my inspiration in everything. Finally, I wish to thank our wise and loving God, who in His providence has ordained all things towards our ultimate good.

Dedication

To *mi esposa querida,* whose unwavering love and support lights my way and gives me life. And, as always, *ut in omnibus glorificetur Deus...*

Chapter I

The House

"It was dark, and not the sort of dark one finds while walking through the dimly lit causeways of a run-down city, or even the darker sort of dark one encounters when alone in the countryside at night. This was a different sort of dark altogether. It was the kind of dark that, rather than being merely the absence of light, seemed to suck the spark out of every luminous soul it enveloped. It was the perfect sort of dark for the mission at hand: the death of a treasonous man."

Or so wrote the bard, Geoffrey of Trastaluche, who was feeling both very out of place and rather important as he crouched behind the thick stone wall that separated this particular street and its inhabitants from the rest of the middle city. Geoffrey had been invited along due to his unswerving loyalty to the ideals of Trastaluche, as well as due to his prominent position as the youngest member of the Committee of Spectacles. His task was to stay strictly out of the way and to record with meticulous detail the events which were about to transpire. Normally his presence on such a mission would have been egregiously illegal; operations such as this were best performed secretly, silently, and with the utmost precision, which meant the least amount of outside involvement. However, the recent rise in unrest and rebellion during the previous two seasons had been anything but normal. Thus, the head of the Committee of Social Order thought it wise to remind the commonwealth of the disastrous effects which resulted from the operations of those who sowed discord throughout Spiraluche, the central city of the immensely prosperous nation of Trastaluche, and of the heroic and immensely necessary role of the Committees in eradicating such maladies and restoring peace and progress to all. Having a prominent bard along who could witness the successful completion of a dangerous mission against the Enemies of Trastaluche and then publicly recite what he had seen in the form of an epic ballad seemed to be an ideal way to accomplish such a goal. Geoffrey had been suggested, vetted, and approved, and a fortnight later found himself squatting in the center of a band of roughly a dozen men, all of whom were silently preparing their armaments for whatever might lie ahead.

Geoffrey had seen the official declaration for the mission at hand earlier that day, emblazoned across the top of the scroll drawn up and authorized by the Committee of Social Order. It had read: "the restoration of peace through the termination of the person, relatives, and possessions of Xavier, designated as a primary enemy of Trastaluche, its citizens, and its Committees." As he scanned the reports that had been secretly gathered against the man Xavier, Geoffrey found himself unsurprised that he had been discovered to be a traitor. Xavier seemed exactly the type of person that one would expect to engage in activities against Trastaluche and its Committees. Father of four and owner of a small shop which sold mostly dried goods and sewing materials, Xavier had not only never amounted to much, but he had also never seemed to care. It was the apathy that had first tipped off the Committee of Social Order: as cluelessly simple as Xavier might seem, he was no fool. His shop was consistently packed with eager customers, and he was well-liked and well-respected by his neighbors. Thus, the fact that he had turned down a prestigious position within the Committee of Ways and Means, the sort of position any sane member of the commonwealth would jump at the chance of having, was practically an indictment in itself as to where the shop owner's loyalties might lie.

Covert surveillance of Xavier's doings and goings, as well as that of his family, quickly proved what had already been suspected: the allegiance of the shop owner and his family to Trastaluche and its Committees was not just apathetic, or even nonexistent; it was downright treasonous. Word was spread, orders were drawn up, and arrangements were quickly made for the execution of an armed raid, sanctioned by none other than Trastivo, Head of the Committee of Progress and Lord of Trastaluche himself, to be carried out by a small group of the Committee of Social Order's most influential Ministers with the purpose of the capture or termination of the persons of the Family Xavier. Such raids were unpleasant but necessary functions of the Committees, as Geoffrey very well knew. Acts of treason against the commonwealth of Trastaluche, such as those in which the Family Xavier were engaged, were widely known to be the cause of much of the disharmony and decay now found in Spiraluche and its six sister cities. Geoffrey leaned back on his haunches, reflecting on an epoch, now nearly a hundred years past, when such traitorous acts had not just been isolated incidents of rebellion against the power of the rulers of Trastaluche and their supporters, but rather had been part of a full-scale assault against the equilibrium and quietude now solidified by the Committees.

Not quite a century ago, the nation of Trastaluche was known under a different name, Hazcaluche, and it was governed by a being referred to only in Geoffrey's time as the Lord of Oppression, founder of the land of Hazcaluche and orchestrator of each and every happening within it. Although the residents of

Hazcaluche had enjoyed a relative era of peace and prosperity under his rule, it had come at the terrible cost of predetermined occupations, stagnated development, and constant conformation to the OverLaw: a stifling set of decrees declared and enforced by the Lord of Oppression and his servants. The Over-Law had not only dictated every facet of the lives, workings, and goals of the citizens of Hazcaluche, but through it the Lord of Oppression had also placed the strictest regulations upon the harnessing and use of the mystical energy *Lucherium,* source of all power, development, and progress in Hazcaluche. It was not until Trastivo, creator and ruler of the Committees, had rebelled against the Lord of Oppression, covertly teaching himself and a small band of followers the secrets to harnessing the full power of Lucherium, that true progress became possible for the people of Hazcaluche. With the explosion of their new-found powers, which transformed them into some of the most powerful beings imaginable (and which, it was whispered, made them virtually immortal, although Geoffrey did not personally believe it), Trastivo and his followers overthrew the Lord of Oppression in the great War of Liberation, reducing his palace to ruin and driving his armies eastward into the mountains. With the collapse of his reign, Hazcaluche, renamed Trastaluche under the benevolent guidance of Trastivo and the Seven Committees, had embarked upon an era of true growth and progress. Its borders had tripled, its wealth and prestige had expanded, and most importantly of all, each citizen was able to choose to pursue whatever work they desired and to seek prosperity in any way they felt beneficial, provided they continually observed the guidance of the Committees and most especially the motto of the Trastaluche: *Progress Before All.*

Geoffrey's own defeat of the illustrious poet Ivan four seasons ago in his bid for membership on the Committee of Spectacles and his continual re-appointment to that position were due to the improvements implemented by the Committees, improvements which had benefitted Geoffrey in ways he would not soon forget. Unfortunately, not every citizen was as quick as he to recognize the benefits of the Committees of Trastaluche. In the years after the fall of the Lord of Oppression, dissenters and those loyal to the path of the OverLaw were not uncommon, but many had been rooted out and destroyed by the followers of Trastivo. However, such unrest was on the rise once again, and with a rather unpleasant trend, if you believed the rumors.

Although most treasonous households were quickly eliminated by the elite bands of Ministers of Social Order whose mastery of Trastalucherian battlefare made resistance futile, there had been some isolated breaks of pattern. The reports were few, varied, and incredibly vague, and their discussion was prohibited by the Committee of Spectacles. However, as a chief bard, Geoffrey had an ear to the ground, and he figured that he had heard as complete of an account of what had happened as anyone outside of Trastivo's inner circle of advisors.

The reports he had heard both scared and confused him: in a handful of situations, the result of the raids had been the complete disappearance and seeming obliteration of not only the household designated for elimination, but also their house, their possessions, and the entire band of Ministers sent out to deal with them. In other words, no one knew what had happened, and no one was left around to figure it out. Speculation abounded about the presence of some new type of

Lucherium or even of the imminent return of the Lord of Oppression, but no official explanation had been offered by any Committee. The most common rumors, however, centered around the presence of a *Conexio*: an ancient, almost magical defense which did in fact still exist. It was a sort of invisible shield, composed of a rare blend of Lucherium and the unified mindpower of the group or family that had woven it, and its impenetrability grew or shrank in proportion to the uniform intentions of its composers. In other words, the more united a family was in their purpose, the stronger and more powerful the Conexio which surrounded their home. It had been a common phenomenon in the days of the Lord of Oppression, Geoffrey knew, as most families were more or less unified in their efforts to comply with the OverLaw. Oh, divisions had existed of course; few shields of any type are completely impervious. Still, in general most families possessed one in some style or fashion.

With the establishment of Trastaluche and the liberation of true individual Progress, the use of such defenses had faded into memory and legend. The OverLaw's binding restraints were lifted, and communal adherence had been replaced by the development of new and more lethal weapons. These days, Conexios were only to be found in two places: encircling the meeting places of the most loyal and powerful members of the Committees or surrounding the dwellings of the most despicable groups of dissenters. And the Family Xavier was one such group, or so Geoffrey had been told by the Committee of Social Order. They were so united in their efforts to resist and destroy the Trastalucherian way of life that their Conexio was one of the strongest the Committee members had ever encountered. It would have been nigh impossible to enter the house, Geoffrey was assured, save for one weak link that had been woven deep into the family's shield without their knowledge.

One of Xavier's sons, Vincente, had for some time now been sympathetic to the Committees and the true Trastalucherian way of life. He had been observed frequenting meetings of the Committee of Progress and was known to be intelligent, ambitious, and perfectly willing to sacrifice whatever was around him to achieve his desires. His leanings of loyalty had been encouraged with promises- and quite valid ones at that- of positions on Committees, of connections, and of glory, and Vincente, young and full of desire, had almost completely returned to the way of Trastaluche. Whether or not he realized it, he had provided the loophole needed to gain entrance to his family's dwelling place, leaving a gaping tear in the house's defenses, which were invisible to the naked eye but starkly obvious to those skilled in the Trastalucherian ways of battlefare and the harnessing of Lucherium. He was to be richly rewarded, Geoffrey knew, if upon learning of the extent of his family's treachery he freely rejected them and swore allegiance to the Committees of Trastaluche. In fact, if he recovered from the shock of the night which lay ahead and landed on his feet, he might be expected to do quite well for himself. The others, the bard reflected grimly, would not be so lucky tonight.

The all-encompassing darkness, coupled with the armor his companions wore, meant it was difficult to discern the faces of those around him. But Geoffrey knew that somewhere nearby crouched at least two senior Members from the Committee of Social Order, several of the Elite Guard which served directly under Trastivo's command, and a half a dozen highly dependable soldiers who in peacetime functioned as keepers of Social Order throughout the city. All of these men were experts in Trastalucherian battlefare, and at least two of them- those who were senior Members- were more than capable of harnessing enough Lucherium to level a house such as this on their own. Each of the soldiers was armed with the traditional combination of a long, curved sword of pale steel and a round heavy shield characteristic of Trastalucherian battle gear, while the Committee Members were dressed in dark robes and grasped ornately carved staves. They were a force to be reckoned with, and perhaps the most powerful that had ever been assembled for such a routine task. The Conexio would still pose some trouble, Geoffrey knew; even with the weakness caused by Vincente's deviance, it was still quite possibly the most complete the Committees had encountered in several seasons. That was one reason so many elite members had been summoned for tonight's mission. The other was the complication he had contemplated in earlier hours: the problem of the disappearances of the targeted and of those doing the targeting in the previous, unresolved cases. It was becoming a thorn in the side of the Committee Chiefs, and they had determined it would not happen again.

The directive was simple. Breach the home's defenses, enter as quickly and quietly as possible, eliminate Xavier and any others who might resist, detain the others for questioning by the Committee of Social Order, gather anything which might incriminate Xavier, his family, or any of his acquaintances, and fade silently back into the darkness.

The night dragged on as the hour for execution inched nearer, and the already soul-sucking blackness grew ever darker. Finally, when Geoffrey was unable to make out even the parchment upon which he wrote and the hand that held his quill, and all that remained visible was a dimly flickering lantern hanging in front of the House of the Family Xavier, the word was given: it was time to move. Geoffrey gathered up his quill and parchment and began to creep, as he had been earlier directed, up a crumbling portion of the wall behind which they had been crouched and on to its narrow upper ledge. From there he could observe and account for all the goings-on of the night. As he reached his perch, a sliver of moon slid out from behind the heavy, rain-laden clouds which pressed upon the earth, and Geoffrey was able to see, albeit unclearly, the scene which unfolded before him.

Below and to the right, not more than twenty paces away, the house of the Family Xavier was nestled between two ancient oak trees and guarded by a smaller, but equally aging stone wall which ran along the opposite edge of the cobblestone road directly below the bard. In the waning moonlight, Geoffrey could scarcely discern the movement of the raiding band; with ghost-like skill they wafted across the road and over the wall, fanning out around the residence until they stopped barely five paces from it.

They had arrived at the shield which surrounded the house, Geoffrey realized. He watched as Samesh, one of the senior members of the Committee of Social Order and leader of the night's raid, strode forward and, with his arms outstretched, began muttering incantations in a low, harsh tone. The wind, growing ever stronger, began to whip in Geoffrey's face, bringing tears to his eyes and snatches of the verses to his ears. The words grew harsh and fast, and suddenly the air itself seemed to catch fire, and there appeared around the house a sort of webbed dome, fashioned out of strands of a mysterious energy, a lightning of greens and blues and pinks blending together and vibrating intensely which danced and hovered in the night sky around the house. Geoffrey, who had never seen anything of this sort before, was stupefied. The Conexio was as well-made as it was beautiful, and he wondered if the Committee of Social Order had made a mistake in assessing the loyalties of the son Vincente. Yet even as such treasonous thoughts formed in Geoffrey's head, he saw the opening: a strand of webbing which throbbed not with the pale rainbow of the rest of the family's tendrils, but with a dark, glaring orange, so completely out of place that Geoffrey wondered how it did not tear itself away from the rest of the shield. It was a more than adequate weakness for the assailants.

As the flaw was made apparent, the second senior Member of Social Order stepped forward to join Samesh, and raising their staves high, they began to unravel the foreign strand, drawing it out into a pulsating orb which illuminated the entire street with a garish, orange glow. It hovered above their heads, growing ever more engorged with its own power, until, having completely separated from the Conexio, it dissipated with a flash and a shower of writhing red flame. Within seconds, the rest of the shield began to waver and fade in potency. A gaping hole appeared in its side, and the band of loyal Trastalucherians wasted no time in pouring through it and converging upon the house.

From then on, Geoffrey could only catch an occasional glimpse through the loosely curtained windows of the home, but he had a fairly certain idea of how this sort of scenario played out. Resistance, if any, would be weak, uncertain, and futile, as the heavily-armed and highly-trained Ministers and soldiers completed their mission with ease. Within minutes it would all be over, thought Geoffrey, glancing down at his parchment to the handful of verses he had written, and imagining the scene that was unfolding before him…

They moved quickly and with extreme precision. Noise was not an issue; they would be in and out in a matter of minutes. Yet so exact were their motions, with so little movement and time wasted, that they nonetheless appeared as phantoms gliding across the last few steps that remained between the boundary of the rapidly fading shield and the entrance to the house. The door provided no delay whatsoever to their advance; a single blow from a heavy mace was sufficient in blasting it off its hinges. Once inside, the raiders wasted no time in filing through the ante-chambers and into the room of hospitality: a central location which served both for dining and entertaining, and one into which all adjacent rooms, including the stairs and the doorway to the main bedroom, opened.

In most cases, the inhabitants would probably be sitting up in their beds, half-dazed and disoriented even as the elite members of the Committee of Social Order closed in to finish their work. The Family Xavier, however, perhaps startled awake by the noise of their door being rent from its frame, had stumbled out into the central room, only just now understanding what was happening. The mother flung herself around her younger children, shielding them while she murmured unknown phrases under her breath. The father and his oldest son, who as of yet was unaware that he was the cause of this late-night invasion, swung around to face the attackers, their faces half-bewildered and half-afraid, their eyes still heavy with sleep. There was no chance to mount a defense. In the time it took for the man Xavier to look upon Samesh, the death-blow had already been cast and the eyes of Xavier became like those of a dead man, his torso contorting and burning as the flames of pure energy coursed through it like lightning. He crumpled to the ground.

Stepping over him, Samesh continued on toward the rest of the home's inhabitants as several guards restrained the oldest son. The mother cried out upon seeing her husband and redoubled her efforts to shield her children as the raiders encircled the *remaining family. Samesh unrolled the scroll which bore the official words declaring Xavier and his family to be Enemies of Trastaluche, preparing to seal the fate of the figures huddled before him, shaking with terror.*

He never had the chance to do so.

As he lifted the scroll, a blinding white light shone out from somewhere behind him, dazzling and burning him with its intensity and piercing every corner of the room. Whipping around, Samesh was able to glimpse what appeared to be a living flame, which emanated energy such as he had never seen. And from its center, gazing at him through eyes set in a face that was at once unrecognizable and all-too recognizable, was the man Xavier, who had lain dead just moments before. Samesh's own eyes would have widened with shock if given the chance, but the flaming being in front of him seemed to both explode and yet take an even sharper form at the same time, growing in power at an unprecedented rate until the house and the raiders within it were completely annihilated (although if Samesh had been given the chance, he would have noticed that the destruction somehow seemed to pass over the family crouched below). Instead, the last thing he saw was a passing glimpse of the eyes of a man he had executed just moments ago, before his own eyes, in their last second of existence, became those which were lifeless and cold....

In his momentary lapse of attention, Geoffrey didn't actually witness the house in front of him begin to glow for a heartbeat before exploding outward in a burst of light and debris which flung the unsuspecting bard backwards and through the air for a good twenty paces and then, as suddenly as it began, vanished entirely. His last clear image of reality was of the barren, charred foundation where the house of the Family Xavier used to stand. Then, in nauseating revolutions of black sky and even blacker ground, he tumbled through the air before slamming into the side of one of the houses which lined this particular street of Spiraluche. The impact knocked him unconscious, returning him once again to an all-consuming, all-enveloping darkness.

Chapter II

The Fall

It was dark, and not the sort of dark which envelopes a person in a comforting, quiet sort of way, nor the lonelier type of dark which one finds in the mysterious caverns of an underground world. No, this was a darkness of another sort. It was the darkness of filth, the darkness created by the waste of thousands of engorged beings who, upon finding themselves fed up with a particular person or thing, cast it away to a hopeless fate. It was the darkness of despair, of fetid consumption, and of half-living, half-breathing garbage.

It was a foul sort of darkness, and Geoffrey the bard was in a sour mood. Not quite a year had passed since his life had been ruined; since he had been chosen, as his Committee's youngest and most ambitious member, to accompany the raid on the House of the Family Xavier; since he had been blasted off his perch by the explosion of energy which had enveloped the house and its surroundings; since he had been unable to explain what had happened to the Committee of Social Order; and since he had lost his bard's commission, his prestige, and his progress. A months-long downward spiral had followed, which he had at first been unable to pull himself out of and later did not care to try, as he was scorned by his fellow Committee Members, ignored in his desperate clamors for work, and all but forgotten by his acquaintances and connections. One thing had led to another, and after one-too-many nights of despair, his ambition and talents frustrated and wasted,

15

Geoffrey found himself on the outskirts of Spiraluche, among the illicit taverns, the whore-houses, and the countless rows of haphazard slums that didn't deserve the dignity of the title of building, lying in the mud, more than a little bit drunk, trading shouted insults with the owner of the tavern in whose bar he had been seated only a few seconds ago.

It had all made so much sense to him only three seasons ago, he reflected. The ones who were ahead were the hard workers, the proud and ambitious sons of Trastaluche who put their noses to the grind-stone for the progress of self and community. Those who felt disin-clined to do so- the lazy, the shiftless, and the ill-humored- found them-selves here, in a barrio so repulsive in its stench and in its occupants that it wasn't even officially recognized as existing. The locals called it Muckland, and the Committee of Public Health had declared it a Gar-bage Heap, where, as "per the records," no one lived, and where no one who valued their reputation, their purse, or their life dared to travel.

It was here, Geoffrey had always heard, that the outcasts of society gravitated: those who had no inkling toward the improvement of self or city, and those who would just as soon take a pint of rank, overaged ale for free as pay for a decent one with honest wages. The Committee of Ways and Means was charged with the care of these "non-existents," he knew. The city might not recognize their lives, but it wouldn't go so far as to explicitly authorize their deaths. Twice a day carts hauling the refuse from Spiraluche proper would slosh their way into Muckland, bringing with them what any madman could still easily recognize as the sorriest possible excuse for food and drink to be distributed to the tav-erns and allotted to the commonwealth in an "orderly" fashion. Any-thing else one might want- medicine, clothing, a shower- had to be worked for. Spiraluche was undergoing an epoch of rapid expansion, and the Committee of Ways and Means was only too happy to employ as many down-on-their-luck citizens as it could get its hands on for the backbreaking work of mining, splitting, and hauling the jagged, ash-colored granite from which rose the buildings and streets of the "new" era of Trastaluche. A brutal day's work could get you a handful of copper, Geoffrey knew, which could be traded in for a decent meal or saved up toward a pair of boots at one of the few shops which sold real goods. "Such a system was all well and good," he thought, "unless you were old, or young, or sick, or injured, or any other combination of circumstances which landed you here in the first place and which sucked you into a vicious circle of finding yourself unable to barter for the goods which you needed to be able to work to earn enough to barter for the goods which you needed to be able to work to earn...."

His oxcart of thought derailed, and he wasn't quite sure if it was because his head was still spinning from his fall or if his mind had caused the symptom itself by pondering one-too-many times how on earth he, one of the greatest and most well-loved bards in Spiraluche, had ended up in Muckland. Yet it was here that he found himself, spitting out grime from between his teeth and cursing the tavernkeeper, the ale which blurred his vision and deadened his legs, the Committees of Whoever and Whichever, and his own miserable self. The grime found its way down his throat, and he retched as he staggered upright, stumbling through the muddy street toward one of the dilapidated "shelters" which lined this river of human waste and worse, and which stank so foully that Geoffrey doubted the stench of his vomit made the slightest difference. He winced as he straightened and ran trembling fingers over the rapidly forming lump on his forehead. He hesitated for a moment, unsure of how one got kicked out of a bar where everything was free. Then he remembered his inebriated tirade against the tavern, its looks, its inhabitants, and pretty much anything else that had come to mind. He grimaced, thinking that perhaps performing a ballad which compared the "seller of ale" to a "decadent whale" and the "smell of the tavern's floor" to the "inside of a whore" was in hindsight not his best work. Everything *was* free there, he thought, including the escort service out the door.

A crack of thunder jolted him back to reality as the first drops of a tempest cascaded onto his face, bringing with them the cold north winds of the rapidly approaching winter season, whose frigid nights and gloomy, rain-filled days would only serve to worsen Muckland in every way possible. He groped his way through the darkness until he reached one of the wooden overhangs which protruded from the faces of the buildings lining both sides of the ever-muddier road and vainly attempted to clean his face and hands on his already impossibly dirty tunic. He stumbled toward the doorway leading to the interior of the shelter, which, while not much better in terms of stench or climate, would at least afford him a slightly drier place to sleep. However, scarcely had he begun to step across the threshold when the owner of the building -a tall, heavy-set man with a deeply scarred face and a staff clenched in his fist- shouted at Geoffrey that they were all 'full up' for the night. Geoffrey started to give a sharp retort... Then he saw the man's powerful biceps and his aggressive, battle-worn glare and thought better of it. Maybe they were full, he thought, or maybe the owner just didn't want another man looking and smelling like the backside of a horse spending the night here. Either way it didn't matter. He backed out the door as quickly as his shaking legs would carry him and continued on what appeared to be a fruitless search for lodging. After half a dozen more refusals, and their accompanying curses and abuses, he was too tired to keep trying.

Turning down a side alley, he slumped underneath a large window ledge and pulled himself as tightly as he could against the rotted wooden wall, doing his best to stay dry. His entire body screamed as its muscles began to unknot… and then it screamed once again along with his mind as his eyes began to adjust to the darkness, and he grew rigid with fear. Around him, piled in heaps on each side of the alley and sprawled across it so that the ground seemed to be made up of a seething mass of putrid human flesh, were dozens of half-living corpses: some missing limbs, some sporting all manner of flesh-eating worms and boils, some coughing and hacking up blood and phlegm and other fluids which looked and smelled even more vile, and some already lifeless, their bodies beginning to melt into the ground below them as the first stages of decomposition and rot set in.

He had unwittingly stumbled into the midst of a nightmare: a waiting room for death. A 'one-way lane,' the locals, with their perverse sense of humor, called it, for it was in alleyways such as these that the doomed, those who were consumed by incurable diseases or infections, spent the waning remainder of their pitiful lives. A curious mix of bile and a howl building in his throat, Geoffrey recoiled in disgust, commanding his mutinous limbs to whisk him away as fast as possible. But his pain-ridden fatigue, combined with the horror of the stench of death rising up all around him, rendered him virtually paralyzed. And then his breath grew even more panicked as he noticed movement in the shadowy recesses of the alley and several figures emerged.

They were wheeling a run-down pushcart before them, and as Geoffrey looked on in horror, several of the shadows began behaving in a simply incomprehensible manner, wading among the jumbled masses of the dead and dying as if they were swine that one would examine before purchase. To some of the diseased they stopped for a brief word. To others they gave bulky packages, and nearly everyone received some sort of disk-shaped object which Geoffrey could not yet make out. A third group, however- those who seemed the worst-off - they loaded into the pushcart. The blood in Geoffrey's veins froze as he came to that final realization, and he imagined that he had stumbled upon the workings of some sort of extermination squad of the Committee of Public Health. His mind was filled with images of indescribable practices and horrors; he didn't know what these people were up to, but he knew it couldn't be anything good, and what was worse, he saw no healthy way out of this dilemma for himself.

Yet, as the first shadow drew nearer to his side of the alley and Geoffrey's eyes continued to adjust to the darkness, he realized that the disk-shaped objects were in reality loaves of bread, and the bulky packages contained cloaks and what seemed to be mixtures of medicinal herbs and salves. His fear abating, Geoffrey's second reaction was one of shock and confusion. No sane person, he knew, would remain a heartbeat longer than he had to in a one-way lane, consorting with plague-ridden individuals such as these. And on top of that, unauthorized distribution of foods outside of the ordered channels of the Committee of Ways and Means was a crime, and not a small one either. Someone caught distributing rations without a seal of approval from the Committees could face serious discipline, as such actions encouraged laziness, disorder, and a disregard for the Trastalucherian Way of Life. These people were most certainly insane, Geoffrey thought, and they were begging to be caught by one of the patrols of the Committee of Social Order that commonly patrolled Muckland to keep the violence and lawlessness down. Now more curious than anything else, he stopped trying to order his defeated body to move and continued to watch the first shadow and its compatriots, who were now a mere stone's throw away from him.

As he- for now Geoffrey could tell that the first shadow was a man- and his band moved closer, Geoffrey was struck by three things. First, he noted with an equal mixture of incredulousness and revulsion that the bodies they were loading into the cart were those of the dead, whose remains were often left to fester in back alleys such as these, with no one to claim them and no one to care for them. Second, and this he noted with astonishment and not a bit of hungry desire; the food being handed out by the shadows was *real* food, not the maggot-infested garbage that was unloaded at the taverns and ration-halls throughout Muckland. His stomach growled in ravenous protest as he smelled freshly baked bread, laced with herbs and melted cheese, along with the stimulating odor of heated, spiced rum. By now, Geoffrey was beginning to think that maybe, just maybe, being stuck in the alley of the dead on this particular night was not such a bad thing after all. The third thing he noticed was a peculiar sensation which he couldn't quite place, but one that gnawed at him almost as poignantly as his hunger whenever he laid eyes on the leader of the band of shadows: a tall, middle-aged man with piercing grey eyes and a face framed by a short beard that was illuminated by the small lantern attached to the end of his staff. Geoffrey's stomach, now thoroughly aroused, growled at him audibly, dispelling any chance for profound thought at the moment, and his mouth called out to the shadows and their tempting aromas almost without him realizing it:

"Oy there! What about some of that special bread for me as well? It's been seasons since I've had a decent meal!"

At the sound of his call, which echoed with a piercing, vital intensity almost completely foreign to a place of such death, the band of shadows dashed out their lanterns and began melting silently back into the darkness. Stumbling to his finally functioning feet, Geoffrey began to grope his way after them, calling out all the while in a comical litany which alternated between cursing himself and the shadows and begging for their help. As he stumbled down the alley, his foot snagged under one of its many inhabitants, and Geoffrey, for the second time that night, fell face-first into the muck, coughing, cursing, and weeping all at the same time.

As he pulled himself upward from the ground, fighting an additional wave of dizziness and despair and trying in vain to wipe his eyes on his gunk-coated sleeve, a spark of light flashed out of the darkness in front of him. Before he could take stock of his situation, the tall, bearded man appeared above him once again, and along with him one of his compatriots: a young woman with midnight hair and skin, whose eyes danced and shone with the mystery of a thousand stars in the glow of the lantern. Both had grim faces and carried unsheathed knives as they approached the disgraced bard who, his stamina exhausted and his brain overwhelmed, quite literally collapsed at their feet, expecting to never awake again. As the world around him faded back into terrifying darkness, he heard the man's voice for the first time, clearly, but as if he were quite far off:

> "Peace and courage, brother; we have no desire to harm you.
> Come with us and we'll make sure you get some proper rest and
> nourishment."

The rest of the night was a blur for Geoffrey, who faded in and out of reality in a semi-lucid state brought about by the overwhelming events of the day. He tried to respond, but everything- the man, the horrid alley, and even his own body- seemed terribly far away and unreachable to him. He faintly recalled more voices and more questions, and the sound of concern which they conveyed was something as foreign to his ears as the heavenly odors were to his nose and stomach. He remembered being carried down and out of the alley, away from the stench of death that loomed over him like the oppressive winter storm that was now departing, its fury spent. He remembered a small, unmarked door in the side of an out-of-the-way street and recalled thinking vaguely that it would be very hard to find a second time. He remembered the sensation of cool, sweet water trickling down his throat, the elegant face of the woman who held the drinking-skin for him, and the stately yet weary bearing of the grey-eyed man whose appearance still nagged at Geoffrey's subconsciousness, though try as he might, he quite couldn't grasp why. Finally, his faculties spent, Geoffrey drifted off into darkness. Yet this was once again a darkness of a different type: a darkness of comfort, of peace, and of slumber.

Chapter III

The Invitation

When Geoffrey awoke, it was a little less dark.

Two tiny bands of light pierced through a small window high in the wall of the room where he lay, illuminating the lazily swirling trails of dust which drifted about, glowing with harmless fire as they announced the arrival of the morning. The rest of the room was still shrouded in shadows, as the rising sun had not yet directed its rays downward to touch the lower regions of the place where Geoffrey found himself.

It took him the space of several heartbeats to realize where he was, or rather, that he didn't know where he was, and several heartbeats more to realize that the bizarre events of the past night had actually taken place. He sat up, shaking his head to clear off the last remnants of sleep and trying his best to ignore the throbbing caused by the lump on his head, a pounding which had lessened in intensity since the night before, but which still threatened to cloud his mind. As he did so, the sun triumphed in its battle against the horizon, filling the room the rest of the way with a soft, golden light. Only then did Geoffrey notice the rows of rotting wooden casks lining the walls around him and the heavy stone cellar arches from which still hung the remnants of wineskins.

A low-hanging doorway at the opposite end of the room opened up into a second chamber, and as the morning rays diffused through it, Geoffrey saw that his room was only a small subsection of what must have been a wine cellar fit for a king. Stacks and stacks of casks, some still intact and sealed, others mere shells of decomposing wood, lined the damp stone walls which stretched past the limits of his sleep-filled eyes, framed by row upon row of massively built arches, whose bulky curves dominated the cellar and made it appear to extend even further than it did.

Voices floated out of the adjoining chamber, as did the smell of newly baked bread. His stomach growling, Geoffrey awakened fully, finally beginning to wrap his mind around the fact that the shadows of the previous night, who had disappeared so suddenly and then returned with knives in hand, had done him no harm and in fact quite a lot of good. The image of the ebony-skinned woman with the sparkling eyes returned to his mind, as did the face of the grey-eyed man and the subconscious tug which persisted in nagging the bard whenever Geoffrey pictured him.

His curiosity now growing along with his hunger, Geoffrey swung his legs off the side of the makeshift bed which he saw had been fashioned for him from a pallet of straw and several discarded cloaks and began to make his way, apprehensively, toward the small doorway which separated him from the reality behind last night's happenings. Ducking to avoid bashing his head on the low-hanging frame, he entered the second room, blinking as his eyes adjusted to its much brighter atmosphere. The first thing he saw, or rather, smelled, was the small brick oven, built up into the wall and tucked between the rows of casks, out of which wafted an aroma similar to the one that had overcome his senses the night before and gotten him into this mess in the first place. His stomach, almost delirious with hunger, announced his presence to the inhabitants of the room long before Geoffrey would have desired, letting out a growl which he thought could have been heard in the streets above save for the rumbling of the early morning food carts. Upon hearing the echoes of his unexpected greeting, four heads swiveled in his direction. Geoffrey felt four pairs of eyes fixed upon him with a stare that was quite serious, but yet which radiated the same deep concern he had heard in the conversations of the shadows that had tended to him the night before.

"Ah, so the dead man has arisen at last!"

It was Grey-eyes who uttered the greeting, pushing back his chair from the simply-built table at which he had been seated and striding over to Geoffrey with a broad smile. He stopped a few paces in front of the bard and looked him over with the same penetrating gaze that Geoffrey had noticed last night, and which was of such intensity that the bard, suddenly conscious of his unkempt and barbarous state, felt almost naked in front of him.

"I must say, not bad at all for a man we drug out of a one-way lane," he laughed, and stepping across the short gap between them, he extended both his hands, palms-upward, in the traditional Trastalucherian greeting. Geoffrey, taken aback by the stranger's amicable welcome and really quite unsure of himself and what he should do, stared back dumbly before remembering himself and awkwardly returning the greeting.

"I... I... wish you good greetings and a prosperous morning, and I want to thank you for your service to me and to apologize for any inconvenience I may have caused you," he began, stumbling over formalities which now seemed artificial and inadequate.

The man nodded in acceptance of Geoffrey's thanks, and then, as if sensing the bard's discomfort, spoke up once again. "But you must find me terribly rude for not inviting you in, especially when you have not yet eaten the morning meal! Come and quiet your stomach with us!" he added, his grin broadening. He led Geoffrey over to the table and offered him a seat, excused himself to the brick oven, and then returned moments later with several hunks of still-warm bread, a pitcher of cider, and a bit of hard cheese.

"You'll have to excuse us," he said in a joking sort of apology. "You see, we weren't expecting company and didn't have time to send out for anything nice."

Geoffrey, however, ignored him completely, for he had already set himself to the task of devouring every crumb of the food set before him, food which to him, after months of measly, rotten city rations, tasted better than the stuffed goose, peppered greens, and candied apples served one a year at his Committee's Feast of Honors, a ceremony he had been lucky enough to attend twice already and which he was hoping to make an annual event in his schedule before his life collapsed around him. Only once he had devoured a loaf and a half of bread, drunk half the pitcher of cider, and completely finished off the cheese did Geoffrey take stock of the outside world again, glancing around the table at its other four occupants who, understanding his hunger, had busied themselves with their own conversations so that Geoffrey would not feel quite so awkward.

The first thing he noticed were their eyes, each of which possessed the same piercing intensity as the tall, bearded man who appeared to be their leader. He sat across from the bard, and Geoffrey was able to take stock of him fully for the first time. Along with his tall stature and his noble yet tired bearing, Grey-eyes appeared for the most part to be a common citizen. His hands were calloused from manual labor, and his forearms showed the finely-toned muscles of a craftsman of some sort. His clothes were simple: dark grey breeches and a matching cloak, as well as a plain brown tunic and simple leather sandals. The only feature of note, Geoffrey reckoned, was a long, winding scar which looked like the roots of a tree that began just below his chin and disappeared beneath the neckline of his garments.

Beside him sat a middle-aged woman whom Geoffrey assumed to be his wife, dressed in breeches, a long tunic, and a cloak of similar color to her husband's. Her eyes, which Geoffrey thought were quite possibly the warmest and most gentle he had ever seen, were a light blue, and despite her sun-hardened face and the streaks of grey in her wheat-colored curls, she was still exceptionally beautiful. She was deep in conversation with a broad-shouldered young man seated to the left of Geoffrey, who had similar features and the same golden hair.

"Probably their son," Geoffrey thought, also noting the height and eye-color which he shared with the bearded man. He turned his attention to the last member of the group: the dark-skinned woman who had helped Grey-eyes tend to him the night before. She sat to his left, with her chair drawn back a bit from the table, nursing a flask of cider as her eyes wandered across the ceiling. She was tall as well and almost as well-built as the son, with a graceful, curving figure and long black hair. She was dressed in trousers of a light tan with a plain green tunic and a matching cloak, and as Geoffrey stared, her gaze suddenly dropped and met his. Awkwardly turning away, he fiddled with the last morsel of bread in front of him, making a show of eating it and draining the last of his mug of cider before looking up once again at the four faces which encircled him, and which had now turned their attention toward their uninvited visitor. For what seemed to Geoffrey to be an unbearably long time (although in reality it was probably only a few moments), no one spoke, and feeling the urge to break a silence that it seemed only he found uncomfortable, he turned to face Grey-eyes and his wife, stumbling through the traditional Trastalucherian words of greeting and thanks:

> "A prosperous day to you, sirs and madams, and I thank you most profoundly for this meal which you have shared with me and the care with which you tended to me this night past. My name is Geoffrey of Trastaluche, son of Joshua, official bard of the Committee of Spectacles, keeper of the Official Tales, and twice honored for service and progress to Trastaluche and its citizens. I am honored to come into your presence and desire that my presence honor you as well."

Geoffrey inwardly cringed as his words echoed around the damp stone chamber before fading into silence. In a banquet hall, before the throngs of eager citizens who had crowded in to hear his tales, such a title seemed to be the perfect way to captivate his audiences and remind them that their evening with him would be one to be remembered and retold for generations to come. Here, it all just seemed absurd and out of place, even if it was the proper Trastalucherian way of greeting. Around him, the other four smiled back and nodded, and Grey-eyes, who, as Geoffrey had assumed correctly, was the leader of the band, returned the greeting.

"We are honored, Geoffrey son of Joshua, for your presence here with us. Truly, we had no idea that such a revered and respected servant of the Committees was our guest today, or we would have prepared a much more appropriate welcome."

This last part was said suppressing a smile, and Geoffrey, never one to miss a joke, laughed along with the others, feeling the awkward tension of the moment slipping away and being replaced with a much more tranquil atmosphere. And yet, despite the outward edginess which was dispelled by Grey-eyes' welcome, Geoffrey's head continued to whirl as an elusive memory darted to and fro in the corners of his mind, defying his efforts to recall what it was about this man that was so familiar yet so remarkably different. Pushing aside his musings, Geoffrey nodded his acknowledgement to Grey-eyes and suddenly realized that he had not caught his name; in fact, the man hadn't offered any names at all, completely skipping that part of a proper greeting.

"Your words of praise warm me, as does your cooking," Geoffrey said. "Might I ask what your name is, as well as the names of your companions, and what noble and mysterious occupation the four of you share?"

He half expected Grey-eyes to answer that the four of them were skilled healers of the Committee of Public Health (the idea of an extermination squad, now that he was in daytime, seemed ridiculous) and that they had been commissioned by their chief to oversee the welfare of the sick in the lower regions of the city. Still, even that answer didn't explain the food they were handing out, nor their presence in Muckland. Instead,

Grey-eyes hesitated, his smile faltering for just a moment, before he answered.

> "My dear sir, as I'm sure you are aware from your encounter
> with us the previous night, our occupation is somewhat of a
> strange one. As such, I'm afraid that we cannot share our names
> with you, at least at this moment. I do hope you understand our
> discretion."

>   "Of course," lied Geoffrey, who didn't understand it in the
> least, "but what exactly *is* it that you do? Are you with the Com-
> mittee of Public Health?"

>   "The Committee for Public Health?" snorted the fair-
> headed man to Geoffrey's left, "Why, you ought to have been
> in Muckland long enough to know that they're a total joke. You
> only end up working for them if you really are quite awful at
> everything else."

Geoffrey, of course, had to agree with him. The Committee for Public
Health, which was, ironically, run by a man who had grown so fat that
he was unable to move around on his own, had long since been nick-
named 'The Committee for the Perfectly Hapless,' and Geoffrey had
never actually known them to take any sort of initiative when it came
to improving anyone's health, including their own.

> "I couldn't agree more," he grinned, "but if not them, what
> about the medicines you were giving out the night before? And
> what about the food? You don't work for the Committee of
> Ways and Means, do you? The rations they give us at the tav-
> erns are pure garbage compared to what you were handing out.

And why were you in Muckland at all if it's not the concern of Committee care?"

"I'm afraid our true occupation is something we'd like to keep quiet about too," answered Grey-eyes, breaking in before the fair-headed one could reply. "You see, not all the Committees know about us, and if some were to catch us at what we do, they'd surely raise hell, seeing as how our work, well... jumps across a few boundaries. We're more effective that way, but I'm sure you can comprehend our desire to avoid the attention of certain Committee heads."

Geoffrey nodded his understanding, thinking about the argument which would be sure to ensue if the existence of this sort of group was even proposed in front of certain members of the Committees. And this band *did* seem quite efficient in the way it operated, he acknowledged; there was obviously some merit in having the same figures hand out both rations and medicines. Of course, he knew, there was a very good reason for it being done the way it was, or else the Committee of Progress wouldn't have set it up just so. However, in this particular case Geoffrey was inclined to agree with Grey-eyes and his band, or at least to sympathize with them.

"Oh don't worry, I give you my word that I won't blab," promised Geoffrey, "but I do feel rather indebted to the four of you, and if I ever get back on my feet I'd be more than happy to propose a ballad in your honor, perhaps to be sung at the festival of the Committee of...."

Geoffrey suddenly felt a hand clamp around his left wrist in a grip he was sure could crush it like an overripe melon. Startled and unsure of what he had done wrong, his head began to turn toward the bulging muscles of the fair-headed man when suddenly his arm was pulled the other direction, dragging his body with it until he was face-to-face with the mysterious dark-haired woman who had reached across to take hold of his arm, and whose gaze, although not quite hostile, was very, very serious.

"That would be a very unwise decision for your health and ours. We work in shadows, with those who, in the eyes of the upper city, do not even exist. Why do you imagine for even a moment that we should want our presence recognized?"

Her voice, which Geoffrey would later describe as one of the softest he had ever heard, yet at the same time so charged with energy that it reverberated in his head like the unfamiliar music of the Northern Regions, filled Geoffrey with a thrill of awe as he tried to wrap his mind around what he had just heard. To refuse the offer of an honor or a promotion was not only an incredibly rude gesture, but also one which called into question the sanity of the person turning it down. Such recognitions were the stepping-stones to true progress, Geoffrey knew, and only through progress could one hope to really improve the Trasta-lucherian community. In his mind the more known you were, the easier it was to influence people, and thus the easier it was to accomplish whatever it was you had set out to do, even if that thing might have been a little 'under-the-table' to begin with. Yet even as he questioned the woman's rationality, he found himself nodding in agreement to her words, although whether it was out of courtesy, fear, or an inkling of a deeper reality they seemed to contain within them, he was never quite sure. She let go of his wrist as suddenly as she had grasped it, and Geoffrey, not realizing that he was straining against her, almost fell over backwards.

"My...my apologies," he stammered, as his eyes searched the faces that surrounded him for any signs of further hostility. "I didn't mean to offend, only to offer some small gesture in repayment for the kindness you showed me. If it pleases you that I make no mention of you, I give you my word of honor as a fellow Trastalucherian that none will be made."

"Peace, friend, no offense is taken, and no harm is meant."

The older woman's voice, gentle and musical, danced its way around the corners of the wine chamber and soothed Geoffrey's bruised ego and bewildered mind.

"And your gratitude is much appreciated," she continued, "as it speaks to the strength of your character. But let me assure you that we are in no need of ballads to call attention to our work, at least for the moment."

Much relieved that he had not insulted his hosts, Geoffrey thanked her for her graciousness and understanding, but his bard's curiosity for a good tale now insatiable, he couldn't resist one last question.

"I... I'm sorry, for I do not wish to pry, but might I at least dare to ask in what sort of place we are in, and what story lies behind a wine chamber as magnificent as this? Why, one could store enough drink in here to satisfy the entire Trastalucherian army a dozen times over!"

That last bit was a gross exaggeration and he knew it, but his ability to charm people with his words and to entice them to tell him their deepest stories, a talent which had always come naturally to him and had allowed him to compose the juiciest of songs, had been nothing short of a burning ruin since he had set foot in this chamber, and the bard in him was now desperate for something to sing about. He couldn't very well use his experience in Muckland unless he wanted his own reputation to sink lower than it already was, and as long as he re-mained stuck near the outskirts of the city and ran the risk of seeing these people again, he thought it best to honor their request and not speak of them publicly. Thus, the room and its history seemed like his last -and safest- bet. At his question, Grey-eyes brightened visibly, and sweeping his arm across the room, declared:

"Now *that* is a question I would be delighted to answer. My dear Geoffrey, you are seated in what was once the greatest store-room of fine wines and ales in all of Spiraluche. These arches once held above them a grand banquet hall, which, in the days before the war, was proudly run by my father's father. It was here that the soldiers of what was then Hazcaluche would re-turn after their campaigns to celebrate their victories with their families and neighbors, and it was here, if my father's grandfa-ther speaks the truth, that a large portion of the forgotten texts, the *Pontilux* as they called it in those days, was transcribed into song. Surely you must have heard of those? You don't encounter them much anymore, of course, but they were once staples in the repertoire of every bard of Hazcaluche."

Geoffrey nodded, albeit reluctantly. He had in fact heard of the *Pontilux Poems*, as they were named: the most integral elements of the forgotten texts of the OverLaw which, in seasons past, had been put to song. Their recitation had of course been forbidden by the Committee of Propriety after the war, and Geoffrey was impressed at the gall of Grey-eyes to even mention them, let alone the fallen name of Hazcaluche or the era before the War of Liberation. Still, during his time as an apprentice bard Geoffrey had served for a few seasons in the Committee of Spectacle's Depository of Texts, and he had once laid eyes on an ancient copy of the work which was hidden away in a dusty corner, most likely long forgotten by anyone who cared. It was a memory which Geoffrey himself had often wished he could forget; accidentally revealing that sort of information to the wrong type of person could ruin one's reputation. Yet, at that precise moment, he was glad of its existence, for it seemed to increase his own standing before his table mates.

The next hours were spent in pleasant conversation with Grey-eyes, a conversation about winemaking, good years, the grapes and grains of the regions, the best distillers of ale, and countless other topics which are boring to most but which bring great pleasure to those who truly appreciate the craft and are always eager to learn more. Grey-eyes seemed to know enough about the wine chamber's history to fill a book of ballads and was more than happy to share it with Geoffrey. An avid wine-drinker and tale-teller himself (for, as you know, the two almost always go together) the bard filed the stories away for future use, although perhaps, he thought, without all the mention of Hazcaluche and the forgotten era of the Lord of Oppression. He had just made up his mind to ask Grey-eyes about his repeated mention of terms and times which, to Geoffrey, all but constituted curses and ill-wishes of the vilest kind, when the young, fair-haired man interrupted their conversation. Geoffrey saw that he had changed out of his cloak and tunic and into an outfit of a dark, earthy tone with a staff in hand, a satchel slung over his shoulder, and a short sword belted to his waist.

"Forgive my intrusion," he apologized, "but the women and myself feel it is unwise to tarry here much longer. Besides, there is another issue which you know we must urgently attend to."

"Oh yes, of course," exclaimed Grey-eyes, "I had quite lost track of the time. Do forgive us," he said, turning back to Geoffrey, "but I'm afraid we have some important matters to look to. It really has been a pleasure having you, although I think I speak for you as well when I say that I hope that if we ever meet again, it won't be in such awful circumstances as last night."

Geoffrey chuckled in agreement, then hesitated, not sure how to put his thoughts into words, and added:

"Thank you for… all of that, you know… last night… if you hadn't come along, I might've… that is…."

But Grey-eyes had already laid a finger on his lips to stop Geoffrey's faltering discourse.

"Say no more, friend," he said, "it was a gain for us all that we found you, and we deserve no more thanks for fulfilling our duties than you do for singing the people's songs. Best of luck with your efforts; I do hope you get back on your feet soon. And speaking of getting back on your feet...."

He motioned to the fair-headed man, who counted out a number of coins from a purse and handed them to Geoffrey.

"I expect this might help a bit," said Grey-eyes, smiling at the astonishment in Geoffrey's expression. "Yes, yes, I know all about the Law of Undue Recompense, but I think just this once we might make an exception, eh?"

He winked at Geoffrey and, before the bard could say another word, either of protest for this highly irregular action or of gratitude for a gift of such significance, he continued.

"I'm terribly sorry about this next part, but we do plan on using this chamber again for our work, and it wouldn't be wise if you, or anyone else, were to know how or where to get in or out. We're happy to get you back up to the surface before we leave, of course, but you'll need to be blindfolded for the journey."

Geoffrey, who in truth had no idea where he was or how to get out, was more than a little taken aback by this request, but he saw no other alternative than to acquiesce. Following a quick goodbye to the fair-headed man and the ebony-skinned woman, he was led, eyes covered with his newly-washed cloak, through the twists and turns of an ancient tunnel by Grey-eyes and his wife. After several missteps and a few head bumps on Geoffrey's part, and just when the bard was wondering whether they would come out in Spiraluche or the next city over, he felt the cool rush of fresh air and, moments later, he sensed the walls of the tunnel give way around him and the darkness of the blindfold grow slightly lighter as the three of them reached the passage's end. The air smelled of flowers and greenery, and Grey-eyes guided Geoffrey down the twists and turns of what felt to be a cobble-stone path until they stopped in what the bard guessed to be the center of a garden, probably somewhere in lower Spiraluche.

"If you don't mind leaving the blindfold on until we're away, we'd be grateful." The words, spoken a few paces behind Geoffrey, belonged to Grey-eyes, and Geoffrey nodded his understanding.

"My thanks to you once again," he responded, "and, if in the future there is ever a time when my services might be employed for repayment, please don't hesitate to seek me out. I know people, you see, high up in the Committees, whose aid might help your work's progress quite a bit…."

"Oh, now I can't believe that anyone in the Committees would want to hear about the happenings of Muckland, but your company and thoughtfulness is repayment enough."

This time it was the woman who answered, her voice a great deal softer and somewhat further away than her husband's, and yet, for all its gentleness, her response slammed into Geoffrey like the hooves of a battle stallion. In the quiet self-admonishment of that unknown woman he saw himself, more starkly than ever before, and he realized that since that ruinous night at the house of the Family Xavier, *he* had been, and in fact was now, just as much of a nobody as the festering sick he had lain next to the night before. His friends in the Committees would just as soon arrest him on some pretext or another than listen to his accolades and adventures, and he may as well be promising his unknown helpers dominion over Trastaluche as the guarantee that anyone who was, well, *anyone,* would ever listen to him again. As he heard the two sets of footsteps fade into silence behind him, Geoffrey was overwhelmed for the second time in as many days by the immense void of failure which threatened to overpower him entirely. Then, quite suddenly, he felt a hand on his shoulder once again, and the voice of Grey-eyes, whose return a despairing Geoffrey had not sensed, sounded in his darkened world once more.

> "Listen to me friend, for I haven't got much time. I don't know by what misfortune you ended up where you are, nor do I care to know, but if 'all this' isn't working out – the Committees, Muckland, the constant fight for every blasted little thing- and if you're wanting to be a part of something *more,* then be here, in this spot, after nightfall in three days' time. I can't promise you'll like what you find if you come, but I can tell you're close to needing this invitation...."

And with that, Grey-eyes was gone again, his final words departing along with him, so that Geoffrey had to strain his ears to catch what he said. All was silent for the space of a few dozen heartbeats before Geoffrey found the courage to remove his blindfold, exposing his eyes to the sudden onslaught of glaring sunlight. He stood there, blinking, for quite a while, as his eyes adjusted to the late morning brightness and his mind whirled, trying to make heads or tails of all that had happened to him in the past day, but especially of the invitation he had received. He continued his deliberations as he wound his way along the worn

paths of the garden- for that was in fact where he had been deposited-
and back into the busy streets and markets of the lower levels of Spiraluche proper. Here, many of the common laborers- the fish-sellers,
the gardeners, and the wood-cutters- would construct make-shift shops
under portable tents to sell their wares during the daylight hours. He
wandered the streets of the city for the remainder of the morning and
well into the afternoon, lost in his own thoughts, until he found himself
on the broad stone causeway that ran along the top of the city's walls.

He paused, more out of exhaustion than anything else, and contemplated the countryside that stretched out before him almost without
noticing it. Something was still nagging at the recesses of his mind;
something that had called up memories from seasons ago; something
that was related to, yet went beyond, the strange events of the past two
days. As his conscious thoughts played a game of chase with his subconscious, his eyes fell upon a wooden door that led to the interior
rooms of one of the many towers that dotted Spiraluche's wall. These
towers were routinely used by the Trastalucherian soldiers as guard
posts, storerooms for weapons, and even temporary prisons. Tacked to
the outside of the door were the most current notices of the Committee
of Social Order advising citizens and soldiers of the names (and badly-
drawn faces) of those unlucky few who, through fate or fault, had become their most-hunted targets.

Suddenly, the musings in his head aligned with lucid precision, and
the memory that had been darting throughout the corners of Geoffrey's
mind came roaring to the forefront. It was the image of a man's face, a
man who Geoffrey had never seen in person, but whose name and like-
ness, set down on a declaration of the Committee of Social Order seasons ago, he had once been intimately familiar with. It was the face of
the dead man Xavier, whose disastrous execution had triggered

Geoffrey's spiral into ruin, and yet, as the memory stared back at Geoffrey, he found himself confronted with a truth which, try as he might, he could not deny. There was no mistaking the fusion of identities before him: the face of Xavier, burned forever into Geoffrey's mind, was the face of grey-eyed man as well.

Chapter IV

The Question

As the full weight of his realization struck him, Geoffrey literally staggered, reeling backwards in shock and almost toppling over the low inner parapet of the city wall. He tried to convince himself that he was mistaken in his conclusions, and that, while Grey-eyes and the traitor Xavier might look very much alike or even be related, there was absolutely no way they could be the same person. His memories from the raid on the house of the Family Xavier replayed over and over again, and most especially the sight he had seen when he had awoken from the mysterious blast that had cast him headlong from his perch: the burning remains of the house, its walls splintered and even the stones of its foundation blown outward by the might of whatever had happened that night. There was no way anyone could survive such a force, reasoned Geoffrey, least of all the man the Ministers of Social Order had set out to kill in the first place.

And yet, despite his attempts to explain it all away, the fact remained that the faces of Grey-eyes and Xavier were almost exactly identical. Grey-eyes was older and more worn, of course, as one would expect to see in the appearance of a hunted man several seasons later. But the regal cheekbones, the piercing eyes, and the thin, bearded chin were all eerily similar, even though it *couldn't* be the same face.

But it was Grey-eyes' scar that terrified Geoffrey, terrified him because it almost guaranteed that his uncomfortable conclusion was in fact the truth. He had seen that type of scar before, he realized, on the burned torsos of the enemies of Trastaluche infamous enough to be publicly executed. Geoffrey disliked having to witness such events, but retelling them was a popular and profitable opportunity for a bard, so he had often gone anyway. The executions were carried out by the Committee of Social Order's Lucherium wielders, and they were quick, clean, and brutally efficient. Once their work was finished, the bodies of the dead were often left on display for the remainder of the day, both to serve as a symbol of triumph for the Trastalucherian Way of Life and as a warning to other rebel bands. The faces and limbs of the corpses were often burnt beyond recognition, but Geoffrey remembered vividly the scars which coursed along the chests and necks of the executed, scars whose pattern had reminded him of the burn-marks on a tree which had been felled by lightning near his home as a child, and scars which were far too close of a match to the mark borne by Grey-eyes to be any sort of coincidence at all.

"But it *had* to be a coincidence," Geoffrey's panicked brain insisted, "or perhaps even a trick of some sort." For as surely as Geoffrey knew that Grey-eyes' scar was identical to those who had received the ultimate punishment for their crimes against Trastaluche, his unpleasant memories of such moments also meant that he harbored no uncertainties as to what happened to the unlucky recipient of such a mark. There was no escape from a Lucherium wielder's death-blow, just as there was no possible way that Xavier could have escaped from the smoldering crater that had his home. And *yet,* there was so much connecting Xavier and Grey-eyes! They couldn't just be unrelated, could they? And if they were related, how would that explain the scar? Did the secrecy Grey-eyes and his band so clearly sought to maintain have something to do with it all?

These questions and dozens of others swirled through Geoffrey's head as he made his way, even more dazed than before, off the causeway of the city wall and back into the rapidly darkening streets of Spiraluche, whose lower levels were cast into the shadow of twilight long before the sun had fully set. At some point during his endless contemplations, he realized that he had not eaten since his breakfast with Grey-eyes and his band and that his head was spinning not only with confusion but also with hunger. Using one of the coins Grey-eyes had given him, he bought two of the small, oddly shaped loaves of bread which the bakers crafted from their leftover dough and sold for half the price of a normal loaf, along with a piece of fruit and a strip of dried pork. He sat down on a section of roughly hewn boulders which served to mark the meeting place between the cobble-stone lane and a large, unpaved space which housed an open-air market during the day. Realizing that he really was quite hungry, he consumed his dinner at a prodigious rate, momentarily pushing aside the crisis within his mind which threatened to break out and possess the rest of his body as well.

As he finished the final crumbs of what he considered to be a satisfactory, albeit dry and rather boring, evening meal, he returned to his musings. They loomed in front of him now in a slightly less dizzying manner, thanks mostly to the full stomach which kept him well-grounded in more ways than one. Struggling with the effort of organizing his thoughts, Geoffrey began to pace around the almost deserted field behind him, muttering to himself in the type of tone that was loud enough to convince his own ears that his experiences were not only in his head and that he wasn't going crazy, but quiet enough to not be overheard so that no one else would come to the conclusion that he *was* in fact insane.

"It seems to me," Geoffrey said to himself, "that there are three possibilities. The first is that Grey-eyes and Xavier are not in any way related, and that the whole connection is just the great-est coincidence in the history of Trastaluche. That doesn't seem likely, especially given the whole scar thing and all the secrecy about his identity and his work which he seemed so anxious to maintain. If it were true, though, that would be the easiest thing. For, you see, it wouldn't matter one bit whether they looked alike or not, and I wouldn't have to worry about this at all. The second option," he reasoned, "which I think is far more likely, is that the two are related somehow. Maybe cousins or long-forgotten brothers, or maybe Grey-eyes is trying to look like that Xavier person for some reason, possibly as a disguise... Could this be true? Now that I think of it, he did talk an awful lot about the comings and goings of Trastaluche before the War, and everyone knows that those are topics you stay away from unless you're drunk, a revolutionary, or worse... and un-less you want to end up beaten, or in prison, or both. Still, Grey-eyes, a traitor?" Geoffrey almost laughed at the thought. The man was odd and a little mysterious, to be sure, but his whole demeanor seemed to be the exact opposite of what one would expect to find in a treasonous revolutionary. "Not a rebel him-self," Geoffrey thought, "but if he were related to one that might explain his conversation choices and his desire to be unknown. I'm sure I'd have to work in the shadows too if I had a blood-lusting traitor for a cousin or something. And if they are re-lated," he wondered, "then what does that mean for me? Even if Grey-eyes and his band are harmless, I've got enough trouble rebuilding my life and my respectability as it is. I don't want to be tied in any way to an enemy of the Committees, especially not Xavier. He's caused enough trouble for me already."

It occurred to Geoffrey briefly that perhaps Grey-eyes was Xavier's oldest son -the one who had unwittingly helped the Committee of Social Order gain access to his own house- but unless he had aged horribly that didn't seem at all likely. After all, this whole incident was barely more than three seasons ago, and the son, whose name Geoffrey couldn't recall, had only just completed the second decade of his life.

"No," he thought, "a brother or a cousin is more likely; someone who knew him well enough to be familiar with the time before the War," (which, as Geoffrey well knew, was only remembered fondly by those still loyal to the fallen Lord of Oppression), yet someone removed enough to be above real suspicion by the Committees." Not that you were ever "removed enough" from a stain on society like Xavier and his family, Geoffrey knew. He'd never met the man and hadn't even witnessed what had happened in the house that night, yet his inability to give an account that satisfied the Ministers of Social Order had led to the loss of his seat on the Committee of Spectacles, the stripping of his bard's commission, and the whole slew of bad luck and worse decisions that had followed. "That's probably why he wouldn't give his name or what he does," thought Geoffrey. "He doesn't want anyone to put two and two together and realize who he's related to. He's managed to do well enough for himself by working quietly in a place that isn't under the oversight of any Committee that really cares, and he wants to keep it that way."

Calming himself considerably as his rationalizations began to take coherent shape, Geoffrey ceased his pacing and started down the streets

of an almost-nighttime Spiraluche once again, his pace quickening with
the adrenaline of one who finally sees a way out of a truly difficult dilemma. The scar still bothered him of course. Grey-eyes was too old to
be a child of Xavier, and anyway, he seriously doubted if such marks
got passed on from generation to generation. Suddenly he stopped dead
and almost laughed out loud.

"A tattoo!" he exclaimed. "Of course! That would make perfect
sense! A sibling or a cousin who loves their brother and wants
to remember their death but doesn't want to be directly associated with his doings or his body- or can't for that matter, with
all that was left of it- goes out and gets a tattoo which more or
less matches the one his brother would have as a sort of memo-
rial."

Anyone who had ever been near the public execution of an Enemy
of Trastaluche would know what such a scar looked like, Geoffrey reasoned, and based on the crimes Xavier was accused of and the state of
his home, it wouldn't be hard for a relative to guess what sort of death
he had faced. Geoffrey smiled broadly, congratulating himself on making some sense out of the whole ordeal and on proving to himself that
the knack of weaving the neatest stories out of the most jumbled, un-
connected threads was still a talent he possessed, despite the months of
disuse it had seen.

Feeling more like his usual self, and warmed by the bread in his
stomach and the jingle of Grey-eyes' coins in the small leather purse he
carried under his tunic, Geoffrey turned away from the now darkened
streets of lower Spiraluche and began the winding climb up toward its
more modest central levels with the idea of finding a well-kept inn there

to lodge in. Perhaps he could find one with a small tavern nestled within, where a weary traveler such as himself could relax and enjoy a pint of home-brewed ale, a luxury that he could in no way afford at the moment but which he found increasingly desirable. In his new-found optimism, he barely stopped to consider the third possibility: that Xavier and Grey-eyes were somehow, through a miraculous twist of reality, the same person. Such an option now seemed ridiculous, and he laughed again, this time at his own confused delusions.

Having reached a more respectable section of the city, he wasted very little time in searching for an inn which would be well-suited for him. After scouring several side streets for such an establishment and haggling with three different innkeepers, he finally settled on *The Twisted Rose*: an ancient-looking stone and plaster building with two stories of rooms atop a tavern and a dining hall, the lot of which was kept immaculately clean by the innkeeper's mother who looked to be about as ancient as the inn itself. It rented rooms with sheeted beds and a pint of ale thrown in at eighteen a night. Geoffrey had talked the innkeeper down to fourteen and could have gone even lower if he'd offered his services in entertaining the other guests for the remaining hours of the late evening, but he was thoroughly worn out. Besides, he wasn't sure if this was the type of place which, when they found out that you had lost your official bard's commission from the Committee of Spectacles, would let you perform anyway, would throw you out without a refund, or worse, would send for the Ministers of Social Order. So he kept quiet about his occupation and paid the fourteen, which, he reasoned, wasn't coming out of his own measly wage-earnings, so the extra few didn't matter all that much.

After paying the fare and claiming his much-anticipated pint, Geoffrey settled down in a rough, wooden chair near the large fireplace that dominated the rear wall of the dining hall. Once there, he set about the task of staring into the dying embers and savoring long, slow sips of the burnt, earthy flavors of the ale, a combination which for Geoffrey was the pinnacle of relaxation. As he did so, it occurred to him, almost in passing, that he had forgotten entirely about Grey-eyes' invitation to meet him in the garden in three-days' time. Unnerved by the secrecy of Grey-eyes and his friends and not wanting to be any more involved than he already was with a man who was quite possibly related to the traitor Xavier, Geoffrey's first instinct was to reject the invitation out-right. Whatever he found would most certainly be shady, he thought, if not blatantly contrary to any number of the Decrees of Progress. It was too much of a risk, both to his reputation and his livelihood, he rea-soned, to make it worthwhile to associate with Grey-eyes and whatever it was he really did.

And yet, as he reclined before the fire, Geoffrey realized two things. The first was that, as much as returning to the garden where Grey-eyes and the woman had deposited him the night before seemed foolhardy, he really had no other place to go. The fact of the matter was that, once the money in his pathetically light purse ran out, there was a decent chance he'd end up reuniting with them anyway, only this time as one of the dead loaded into their push-cart to be taken away for a decent burial. This sobering fact was one of the few Grey-eyes had been able to tell him about the true nature of his band's occupation during their long conversation earlier that day. Without his bard's commission, he had no real chance of getting any sort of work other than the menial tasks which any ignorant peasant off the street could do for a wage that barely covered an evening meal. Of course, one could almost always buy their commission back if they knew the right people, but that re-quired a sizable sum of money that Geoffrey just didn't have and didn't see himself having anytime in the near future. All sorts of taverns and markets in the lower city didn't care about these sorts of things, he knew, but they weren't the sort that you frequented if you were trying to make it somewhere in the Trastalucherian world; he had experienced his fair share of these in the previous months and knew that you were just as likely to leave at the end of the night with your purse- and possibly your throat- cut as with it any heavier than when you came in. The second realization was much more subtle but clear nonetheless: a gentle tugging at Geoffrey's mind that, when he focused on it, grew into a restless desire to learn more about his mysterious saviors and their obviously unorthodox way of life.

"In fact, Grey-eyes might be just like me," thought Geoffrey, draining the remains of his pint in a long, satisfying draught and sitting the mug upended on a small wooden table next to him, "a man of great potential who was forced to make his living in the shadows because of the stain of being related in some way to an Enemy of Trastaluche."

The more Geoffrey contemplated his situation, the more appealing the idea of returning to the garden sounded. It was obvious that Grey-eyes and his band had money and resources, and if he won their trust and was accepted into their little group, they might be willing to lend him enough to restart his once promising future. If nothing else, it was an opportunity, and Geoffrey was too astute a person to blindly turn it down without at least having a second look. A part of him was still worried about how little he knew of Grey-eyes' work and his potential relationship with Xavier, but he waved those thoughts aside, telling himself: "if it turns out that their occupation is too 'under-the table,' I can always back out again and turn them in to the Ministers of Social Order for a hefty reward and everything needed for the writing of an epic ballad about my own adventures." Either way it was a profitable endeavor for himself, Geoffrey concluded, and, feeling quite pleased with his reasoning skills for the second time that night, he decided to indulge just a little bit more and ordered a second pint of ale.

Chapter V

The Realization

And so it was that, three nights later, Geoffrey found himself trekking through the poorly-paved streets of lower Spiraluche, searching for the entrance to the walled-in, overgrown sanctuary that he hoped was to be his gateway to a greater life. It took him some time to find the garden, despite the fact that he had a good knowledge of the lower levels of the city and had made sure to mark its location in his memory, and also despite the fact that so few of these floral courtyards remained. The Committee for Ways and Means had been slowly but surely demolishing them over the years and constructing all manner of storage rooms and workhouses in their place, which could be utilized, they said, "for the betterment of all of Spiraluche." As a result, the few gardens that did still exist in this part of the city were well-hidden and long since forgotten.

After nearly an hour of searching, however, Geoffrey came upon the place almost by accident. It was nestled in the shadows between an old grain bin which rose to the height of half-a-dozen spear-lengths and an abandoned two-story home, once probably belonging to the chief Minister of some sort of local branch of a Committee, but now completely run down and all but abandoned. The garden itself was (as Geoffrey had suspected) concealed from view by a crumbling brick wall practically invisible itself due to the dark green curtain of ivy that covered it and which hid well the small, iron-wrought gate near its center.

Geoffrey entered through the gate with excitement and not a little bit of apprehension. Unsure of where to go, he decided his best option was to retrace his steps to the place where he had bid farewell to Grey-eyes and his wife. Stumbling over the uneven cobblestones lining the twisted paths which wound this way and that throughout the overgrowth of brambled roses, creeping vines, and lilac bushes, he pushed himself forward until he finally reached a small clearing near the center of the garden which he recognized to be the place. Sitting on a low stone bench which was nestled up against the trunk of an ancient, dying ash, he resigned himself to a long wait, as he really had no idea when Grey-eyes or whomever he sent would arrive.

As the minutes stretched into hours and the loneliest part of the night drew near, Geoffrey's speculations began to waver between *when* Grey-eyes might appear to *if* he would appear. It suddenly occurred to him that he had no real reason to trust Grey-eyes or any of his associates. On the off chance that someone did come to meet him, they might just as soon decide he knew too much and slip a knife between his ribs as invite him to a late dinner. Completely forgetting (as one often does when one is alone in an unknown place at night) that Grey-eyes had most likely saved his life, and that if he had wanted Geoffrey out of the way it would have been a much easier task to get rid of him several days before, he began wondering why he had ever thought it was a good idea to come here and how wise it would be to get out as soon as possible. These thoughts grew in force and frequency as the hour grew later and moonhigh came and went. Geoffrey was almost to the point of succumbing to them when from somewhere behind him came the grinding of rock on rock and the distinctive creak of rusted metal hinges. He half-jumped, startled by the suddenness of the noise, and spun around to face the direction it came from, adrenaline surging through his body and the contrary impulses of caution and curiosity waging war within his mind. He heard the soft crackle of twigs snapping as a shadow moved toward him, and moments later the tall, fair-headed man whom Geoffrey had met the previous day and assumed to be Grey-eyes' son stepped out into the pale, wavering moonlight. He seemed surprised to see Geoffrey, as if he hadn't expected him to actually come, but it was a pleasant sort of surprise, and one which was quickly accompanied by a broad smile and two palms extended in greeting.

"Geoffrey! Good evening my sir, or shall I say morning at this point? I really didn't think you'd have the guts to show up, but I must say I'm thrilled you proved me wrong. You made quite an impression on Father the other day, and he was fairly certain you'd be here. So sorry to keep you waiting so long; it's been a very busy night. Say, have you eaten? Here, I've got a bit of bread in my bag yet to tide you over; help yourself to whatever."

Geoffrey was taken aback by the young man's torrent of words. He thought he ought to feel indignant at the other's suggestion that he didn't have the courage to return to the garden, but the son's (for Geoffrey now knew that he was indeed Grey-eyes' son) easygoing, optimistic personality helped the bard feel almost instantly at ease. He hadn't had the chance to converse much with him during their encounter a few days before, apart from a shared joke about the state of the Committee of Public Health, and he was interested in the opportunity to do so now, especially since he did not seem quite as guarded as his father. He returned the greeting and thankfully accepted the offering of bread while the son began the process of blindfolding Geoffrey once again.

"It's best this way for the time being," he said apologetically, "at least until you understand what exactly it is we do and we get to know you a little bit better. Think of it as our shield of se-crecy, and your shield of protection as well."

'Protection' from what, Geoffrey wasn't sure, but he allowed him-self to be blindfolded and led once again to what he assumed to be the entrance of a tunnel, most likely concealed within a section of the gar-den wall somehow. With the son's hand on his shoulders as a guide, they began the descent under the streets of Spiraluche. The trip seemed much longer to Geoffrey this time, and he wondered if they might be traveling to a different room, although between the deprivation of the blindfold and his jumbled recollection of his journey three days prior, he really couldn't say with certainty. His suspicions were confirmed, however, when after what he judged to be about an hour, he felt the rush of cleaner air on his face and, having been freed from his blindfold, opened his eyes to behold the hidden world of Grey-eyes once again.

He saw at once that he was indeed in a different location; bare, cleanly-fitted granite walls, a plain wooden ceiling, and a smooth, hard-packed dirt floor formed the borders of a roomy chamber which Geof-frey guessed to be the cellar of an unused warehouse, perhaps one where lumber had once been trimmed and cut to size, judging by the occasional piles of sawdust that lingered in the corners and along the edges of the room. It had no windows at all that Geoffrey could see and was instead dimly illuminated by the glow of around a dozen lanterns suspended from the ceiling or fastened to the walls in a haphazard pat-tern. However, the refreshing breeze which played across his face was evidence of at least one hidden air shaft to the outside world. A single doorway set in the opposite wall led to what appeared to be another chamber of similar size. "Probably a former finishing or drying-room for the lumber," thought Geoffrey. What caught his attention most of all, however, were the contents of the storage room.

To his left, stacked in double rows, were several dozen ornately crafted clay urns, the type used for storing all manner of foods and drinks. However, it was not their presence that astonished Geoffrey, or even the large quantity of such an expensive piece of work. Pottery-craft was a common enough occupation, given its few initial costs and its potential to pay well. What left Geoffrey speechless was the quality of the urns. Their glossy sheens of deep reds, blues, and purples, combined with the intricate curves and shapes tastefully crafted into their surfaces, were by far some of the best he had ever laid eyes on. They were the sort which one might expect to find in the house of one of the seven Committee Chiefs, to be used only on special occasions, and which cost nearly as much as the yearly wages of the cook and the table-helper combined. And yet, here were dozens of them.

Beyond the clay urns, in the far corner of the room, he could make out the awkward, spider-like shape of a loom, already rigged with strands of finely spun wool, its arms rhythmically rising and falling as a figure who Geoffrey was unable to see from his vantage point near the entrance was weaving with incredible speed. Beyond the loom he could glimpse spools of dyed and undyed wool and finally, hanging from the rough-hewn rafters of the ceiling, a great number of rugs, blankets, and drapes, all fashioned with the same skill and exquisite quality as the urns.

And to Geoffrey's right were more "work-shops" of the same type. One corner was filled with tables, chairs, shelves, and benches, all fashioned so perfectly that it was almost impossible to tell where one plank of wood ended and another began, and each adorned with ornately carved patterns of leaves and vines and flowers. In another he saw a heavy brick oven similar to the one he had noticed in the wine chamber, its narrow, iron smoke-pipe snaking up through a secret hole in the ceiling. Even at this late hour it was still in use, its hidden contents releasing a delicious odor which seemed to brighten the room all by itself.

Lastly, and perhaps most peculiarly due to its contrast with the rest of the cellar's contents, was a plain, rough-hewn table located near the middle of the room. At it sat a solitary man, who was hunched over a long roll of parchment, his quill pen dipping and then scribbling and then dipping again with the ease and precision of a practiced scholar. Around him, covering every corner of the table and spilling out onto the floor, were bunches of unused parchment and stacks of leather-bound books. The man had his back turned to Geffrey, but he could tell from his short, bony figure and the silvery-grey hair which reached down to his shoulders that it was no one he had met. Turning once again toward his guide, he noticed the fair-headed son's smile at his awestruck gawking, a smile which broadened when he saw Geoffrey looking back at him.

"Quite a haul, isn't it? Everything here was crafted by a member of our little band, and we use the profits to fund, well, our other... activities, such as our work in Muckland."

Geoffrey nodded in understanding, but inwardly he felt an alarm bell beginning to ring as the sensible side of him cautioned that there was no way a group like this could legally acquire such a large quantity of treasures, especially without an official commission from the Committee of Ways and Means, a document which he seriously doubted Grey-eyes had, given his evasiveness around the topic thus far.

"It's all very impressive," he admitted, "but where does one find the craftsmen and the space to put all of this together? Do you have a firing kiln and a carpenter's workshop down here as well?"

"Well, no kiln," the son laughed, "but the carpentry tools are in the next room over. Some of this," he gestured at the pottery, "is made in our peoples' own shops; many of them have daily occupations as well. However, some of the more serious members have to spend almost all of their time down here, so my father had this area set up a few seasons ago to make it easier for them to continue their work."

The words *serious members* and *have to* rang in Geoffrey's ears, and the suspicion that Grey-eyes might be involved in the notorious underground market of Spiraluche, an organization almost as much of a thorn in the side of the Committees as the treasonous followers of the Old Era, although not nearly as despicable, seemed even more plausible. Still, Grey-eyes and his family didn't seem to be the sort to run such an operation, and furthermore, Geoffrey found the notion of the chief of an underground marketeering branch spending his valuable time waltzing about Muckland and risking discovery while slipping food to a bunch of premature corpses utterly inconceivable.

"So, what's the point of it all?" he asked, moving his hand in a sweeping gesture across the room; "I mean, what it is that you *do* with the profits from all… this? It surely doesn't all come back to you, right? Not to sound rude, but if it did, I'd think you could establish yourselves in a little nicer place…" ("If it did, you could buy the whole city," he muttered under his breath.)

"No, no, it doesn't all come back to us," the fair-headed son answered. "Some of it, as I already mentioned, goes toward our work in Muckland and other similar initiatives. As to the rest… well I'm afraid that's something I can't tell you just yet. But come in with me and take a look around. There's someone here that Father thought you especially should meet."

He motioned toward the older man writing at the table in the middle of the chamber, who, apart from a brief, unconcerned wave over the back of his head when Geoffrey and the son had entered, had not shown the slightest interest in the newcomer behind him or any of the other goings-on in the room. Geoffrey followed the son down the last few stone steps of the tunnel entrance and across the well-packed floor to the table where the older man sat. As they drew near, he held up his left hand as if to forestall any conversation, while with his right he scratched out the last few words on a line of parchment in a bold, flowing print that reminded Geoffrey of the style of the official Decrees of the Committee of Progress. His sentence then finished, he carefully set down his quill and, sliding his chair backwards, stood and turned to face the two of them.

He was not quite as old as Geoffrey had first thought- perhaps only in his 50th year- but his face and hands were weathered with the look of a man who had seen and done more in his lifetime than most. He was brown-skinned, with a wrinkled brow and the squinting eyes of a scholar or a writer of some sort, and was dressed in a simple, dark green tunic and brown trousers. He was shorter than Geoffrey by a fair amount, but his seafoam-colored eyes shone with a brilliance that indicated a sharpness of wit and intellect which could easily match that of any man.

"Geoffrey, this is Trentius," said his fair-headed companion. "He's our scribe and all around 'man-of-letters,' and one of the cleverest men you'll ever meet. Father thought the two of you would get along well, and Trentius is just the man for answering and not answering any questions you might have about 'all this.'"

"An honor to meet you, Trentius," said Geoffrey, who was a little taken aback by such a casual introduction, and one bereft of the litany of titles and occupations which he knew were almost obligatory these days in Trastaluche. Nonetheless, he bowed slightly and extended his palms outward toward the older man. "I look forward to hearing about you and your occupations."

"And likewise to you, Geoffrey," answered Trentius, as he completed the greeting in a low, resonant voice. "I hope I can be of assistance in answering those questions which are proper at this time, and I look forward with great interest to asking you some of my own."

This last bit confused Geoffrey, as he wasn't sure what he could know that would possibly be of interest this person who appeared to be a marketeering scribe, but he smiled and gave his assent politely, thanking both Trentius and the fair-headed man, who had darted away momentarily to fetch Geoffrey a second chair from the pile in the corner, and now returned with one which seemed fit for the owner of a merchant fleet or a ruby mine. Geoffrey settled into it quite gingerly as the son began to excuse himself again, saying: "I think I'll leave you two to your speculations now; I'm in charge of the baking tonight, and I also have to see whether the weavers need any help."

He pointed in the direction of the loom, which Geoffrey could now see was manned by Grey-eyes himself and the lithe young woman with the dark skin and the startling eyes. Grey-eyes saw him and smiled momentarily in his direction before turning back to his work, and Geoffrey smiled back in spite of himself and his own apprehensions.

"My thanks for your guidance and for coming to collect me," he said to the fair-headed man, and, taking a chance, added: "and if it isn't too much trouble, I don't believe that I ever caught your name."

The other grinned and, leaning in, said in a low voice, "My pleasure, good sir, and I must say that your courage in coming is a great testament to the type of man you are. It is an honor to make your acquaintance; my name is Vincente, and I hope to see you again in the future."

And with that the fair-headed man bounded away toward the loom, leaving Geoffrey alone with Trentius, a stack of parchment and books which he thought would take him the better part of a year to go through, and the sound of the name 'Vincente' hanging in the air, a name which, upon hearing it, struck Geoffrey as remotely familiar, although he couldn't quite say why. Shrugging it off, he turned back to the table and the man seated at it, and struggling to find a way to break the silence, he gestured at the stacks of parchment in front of him, asking:

"And where is your work taking you tonight, good sir? Which of these exquisite items are you cataloguing in such an impressive script?"

He guessed that Trentius was most likely in charge of recording the number, type, and price of the goods which surrounded him, an assumption which he almost instantly regretted as the older man answered:

"None of them, in fact. I do help out with their records occasionally, although there are plenty of people here who can do that. No, I'm cataloguing something of a far different sort tonight. Have you ever seen this?"

He slid an ancient-looking book over to Geoffrey, the one from which he had been copying, and which Geoffrey had assumed to be last year's ledger. Carefully opening its cracked, leather cover, he turned a few pages until he came to the title: *Verses of Light and Life*, and in a smaller, faded text under it, a single printed word: *Pontilux*. Geoffrey almost dropped the book as his mind absorbed what he was reading, and all of his misconceptions about who Grey-eyes was and what he did came surging back. This book, if it was indeed what it claimed to be, was perhaps the most forbidden text in all of Trastaluche, for in it were contained the poems and songs which summarized the very core and methods of the Lord of Oppression, his OverLaw, and his reign.

Faking a smile, he turned back to Trentius, and, trying to mask his trembling hands, inquired, "Is... is this really what it says it is?"

"Very, very good," responded Trentius, nodding in approval. "The man you met a few days before said you knew about this text. Very few do these days; in fact, this is one of the last remaining copies of it, and parts of it are faded almost beyond recovery. Hence it is the object of my attention tonight. But tell me, Geoffrey," he leaned in toward the bard suddenly, "what do you know about the contents of the *Pontilux Poems*? What have they told you it holds?"

Geoffrey was taken aback by such a direct question and, not wanting to anger his hosts, wasn't quite sure how he should answer. "Truthfully…," he stammered, "I don't know much more than the name. They don't teach it to the bards anymore. The most I can say is that it comes from the time before the war; you know, during the era of…." He trailed off, not wanting to actually say it.

"You mean the Era of Joaquin? Or the so-called Lord of Oppression?"

This time Geoffrey actually did drop the book onto the table, where it fell with a dull thud which did little to mask the pounding of his heart in his ears and mouth. He had seen the actual name of the Lord of Oppression put down in writing only twice in his life: once, in the text of the First Decree of Progress, which was housed in the fortress of Trastivo, and which declared the death of the Lord of Oppression and the end of his rule, and a second time in a different copy of the very text he had just been holding, which he had glimpsed only briefly during his younger years. As for hearing it spoken aloud… that had occurred only one time: on the lips of an Enemy of Trastaluche who somehow managed to chew through his gag and had shouted it in the moment before his particularly brutal execution. It had haunted him then, and it haunted him now, but he nodded weakly in assent to the question Trentius had posed.

"Yes... that one," he answered.

Trentius smiled for the first time since the two of them had met, while his eyes shot Geoffrey a look which showed that he understood full-well what was on the bard's mind. Then he opened the *Pontilux* and turned to a page near the end of the text. Handing it back to Geoffrey, he said:

"Here. Read this. Don't worry; no one can find you here, and no one here is looking to harm you."

Shaking more visibly than before, Geoffrey glanced down at the heavily illustrated page, which contained only a few lines of verse:

Turning, as man does, as if a wheel;
a wheel which, like the seasons, never ends;
a time will come when Truth man shall conceal,
when into death and war all life descends.
When man's own person, other men will steal,
when man's own Guidance, rule and might upends;
when humble verse as this shall lose appeal,
and stagnance under form of growth ascends.
Then keep in secret what Verse may reveal,
until man's Life, like season, re-descends.

The verses, which Geoffrey recited out loud with a practiced, albeit nervous, tongue, seemed to fill the room where he sat and linger in the air as if tied to the tantalizing aroma of the bread that was still baking over to his right. As the final words rolled off of his lips, a thrill coursed through his body; the type that fills you with excitement and yet makes you shiver with awe all at the same time, and the type which remains within you long after the moment is past, unsettling you and also orienting your senses and your mind to narrow their focus in on one single thing; one matter which is the only one that matters.

Geoffrey set the book back down, more gently this time, and turned his gaze expectantly toward Trentius, who had closed his own eyes while Geoffrey was reading. After a moment, he opened them and, gazing directly at Geoffrey, recited from memory the last two lines, his voice rising and falling as expertly as Geoffrey's own:

"*Then keep in secret what Verse may reveal/ Until man's Life, like season, condescends.* My dear Geoffrey, that is exactly what we are doing here. Now, I don't know what the Committees have told you about the Time of Oppression and about what this book contains, but what I do know is that every tale, every season, comes to an end, and just like the one before it, so will the epic of Trastaluche. And when it does end- and, believe me, it won't be a prettier end than the way it began; if anything it'll be worse – something else will have to be built upon its ruins. And when that happens it may very well be quite valuable to know what came before it, both the good and the not-so-good, the acceptable and the unacceptable. We, dear Geoffrey," he gestured around the room, "are keepers of traditions past and present, and it is here that we put them into word, into art, and even into eating. What traditions we keep alive and how exactly we do so is not something that can be explained in a night, nor is it something which you are prepared to learn at this time. But *you*, my bard, should know better than most that many things which are not quite so proper or so agreed upon by the powers of the world are still worth remembering and, indeed, retelling when the time is right. And *that* is what we do here, and what you would do as well, if you seek to work with us."

Geoffrey's head was spinning so fast now that he was unable to fully process what he was hearing. Part of him, still resonating with the verses he had just read, seemed to understand perfectly what Trentius was saying, as if half of him were a lock which had just been fitted with a perfectly matching key. His other half, however, the half which had been wary about Grey-eyes and his connection to the treasonous Xavier, about the unbelievable contents of this room, and about Trentius and the forbidden knowledge he possessed, was screaming at him to get away as fast as he could from such people and their ideas. Ideas which, he knew, could only lead to ruin if one got too close to them. When Trentius, who once again seemed to be able to read Geoffrey's emotions as easily as the verses before him, stood up to indicate a change in theme, his sudden movement caused Geoffrey to almost jump out of his skin. His nerves fraying, he quickly followed suit, eager to get away from the lines in that book which were burning their way through him as if they were a red-hot coal which had been placed on his head and wouldn't stop melting him away until it reached his feet.

"But my apologies, Geoffrey," smiled Trentius. "I had forgotten how late it was for you, and how overwhelming this might seem at first. Come, let's have ourselves a little feast and then perhaps you might enjoy being on your way for the night."

Leading Geoffrey over to the oven, he lifted two loaves off of a cooling rack and handed one to the still dumbstruck bard, along with a mug of cool water, an apple, and a small piece of roasted meat which smelled a little like duck. The two of them took their plates back to the writing table, where Trentius cleared a space and they ate in relative silence. Geoffrey tried his best to push away the tightness in his stomach long enough to savor the tenderness of the meat and the crisp, buttery crust of the bread, but with little success. Trentius asked him a few questions about his former occupation, and Geoffrey answered them politely enough, but his attention was nowhere near the present moment. Looking back later, he found that he had no specific recollection of what his answers had been. After their late-night meal, Trentius, who had informed Geoffrey that it was his task to lead him back to the surface of Spiraluche, was putting up his work for the night and readying a lantern for the journey when Grey-eyes, his task at the loom having been completed, made his way over to the two of them, calling out a greeting.

"Geoffrey! I'm delighted that you returned! I'm sorry for my absence; Ayila and I- that's the young woman you met a few days ago- had fallen a bit behind on that rug you see over there, and we've been trying to get caught up for the last few nights now. I trust you found your conversation with Trentius stimulating enough?"

"Yes, yes, more than enough, thank you," stammered Geoffrey, and Grey-eyes, noticing his nervousness, smiled.

"It's all a bit much and also rather mysterious, isn't it? We're sorry about that, but we've found that when it comes to sharing who we are with people such as, well, yourself, it helps to do it a little bit at a time. I do hope you'll come back to see us again, though. I'd love to have someone like you for our expeditions into Muckland; I'm positive you'd be a huge help." He

clapped a now even more uncomfortable Geoffrey on the
shoulder and, turning to Trentius, asked: "Are you about to
take him back up top, then? Do you mind if I join you for the
journey? I've been sitting at that loom so long I think my back
is as twisted as that rug."

And so it was that a very bewildered Geoffrey found himself blindfolded once again and being led through the tunnels by Grey-eyes and
Trentius, who were perhaps the two most enigmatic people he had ever
met. The route to the top was much shorter this time, and Grey-eyes
informed him that they would be taking him to a different spot than
the last, both due to its proximity and "so that no one should see you
entering and exiting the garden and wonder what goes on in there," he
explained.

Upon reaching the surface, the two led Geoffrey a short way along
what felt to be a wet, sandy sort of path, maybe in the lower city along
the edge of the creek which wound its way through Spiraluche, before
depositing him, as before, with the instructions to wait a few moments
before removing his makeshift blindfold. Grey-eyes pressed a small
pouch into his hand, and Geoffrey felt within it the hard, round edges
of a sizable quantity of coinage.

"To show our appreciation," he whispered, "and to keep you
out of trouble. I know you've been thinking about my offer to
get into something more, and I hope that, even if it scared you,
tonight showed you that it's possible. Best of luck to you either
way, Geoffrey."

He heard Grey-eyes' footsteps receding into nothingness, and he was left alone once again with Trentius. The grey-haired man grasped his shoulder and, leaning in closely, breathed one last piece of advice into his ear.

"Think about what you learned tonight, Geoffrey, and think about the offer we've made you. If you want to meet again, be here tomorrow night, dressed in something dark. There'll be a man- a low ranking Patroller of the Committee of Social Order who works with us as well- who will come by not long after moonhigh. He'll notice you, and he'll ask you why you're here; you'll know it's him because he'll use the phrase, 'What in the name of all that is light are you doing lurking about in such darkness?' Until then, a good day to you, my friend," he said, as he began his departure.

"Wait!" called out Geoffrey, who had finally found his voice. "What do I say to the man when he asks why I am here?"

"Say you're here to be taken to meet *him*, of course," replied Trentius, his voice rapidly fading as he made his way back toward the entrance of the tunnel from which they had emerged, most likely one of the dozens of old flood drains that crisscrossed below the city. Pulling the blindfold away from his face, he strained his eyes into the darkness, but the figure of Trentius was already out of sight, his footfalls rapidly becoming one with the rippling of the creek and the nighttime noises of Spiraluche.

"And who is *him*?" inquired Geoffrey, not quite knowing why he was asking all these questions in the first place.

"Why, you've met him already. The one who found you in the first place, and who was here tonight with us. Ask for Xavier."

And then Trentius was gone, leaving Geoffrey the bard alone with his thoughts in the darkness, thoughts which had passed from confusion to curiosity, from curiosity to desire, from desire to astonishment, and now from astonishment to rapidly growing horror.

Chapter VI
The Horror

It was dark, and not the sort of dark which envelopes the nighttime lovers, shielding their passionate trysts with its blanket of secrecy, or even the desolate sort of darkness which comes when one has lost someone or something very dear to them and cannot see the beauty of the light no matter how brightly it shines. This was a darkness of fear; a darkness of creeping things, of unknown forces conspiring in the shadows, and of unsurmountable powers plotting to confuse and upend the lives of pitiful mortals.

It was a darkness of horror, and it was into this darkness which Geoffrey the bard found himself suddenly plunged, as Trentius' parting words fell upon him like the black, soul-sucking waters of a deadly flood. *"You've met him already; ask for Xavier,"* he had said, and with those words he hurled Geoffrey back into the nightmare he had been trying to claw his way out of ever since that night when his future had been ruined, that night when the house of the Family Xavier had been raided and then, through some mystery of nature, had been wiped from the face of the earth, annihilated in the most literal sense of the term along with everyone and everything inside.

Or so he had thought. Yet here was *proof*, undeniable proof, that his earlier suspicions were true. Grey-eyes was indeed the man Xavier, the infamous enemy of Trastaluche who had been sentenced to death for his abhorrent adherence to the Lord of Oppression and his laws, laws which Geoffrey had read even tonight and a Lord whose name he had just heard spoken for only the second time in his life. And it wasn't just Xavier who had escaped, he realized. Had he not met his wife and son? Suddenly, the significance of the name Vincente came rushing back to him, and for the second time he cursed himself for his lack of memory. It was the name of the eldest son of Xavier, the one whose attraction toward the Trastalucherian Way of Life the Committee of Social Order had used to breach the family's defenses and break into the home. Obviously, he had not been quite so disloyal as the Committees had thought.

Geoffrey's veins felt as if they were filled with ice, as if he were back in the diseased alleys of Muckland. However, this time the shadows creeping nearer had not come to save him, but to drag him away to a fate far worse than he could imagine. He shuddered as all of the stories and lessons he had learned about the followers of the Lord of Oppression came flooding back. The OverLaw had not only been a crushing force which bound the common person with shackles of iron to a lot in life in which they had no say, but it had commanded worse than that. Tales were whispered in dark corners, Geoffrey knew, of the far more sinister actions this Law prescribed, practices which were continued even to this day by traitors such as Xavier: tales of blood rituals, of mangled, rotting corpses worshipped and caressed, of the sounds of endless pain made by the captives being sacrificed, and worse, of the unspeakable banquets which followed, after which the bones of the dead were left clean and dry to serve as the bed upon which would be lain the next round of victims.

He staggered away from the edge of the creek and began stumbling up its steep banks and onto the darkened roads of Spiraluche where he fled blindly, all the while fighting the looming terror which welled up inside of him and pressed up against his sanity until it perched precariously on the verge of a long plunge into endless panic.

He ran. Ran faster and harder than he ever had before, not knowing where he was or where he was going except that he must put as much distance between himself and all of 'that' as possible. He ran for what seemed to him to be an eternity, spurred on by the fear of a shadowy malice pursuing and overtaking him, until at last he collapsed, chest heaving, on the wide stone steps of a Hall of Performances and Spectacles, built for the entertainment of the citizens but at this time of night devoid of all activity.

He tried to process what had happened, what *was* happening to him, but his body felt as if it were about to be torn in two by its own ragged heaving for air. He dragged himself up into a sitting position, his elbows resting on his knees and his hands gripping the sides of his head, willing the nightmare which whirled around within to stop.

"Breathe, Geoffrey, breathe! You made it out; you're alright now. They can't get at you here; it's too open. Too much of a chance someone would spot them."

As he gulped in breath after breath of the fresh night air and his gasps grew less life-rending, the terror within him began to subside just a little, becoming a raging torrent which tore at his subconscious but left the rest of his mind free enough to think and to process what he had just seen and heard.

He knew what he had to do, of course. "There's nothing else for it," he said aloud. "I've got to go straight to the chambers of the Committee of Social Order and report everything. They've got to know that…. that *man*… survived. And if he did, then it's quite probable that in those other cases like his, they survived as well."

Dawn was drawing near as Geoffrey reached his inevitable conclusion, and the first hint of greyness began to streak across the eastern horizon, bringing with it a second round of ebbing in the bard's terror. His breath began to slow even more, and his heart pounded a little less frantically as he considered his situation.

He had escaped from them, he realized, escaped from the destruction of Xavier a second time. He felt waves of adrenaline coursing through him, and almost in spite of himself, in a burst of courage he let out a short laugh.

"They had no idea how much I knew," he thought, "Trentius and the others, with their mysterious poems and their forbidden books and their fancy crafts. They were blind fools, all of them, and this time it's going to cost them dearly. This time it won't be me who goes under."

He smiled now, thinking of the astonishment of the Committee members when he revealed his shocking truth and their gratitude toward him when it was confirmed that a secret world of incomprehensible magnitude was pulsing and growing beneath their very feet.

"In fact, this is exactly what I needed," declared Geoffrey to no one in particular. "If I reveal this to the Committees and lead them to where I was dropped off- they'll find the passage of course, they always can- they'll be forced to grant me my bard's commission again and even another spot on the Committee of Spectacles. And once this is all said and done, and the honors and rewards have been received and the apologies have been made, I'll sit down and compose the ballad of a lifetime about this adventure, the type of ballad that'll be sung for seasons in every tavern and inn and banquet hall throughout Trastaluche. It's perfect; it really is!"

Congratulating himself for making such a profitable ending out of a truly horrifying situation, he hoisted himself to his feet and set off toward the upper levels of Spiraluche where the central chambers for the seven Committees were located. There were many other guard-houses and meeting places for the more local Ministers of Social Order along the way, he knew, but this information was the sort which you took directly to Jania, the Chief of the Committee of Social Order her-self, or at least to one of her immediate advisors.

He quickened his pace as sunrise drew nearer, and his steps grew surer as the first true light of the morning crept over the rooftops of the houses and towers of Spiraluche and the rough, winding roads of the central levels widened out into the immaculately paved highways of the upper city. As he walked, he briefly considered what would happen if the Committee Ministers didn't believe him, but he shook such worries aside, assuring himself that his skill with words and the sheer weight of the news he carried would be more than enough to sway his listeners.

"After all," he reflected, "they threw me out before because I couldn't explain what had happened to Xavier, and now here I am, bringing not only an explanation but lots more besides. Once I lead the Ministers to the garden and they find the

entrance, they'll know I'm telling the truth. And what a prize
I'm bringing them! The enemy Xavier himself, his family, the
man Trentius, that woman Ayila...."

His internal boasting trailed off for a moment as he remembered
the brilliant eyes of Ayila and the tenderness with which she had cared
for him... "Surely she couldn't be all that horrid, could she? Perhaps
she's a prisoner there, or under some sort of evil trance...." Geoffrey
shook his head to clear such treasonous ideas. After all, she'd behaved
just as strangely as the rest of her band, and many of them he knew to
be traitors.

"Anyway, the Committee will sort it all out in the proper way; they
always do," he said to himself, and then recalled that the whole reason
he had fallen into this mess so many seasons ago was the Committee's
failure to do just that. He shook his head more violently this time, commanding his mutinous thoughts to subsist and glancing warily around
as if someone could have heard them.

> "It's just the shock of it all," he reassured himself, "and
> all of that twisted, confusing talk with Trentius. It's ad-
> dled my brain so that I can't think straight."

He quickened his pace once again as if to outrun his uncertainties
and soon found himself surrounded by the towering granite columns
and mighty bronze doors which adorned the facades of the Courtyard
of Committees, a massive stone plaza which was bordered on three
sides by the central meeting halls for six of the seven Guiding Committees of Trastaluche: Social Order, Ways and Means, Wealth, Propriety,
Public Health, and Spectacles. The western side of the courtyard was

dominated by the exterior walls of a gigantic fortress, the central defense of Spiraluche and the heart of the city, within which could be found the meeting halls of the chief and seventh Committee of Progress and the chambers of its leader: Trastivo, Overseer of Trastaluche and vanquisher of the Lord of Oppression.

Despite his hurry to report what he had seen, Geoffrey was forced to stop, as he always did, and to marvel at the sheer power which the Courtyard of Committees emanated, a power which seemed like no other on earth. It was here, Geoffrey knew, that the future of Trastaluche was made a reality, and its inhabitants were kept safe from the barbarous practices of folk such as Xavier. He turned briefly toward the southern edge of the courtyard, where the meeting halls for the Committees of Public Health and Spectacles were located, remembering fondly a time when he had occupied a place of honor within the walls of the latter as one of twelve senior members, a position that had been awarded him due to his undisputable talent and his service to the ideals of Trastaluche. Then he headed in the opposite direction toward the northern side which housed the Committees of Social Order and Wealth.

The sun had fully cleared the horizon, and although it cast its warm morning glow across the city, it spared the courtyard where Geoffrey walked, as of yet blocked out by the immensity of the buildings surrounding the bard. As Geoffrey drew nearer to the entrance of the central meeting hall of Social Order, he noted without surprise the presence of several guards outside its main doorway. Striding confidently in their direction and up the stairs of the building, he held out his palms and, bowing, addressed them in proper Trastalucherian style:

"A prosperous morning to you, good sirs. My name is Geoffrey of Trastaluche, son of Joshua, Bard of the Committee of Spectacles, keeper of the Official Tales, and twice honored for my service to Trastaluche and its citizens. I bring urgent news for the Committee of Social Order, regarding...."

He got no further in his greeting before one of the guards, a broadshouldered, heavyset man with small eyes and a misshapen nose interrupted him. "Your papers of commission, Bard," he stated flatly, while stepping in front of Geoffrey and leveling his spear at the other's chest. Geoffrey felt his heart sink. He'd hoped to be able to avoid that question, at least until he made it inside. Sizing up the guard's stare, and the spear whose point hovered less than an arm's length in front of him, Geoffrey opted to try for the bluff.

"No, no, you see, I must see a Committee member at once. I apologize; I left my papers at home in my hurry to get here. This really is an urgent matter...."

"Not so urgent that you can't go back and get them," replied the guard obstinately, his feet rooted firmly in front of the entrance to the meeting hall and his spear unwavering in its aim. "No one is allowed to enter without them, especially not for an audience with a senior Committee member; surely you should know that. Run along and get your papers of commission, and we'll see who you are and what we can do."

"I already *told* you who I am," replied Geoffrey, his frustration growing as his bluff was called. "Geoffrey of Trastaluche, former senior member of the Committee of Spectacles. My news is too important to wait, I tell you. It concerns a certain...."

"No papers, no admission," barked a second guard, who, from the braid around the edges of his tunic and the detailed metalworking across his breastplate, appeared to be an officer of some sort. "Now, are you going to go fetch them, or do we need to have you arrested for making a disturbance?" Geoffrey felt his heart sink even further as he realized now that he had no choice but to come clean, an act which would seem ridiculous and more than a little bit suspect after his insistence that he'd left his documents at home.

"Actually," he stammered, "my commission was... suspended... a few seasons ago. It was all a mistake, I assure you. The information I'm bringing is credible and essential for the Committee of Social Order...."

He faltered as the guard with the spear took a half-step closer, thrusting the point of his weapon forward until it was only a finger's width away from the bard's chest.

"No Commission, you say?" The second guard spoke again. "I'm sorry, but I'm afraid we can't allow you in. Try your local branch of Ministers of Social Order, and if they find your story worthwhile, they'll bring you back here...."

"No, please," blurted Geoffrey before the guard could continue, "this is too important to wait, and besides, the local Ministers never will never believe me...."

"That's enough," snapped the first guard; "be off with you, Bard! You've wasted more than enough of our time today already. If you can't prove who you are, and even *you* admit that the Ministers won't find your story credible, then there's nothing to be done. I'm surprised you had the gall to come here in the first place; deception of one's identity is a crime, you know...."

The second guard began moving toward Geoffrey as well, his hand on his sword hilt, and Geoffrey stumbled back quickly, almost losing his balance as his feet slipped on the edge of the first stair. Desperate to be admitted, he played his final card.

"Wait! I bring news regarding the whereabouts and activities of an Enemy of Trastaluche and a follower of the Lord of Oppression. You *must* allow me in to speak with a Committee Member; it's vital that they hear my message!"

Almost as soon as he had blurted out his message, Geoffrey bit his tongue and cursed inwardly at getting ahead of himself. He knew that, by decree, the guards were obliged to allow him in to speak with someone, given the gravity of the information he claimed to have. However, with his credibility destroyed and his reputation nonexistent, he didn't see any way they would take him seriously. If anything, he ran the risk of being flogged for publicly lying and abusing the time of a Committee Member before being kicked back out into the streets again.

"What's even worse," he realized, "is that I don't even know where I was last night, or how I got there. Of course, if someone were to believe me and go looking for the secret entrances, they might find them, but without proof that I should be believed in the first place, how is that going to sound? Other than the names of a few people that the Committees believe to be dead and their involvement in some illegal activities, none of which I can prove, I've got almost nothing. Why should they listen to me at all? After all, they threw me out because I couldn't tell them exactly what had happened that night at the house, and now I show up with this insane tale which has more holes in it than a beggar's shoes... Still," he resolved, "there's no other choice. I've already opened my mouth, and they've got to be told that there's a secret world going on beneath their very feet. And the reward is easily worth the risk."

In front of him, the guards, who appeared more annoyed than anything else that the nuisance before them had chosen to invoke his right to report an act of treason against Trastaluche to the Committee of Social Order itself, conversed briefly in lowered tones. Finally, the leader of the group, with a smile that seemed to be simultaneously false and yet genuinely enjoying the humiliation he foresaw in Geoffrey's future, motioned to the bard to follow him.

"At your insistence, Bard," he said, leading Geoffrey through the massive bronze doors and into a long, arched hallway. The guard strode silently down it with Geoffrey following a few paces behind until he stopped in front of one of several small doorways which branched off into various other chambers. "You'll wait in here until we find someone to deal with you," he continued, shoving Geoffrey into a nondescript room whose only furnishings were a plain wooden table and matching chair, a small collection of chests and boxes piled haphazardly against one wall, and a tiny window which overlooked a sort of enclosed patio occupying the space between the building he inhabited and the central meeting hall for the Committee of Wealth.

"Make yourself comfortable," the guard half-jeered, and then added on a much more serious note, "and don't go poking around. You'll be seen soon enough." With that he left Geoffrey on his own, slamming the door behind him with a menacing 'boom.'

Geoffrey slumped down into the chair and resigned himself for a long, anxious wait. If the quality of the room they had just deposited him in said anything, he thought, it was that he was in trouble. There was no way now that he'd get to see anyone of any importance, nor was anyone at all likely to be bothered to see him for the next several hours. He reflected grimly that, if he was lucky, he'd be met by a low-level Minister who would listen to his story, promise to follow up on it, show Geoffrey to the door, and then forget completely about the whole thing. If he were *unlucky,* he thought, he'd end up with some slightly higher-ranking official who, annoyed that Geoffrey had wasted his time, might care just enough to have the bard officially written up or even jailed for spreading falsities. Either way, Geoffrey thought, the prospects of a re-ward and a glorious return to fame seemed just as far away now as they were that night in Muckland, and he felt the all-too-familiar sentiments of helplessness and despondency began to settle once again on his shoulders.

Looking for something to distract himself from the uncomfortable corner he had backed himself into, he rose and made his way over to the stack of chests which the chief guard had expressly told him not to nose around in. "Not that anyone will be showing up soon to discover me," he muttered, and began to work at the heavy leather clasp that held the top chest closed, partly out of boredom and partly out of a desire to defy his captors and their insufferable smugness. The clasp, which was faded and cracked with age, nevertheless appeared to have been opened only a few times before, as the leather still bore the stiffness which comes with a glove or a pair of boots that hasn't been broken in. After a fair amount of twisting and pulling, however, it came undone, and Geoffrey opened the lid of the chest to find it filled to the brim with books, some of them obviously newer acquisitions, but the majority of them so old that their binding had come loose and their covers were falling off.

After moving the first chest onto the table, Geoffrey opened the two below it to discover that their contents were virtually the same. Curious as to why the Committee of Social Order would house three boxes of falling-apart books in an out-of-the-way waiting room, he returned to the contents of the first box and began leafing through the different texts. He was surprised to find that he had read a great deal of them; in fact, almost all of the books were compilations of poetry and musical lyrics, many of which he had memorized and recited in his younger days as a bard to help him master the art. An especially old text near the bottom of the chest caught his eye, and he dug downward through the shifting piles of pages until he was able to get a hand on it and pull it to the surface.

Its calfskin cover was badly damaged, and the entire book was quite small in size; in fact, it was only about as long as Geoffrey's palm. He wasn't quite able to make out the name of the text, but the ornate lettering and exquisite illustrations that adorned its front and back seemed to him to somehow be familiar. Sitting down, he opened the book to its interior title page and quite literally fell out of his chair in shock: there in front of him, for the second time in as many days, was a copy of the most forbidden book in Trastaluche: the *Pontilux Poems*.

Glancing fearfully over his shoulder as if someone might be watching, Geoffrey quickly closed its cover and set about repacking the chests and moving everything back to exactly where it was, lest someone might enter and see him not only meddling where he shouldn't be but also holding a text which described in vivid detail the laws and rituals of the Time of Oppression. He had just finished re-ordering everything and had only to put the *Pontilux Poems* back in the uppermost chest and close it up again when a thought struck him.

"Perhaps there's something in here I can use to convince the Committee that what I'm saying is true," he realized. "After all, no one knows that I found this copy, and I can say with total certainty that Trentius showed me the same book and read to me from it. Maybe I can find some information that could only come from having seen this book or been in contact with its followers. I've got time, after all, and as long as I replace it before anyone comes to get me no one will be the wiser."

Intrigued by such an idea and happy at the prospect of having something to do for what he knew would be a rather long wait, Geoffrey settled down once again in his chair with the book laid out in front of him and began leafing through the first few pages of titles, dedications, and all the other nonsense which seems to take you far too long to get through when you are really quite eager to read a certain book.

However, scarcely had he set his eyes on the first line of text when a violent commotion arose which seemed to come from both outside the door to his room and outside the window in the yard below. Amidst the indistinguishable commands being shouted on all sides, Geoffrey didn't hear the footsteps rapidly approaching the room where he was being kept until they were only seconds away. Realizing that he had no time to return his contraband to its rightful spot, and almost panicking at the thought of the consequences which might ensue if he were caught with it, he dashed over to the window to toss it away before realizing as he looked outside that the sounds were indeed coming from both sides of his small enclosure, and that trying to get rid of the book that way was quite literally equivalent to throwing it at a guard. Moving quickly back to his seat, he stuffed the book into his tunic and, putting his feet up on the table, leaned his head back with his arms crossed over his now box-shaped chest as if he were napping.

Scarcely had he done so when the door flew open, slamming against the wall with a noise so jolting that it made it quite easy for Geoffrey to fake being startled awake. He opened his mouth to greet whichever Minister of Social Order had come to speak with him, but before any sound could come out three guards burst into the room, clad in tunics of crimson and breastplates and helmets of grey and armed with long, curved swords. They strode toward Geoffrey with the look of soldiers about to perform an execution, and he wondered in fright how they could have known about his looking at the book and if they didn't, why on earth they were here. His arms still locked almost mechanically in front of his chest, he opened his mouth again to apologize for his wrongdoing and beg for clemency, but by that time the guards had brushed past him, heading instead for the three chests stacked up in the corner. Before Geoffrey could react, each had taken ahold of one and hoisted it up on their shoulders; then, they filed out as quickly as they had come in.

Geoffrey breathed a sigh of relief, uncrossing his now shaking arms, and wondered what on earth was going on. The shouting both inside and out was still continuing, but the general chaos had subsided somewhat. Tossing the book back onto the table and creeping over to the window, Geoffrey peered out into the yard below and saw a regiment of guards of the Committee of Social Order, all dressed for battlefare like those who had barged in on him, stationed in lines on either side of the open space. Between were several more guards, holding something which Geoffrey couldn't quite identity, and several high-ranking Ministers of the Committee of Social Order, who were easily identifiable by their long, ash-grey tunics clasped at both shoulders with a bronze pin in the shape of the Trastalucherian Seal: a seven-pointed star with its upper point thrust out further than the others to symbolize the seven Committees and the Trastalucherian motto of "Progress Before All." There was a commotion at the far end of the yard, and the line of soldiers parted to admit the three guards who had been in Geoffrey's room just moments ago, still carrying their burdens and now accompanied by the officer which Geoffrey had encountered earlier that morning. They tossed the chests down roughly onto the wide stone slab which occupied the center of the patio, and then all but the officer took their places in the two ranks facing inward on either side.

A horrible silence fell suddenly on the scene before him as each figure stood motionless, awaiting further direction. Then one of the Ministers, a tall man with a full, dark beard and a balding head, spoke in a tone which rang out clearly across the enclosure and which was at once charged with energy and yet devoid of all emotion:

"Bring forth the accused!"

At this the two soldiers holding the unrecognizable object stepped forward, and Geoffrey saw that the thing supported between them was in fact an elderly man, so hunched over from age and pain that he seemed like no more than a cloth-covered stone, and so badly beaten that his face was little more than a formless pulp of oozing, bleeding tissue. Geoffrey staggered backwards a little at such a repulsive sight, and he wondered what evil this man must have committed to have deserved such a punishment. He wouldn't have to wait long to find out, he realized, as the two guards shoved the man down roughly onto a plain stone bench and pulled his arms across the matching table before it, tying his wrists and legs so that he remained in a half-sitting, half-crouching position with his lower body pinned to his seat and his arms stretched out in front of him. The Minister was handed a scroll by the officer Geoffrey had spoken to earlier, which he began to read from once the prisoner was secured.

"Hear this, all loyal citizens of Trastaluche who are gathered here today in the name of Social Order to witness the proclamation of the sentence to be carried out upon this accused here present in restitution for his crimes against the Decrees of the Seven Committees and the Trastalucherian Way of Life. I, Emore, senior Member of the Committee of Social Order, keeper of the peace of Spiraluche, and advisor to Jania, Chief of the Committee of Social Order, do hereby affirm the accused's guilt of the crime of treason of the second order against the Nation of Trastaluche. Therefore, I proclaim *you*, Eldrige of Trastaluche, former bard and Keeper of the Depository of Texts of the Committee of Spectacles, an Enemy of Trastaluche, and thereby strip you of your titles and occupation...."

The Minister went on for some length further, prattling on about the official titles of the accused and why and by whom he, Emore, was authorized to remove them and what all this meant, but Geoffrey listened to little of it, for upon hearing the name of the elderly man he realized that he knew him, and not just vaguely, but really rather well. For it was Eldrige whom Geoffrey had studied under for several seasons, gaining experience by reading, copying, and discussing different writings during his time as an apprentice bard working in the Depository of Texts. Eldrige had been the closest thing he had to a mentor during that time, and Geoffrey still remembered with fondness and quite a bit of gratitude the many afternoons he had spent with the grizzled old bard in the lower chambers of the Committee of Spectacles, reading through ancient books, laughing at their oddities, discussing their profundities, and puzzling over their trickier sections. In fact, he still employed many of the crowd-pleasing tricks that Eldrige had taught him in his own composition and performances. "What could the old man have possibly done to deserve this?" he wondered, and turned his attention back to the pronouncements of the senior Minister Emore.

> "... and hereby dissolve them for the foreseeable future, their dissolution a result of the formal accusation and guilt of the accused concerning the following crimes against Trastaluche: the owning and harboring of forbidden texts, foremost among them the *Pontilux Poems,* the *Rituals and Music of Hazcaluche,* the...."

"But he didn't know they were there!" Geoffrey wanted to cry out. His head was spinning once again as he contemplated with growing horror the scene unfolding before him. He was almost positive that Eldrige had no knowledge of the book which now sat only a few paces from Geoffrey; the younger bard only knew of its existence within the Depository due to the fact that he had discovered it, quite by accident, along with a few similar books in a secluded corner of the lower chambers while chasing down a rat with a broomstick. The book had scared him then as much as it scared him now, and he'd left it where he'd found it. As for the other books, why, Geoffrey had read the *Music of Hazcaluche* while training to be a bard! No one had ever told him it was a forbidden text; in fact, many of his instructors admitted to using and teaching from it frequently, albeit after doctoring the cover to change its name. "And anyway, even if it were, was the possession of forbidden books enough to merit this sort of brutal humiliation?" Geoffrey pressed his face up to the window again, his mind whirling as he tried to conceive of a plan to exonerate his former mentor.

"... in keeping with the Decrees of the Committees of Progress and Social Order, I order these and all books confiscated from the house and place of occupation of the accused to be burned, and their ashes scattered, so that such treasonous lies may no longer be preserved intact within the nation of Trastaluche. As for the punishment of the accused, the severity of his crime demands that I pronounce the following sentence: that his tongue be cut out and his fingers removed before being cast out into the streets, so that nevermore may he pollute our prosperous land with his treacherous deceits in writing or in voice...."

Geoffrey felt his throat constrict with disgust, and his body seemed unable to move as he heard the sentence being pronounced.

"It can't be possible!" he thought, "All that just for owning some books?? But this man served for years on the Committee of Spectacles; why, he was even its Chief Member for seven seasons! There's no way that he could be a traitor!"

He wanted to cry out in protest, but fear and the grotesque anticipation of what was about to happen kept his mouth tightly shut. In the courtyard below he could hear the soldiers pounding the butts of their spears against the flagstones in approval, while Geoffrey stood at the window, muscles rigid, his mind trying to grasp the scene unfolding before him. The noise from the soldiers died as suddenly as it had arisen, and the only sound was a quiet whimpering from the old man, insisting that this was all a mistake, claiming that he didn't know about the books, pleading for mercy, but all to no avail.

His feet frozen as if rooted into the ground, Geoffrey found himself unable to turn away as the guard who was designated to carry out the sentence stepped forward, wielding a pair of barbed tongs, a small metal contraption which Geoffrey didn't recognize, and a short, curved knife which glistened in the late morning sun as he approached Eldridge. It was the same broad-shouldered, small-eyed guard who had threatened Geoffrey earlier, and the bard now watched helplessly as he pulled the old man's head back and inserted the metal object he carried, which Geoffrey now realized was a modified clamp used to hold the accused's mouth open.

The guard bent over Eldrige, and Geoffrey saw the tongs reach down, clamp, and pull upward; then the knife flashed quickly in and out and the old man let out a guttural scream that was rapidly choked out by the gushing of his own blood, which filled his throat and came spilling out the sides of his mouth. The small-eyed guard dropped the tongs and tongue on the table without fanfare and released his grip on Eldrige's head, who immediately bent over and began coughing out massive globs of blood every bit as crimson as the tunics of the guards which surrounded him.

Geoffrey's throat filled with bile at the sight, and finally able to move, he slumped down beneath the window ledge and buried his head in his hands as the guard moved on to Eldrige's fingers. More screams filled the room where Geoffrey crouched, unable to go on watching, and based on the number of the cries and the length of time they went on for, he guessed that the guard wasn't doing an entire hand at a time. Geoffrey shuddered at the thought of what was occurring on the other side of the wall, and he pressed his palms against his ears in a vain attempt to blot out the screaming.

After what seemed to him to be a lifetime of ages, the cries ended, replaced only by a quiet weeping, and Geoffrey found the courage to rise again. The yard was silent once more apart from Eldrige's sobs of pain, and Geoffrey saw that one of the files of guards had dispersed and were now gathered near the low granite wall which separated the scene from the massive courtyard outside, breaking open the chests of books and tossing their contents onto a rapidly growing fire. Eldrige was bent over, still bound, his hands, face, and upper torso a mess of dripping blood. The urge to vomit surged within Geoffrey once more, and his knees began to feel weak. So focused was he on Eldrige that he failed to see the soldiers in the remaining row- those behind the prisoner- each of whom now held a loaded crossbow.

Neither Geoffrey nor Eldrige saw the arrows coming; there was only a sudden 'hiss, thwack!' and the old man went rigid, letting out one last cry as his back seemed to sprout in a forest of tiny, dead saplings.

Chapter VII

The Choice

Geoffrey reeled backwards, taken completely unaware by the on-slaught of cruel, barbed shafts which buried themselves into the back of his former mentor. Only then did the full brutality of the situation hit him: the Committee of Social Order had not told Eldrige that he was to be killed, allowing him to be tortured not only by the knife-wielding guard, but also with the fear that he would be cast out in the streets, unable to talk, to work, or to fend for himself. Instead, they had finished the job from behind, in the most cowardly way possible. Geoffrey sank into the chair in the center a room which was rapidly seeming more and more like a prison cell. He was shaking all over, although he couldn't tell if it was from the horror of what he had just seen or from the destruction of his entire world before his eyes.

If there had ever been a loyal citizen of Trastaluche, Eldrige would've been a shoo-in, Geoffrey thought. His long years of service on the Committee of Spectacles and as instructor to the countless young bards who had studied under him and who now roamed the streets and hills of Spiraluche and the surrounding towns, reciting and re-living Trastaluche's greatest moments, was evidence enough of the unmeas-urable contribution he had made to the Trastalucherian Way of Life.

"Even *if* he had known about the books," thought Geoffrey, "which I highly doubt, does such a small fault erase all that he did over the years?"

And then there were the unspeakable tortures which Geoffrey had witnessed, acts of bestial savagery which seemed far worse than anything he could have imagined from the Committees. It all seemed so surreal, so awful, that he could hardly believe it. Geoffrey moaned, letting his head down into his hands, wanting to hide from it all, when he was struck by another horrifying realization:

"It could have just as easily been me!" he exclaimed to himself. "After all, I came across the *Pontilux* in the Committee cellars all those years ago. What if someone had noticed?"

In fact, Geoffrey thought, it could *still* be him; had he not been reading the very same book in the company of several Enemies of Trastaluche only last night? He felt a sinking sensation in his chest, and suddenly he was very unsure of his decision to report what he had seen the day before. He shivered at the thought of himself in Eldrige's place, his face beaten beyond recognition; his hands stretched out in front of him awaiting dismemberment; his head forced back and his jaws pried open; his tongue hooked and yanked forward, the knife descending… He forced himself to stop, unable to contemplate what would happen next. Then, in a moment of revelation, he realized that he wasn't sure that he could bear to see such atrocities worked out on Ayila either, or on Trentius, or Vincente, or even Xavier, at least not without very hard proof that they had done much worse than Eldrige had, proof which he might suspect to exist but definitely didn't have.

It didn't seem human, he thought; none of it, none of what he had seen and heard and experienced at this place, felt the least bit human. He gave a guilty start as he heard voices somewhere outside and realized that he'd left the deadly *Pontilux Poems* sitting open on the table,

in plain view of anyone who walked in. He breathed a sigh of relief as
the voices passed by his doorway and continued on down the hallway;
then, he turned to the book in front of him. He was wondering where
on earth he could successfully hide it when a title from the open pages
caught his eye: *False Truths, Dying Life.*

His first impulse was to snort at the obviously flawed logic of the
followers of the Lord of Oppression and to continue searching for a
hiding spot for the book, but an unknown urge kept drawing him back
to its contents. Looking back in seasons to come, Geoffrey was never
quite sure why it called to him so strongly. Perhaps it was because at
that moment his own life was such a mixed-up disaster that everything
he'd once accepted as reality and truth was now thrown into doubt. Or
perhaps his addled brain just needed some sort of, any sort, of puzzle
to wrap itself around in order to distract itself from the horrible realities
it had just witnessed. Whichever it was, Geoffrey found his curiosity
irresistible, and after glancing around quickly to make sure he was still
alone, he set about reading the verses which bore such a contradictory
title.

> Beware a truth which shines like precious gems;
> for hardness, like a diamond lies within
> and crushes that from which its beauty stems.
> From such seduction, truth is often thin,
> and harbors evil things that dwell therein
>
> But hark the word which takes no brilliant stand,
> which to itself attention does not call;
> for that which needs no forces to command
> is truth that needs no falsehoods to enthrall.
> To such a truth, then lend your beck and call.

Beware a Life which Living does proclaim,
where Living is for Living, and no more.
For such a Life is Death by different name,
which gives no thought to after or before.
For Living is not Living and no more.

The words were dizzyingly twisted, and yet they seemed to make more sense to Geoffrey than any of the Decrees which he had observed being followed throughout the morning or the retribution he had seen carried out in the name of Trastalucherian Progress. For a fleeting moment, they even seemed to make sense out of the whirlwind of encounters Geoffrey had experienced during the last week. He recalled his despair in Muckland and his rescue by Xavier and his band, and he realized that he had in fact been kept alive precisely by this group of "dead" ones, this group of companions who by all accounts shouldn't be alive, and by all that Geoffrey had ever been taught, were the type of people who wallowed in death and malice.

And yet he had seen *none* of that in the smile on Xavier's wife as she watched the famished bard enjoy her baking, or in the joking tone of Vincente, or in the passion of Ayila, and he realized that Xavier was correct. There was *more*; he, Xavier, *was more*. He lived more, he accomplished more, and he meant more in every gesture than Geoffrey had ever thought possible. And as for what he had seen today… Geoffrey shuddered once again at the memory of the small-eyed guard who seemed just as capable of slicing out a man's tongue as informing a visitor that they needed the proper papers to enter, and of the toneless, impassive Minister who had not only condemned a man to torture and death but had intentionally made it as horrific as possible for the victim.

For all that the Committees claimed to be, for all the progress they said to uphold, and for all the bloodshed they claimed to have overthrown... *there* was death, Geoffrey realized; there in the yard right outside his window, but also in the eyes of nearly every guard and every officer and every Minister he had seen. And he wondered why he'd never noticed it before. In that moment, Geoffrey made a decision. It wasn't a rejection of the Trastalucherian Way of Life- he was still far too confused, far too frightened, and far too stuck in his ways to do such a thing- and neither was it an embrace of Xavier and the *more* he had promised. But it was a monumental choice for Geoffrey nonetheless, and he breathed deeply to steady his resolve.

"Whatever happens today, I won't say a word about Xavier and his band," he said to himself, "at least not yet. Maybe they truly are the lying spawn of demons and deserve to be tormented and killed, and maybe they're not... but I can't report them, not until I know more, not until I see for myself who they really are and what they stand for. If I make it out of here alive and well, I'll go back there tonight, and I'll bring this book with me and ask Trentius and Xavier and whoever else to tell me what this is *really* about; damned if they think I'm prepared or not! I need to know *more*.... "

In the distance, another door opened and shut, and Geoffrey heard voices heading his way once again. Stuffing the book down the back of his tunic, he sat up straight in his chair, thrusting back his shoulder blades so as to conceal the bulky object hidden between them. He had time to breathe deeply once more, and to notice, just for a heartbeat, a sense of peace and purpose which he had not experienced for a very long time, when the door opened and in stepped Emore, the same

Minister of Social Order who not an hour ago had ordered the torture and execution of Eldrige.

Geoffrey tried to mask the shock and fear which rose up within him; Emore was a senior Member of the Committee of Social Order and known for being extremely intelligent and relentless in his interrogations. He was not the sort of man Geoffrey had hoped to converse with under normal circumstances and especially not now that he had just witnessed the Minister's bloody handiwork in the yard outside. Emore strode toward Geoffrey, smiling, as he held out his palms in greeting.

"Ah! Geoffrey the bard, isn't it? I seem to remember you from the whole unpleasant incident with the vanishing house a few seasons ago. You struck me as an ambitious, clever sort of fellow then. Please do allow me to introduce myself: I am Emore, senior Member of the Committee of Social Order, keeper of the peace of Spiraluche, and advisor to Jania, Chief of the Committee of Social Order. Greetings and a prosperous morning to you! I do apologize for the wait; there were some routine chores I had to attend to before I could see you. Unfortunate I know, but it couldn't be helped. I trust you are doing well?"

The Minister's disarming smile and casual tone caught Geoffrey by surprise, and if he hadn't just witnessed the "routine chores" out his window, he most likely would have been flattered into telling Emore everything. As it was, the tension within him surged before such obvious lies, putting his entire body on edge. He swallowed and managed to return the gesture of greeting.

"Greetings and a prosperous morning to you as well, Minister Emore! Yes, I am Geoffrey, son of Joshua, former Bard of the Committee of Spectacles, keeper of the Official Tales, and twice honored for my service to Trastaluche and its citizens. May I say, it is an honor to meet you."

The routine of the words of greeting, which Geoffrey had uttered thousands of times throughout his life, helped him overcome his fear, and the stilted nature of the proper terms served as a mask to the awkward, stuttering croak which was all that he could muster. If Emore noticed anything off in the bard's behavior, he didn't show it. Rather, his smile broadened, and he sat down on top of the table, his body facing the door and his head turned to the side to gaze at Geoffrey.

"Why thank you, my good bard. Now, the captain of the guard- I think you met him on the way in- was telling me that you had the most interesting news for me, and I must say I can't wait to hear it. Why don't you tell me what you heard and saw and afterwards I'll ask some questions and we'll... discuss it for a while?"

"Well, it was nothing really...," stammered Geoffrey, his mind racing to come up with a lie that would be plausible enough to get him off the hook, mild enough that no one would follow up on it, and yet serious enough that Emore wouldn't be angered at Geoffrey for wasting his time. "You see, I was down at the fish-market first thing this morning, and I overheard two fellows arguing. One of them said something which I couldn't quite make out, but it sounded like the name of, you know... the name of Trastaluche before the War of Liberation, during the Time of Oppression and all that. Well, the other fellow got real angry and began shouting at him, and then a couple of other folks began to get involved, and I couldn't really see what was going on or hear real properly, you know? They all converged on the one fellow who had shouted the cursed name, and for a while there was a lot of hitting and punching and shouting, but when the dust cleared... the first fellow was gone. No trace of him at all; I swear it seemed just like magic. Well, I'm a little ashamed to say it, but I'm afraid I worked myself up into a real state of terror over it all, and thinking how important it was that someone in the Committees knew, I ran right up here as quick as I could. Didn't even think about going to a local chamber of Ministers until I was already here. I really didn't cool down and start to see things clearly till they showed me to this room and I had a bit of a nap. I'm terribly sorry if I've wasted your time, Minister Emore. You see, it all seemed so awful at the time that I thought it must be the work of, well, the Enemies of Trastaluche."

Geoffrey studied Emore's face as he added the finishing touches onto his tale, inwardly thanking his bard's ability to come up with a story on the spot. The minister stroked his beard, his smile fading somewhat, and Geoffrey could tell that he didn't quite buy it. "He might not know what's wrong," Geoffrey thought, "but he knows something's off." As if he could read the bard's thoughts, Emore stood suddenly and began pacing back and forth in front of Geoffrey as he addressed him.

"No, not at all, Sir Geoffrey. My time is never wasted in talking to a concerned citizen of Trastaluche. Now tell me, which fish market was this? As I'm sure you know, there are several in the lower city."

"It was the west market, Minister Emore. I go there almost once a week to purchase dried Lake-Haddock."

"I see, I see. And this commotion; you say many people were involved. Can anyone else bear witness to your story?"

"I'm sure they can, sir," replied Geoffrey, "but the thing is, most of them fled when they discovered the first fellow had mysteriously vanished, and I didn't stick around to ask questions myself." "That should be tough to prove false," he added to himself. There are always brawls going on in the western fish market, and people scatter as fast as they are able in the aftermath to avoid the patrols of the Ministers of Social Order."

"Of course, of course, I understand," continued Emore. "But, dear Geoffrey there's one thing I'm confused about. You see, the guards outside this building say that they told you to go to the chambers of one of the local Ministers of Social Order and tell them the story. I can understand your forgetfulness in coming here first, but why did you insist on staying after you were reminded of your options? And why did you say the local Ministers wouldn't believe you?"

Geoffrey felt his throat constrict with nervousness. This was his story's biggest hole, of course, but in the moment of telling he hadn't thought of any way to patch it. He let out what he hoped sounded like a nervous, embarrassed laugh and replied hesitantly:

"Oh, that. I'm very sorry Minister Emore. It's just I was so worked up that I didn't quite understand what they were saying

at first. It sounds silly, I know, but as I told you, I didn't realize
how foolish I was being until I had some time to reflect in this
room. As for that part about the local Ministers not believing
me..., I have to apologize again, I'm afraid. The truth is that I
was too scared to go back down near where it all happened, and
I thought that if I said what I said then the guards would have
no choice but to let me in...."

Emore nodded sagely and said that of course he understood, but
Geoffrey could see in his eyes that he still wasn't convinced. "He hasn't
caught me in the lie yet, though," reflected the bard. "As long as I don't
misstep then the worst he can do is have me reprimanded for wasting
his time... I hope." The book felt heavy and awkward against his sweaty
back, but he dared not shift, lest somehow it come loose and slide down
onto the seat of the chair with a thud. Emore stopped his pacing and,
sitting back down on the edge of the table, turned to Geoffrey, his face
plastered with a fake smile.

"Well, Sir Geoffrey, thank you for your diligence and... courage... in reporting this matter to us. We will of course look
most closely into *all* parts of it."

Emore's last words made Geoffrey shiver, and he realized that
Emore not only suspected that he was lying, but that there was much
more going on than Geoffrey was telling. The Minister, meanwhile,
continued as if he hadn't noticed a thing.

"Of course, if you were ever to witness something like that
again, or perhaps something a bit more... substantial, I do hope

you'd come back here and report it. You won't get in trouble for any part of it; I give you my word. Just tell the guards outside that you're acting on my orders, and there won't be any problem. That sort of thing would be greatly appreciated, of course. In fact, I expect it might be enough to get back your commission and perhaps even a chance at a chair on the senior Committee of Spectacles again. It makes keeping your eyes open very worthwhile, eh?"

"My... my commission?" Geoffrey stuttered, taken aback. He hadn't expected this, at least not until he had given the Committee of Social Order something concrete enough to lead to the apprehension of Xavier. For a moment he felt an almost inborn surge of ambition begin to rise up within him, but it got no further than the memory of Eldrige, mangled and bloody, his body riddled with arrows, before it dissipated. The performer in Geoffrey, however, did not.

"Why... why that would be ideal, Minister Emore! My thanks to you for such a generous offer; I will be more than sure to stay vigilant in my contributions to the progress of Trastaluche!"

He was laying it on a bit thick now, he knew, but he figured if he were really as addle-headed as the tittering citizen he was pretending to be, then his response would probably be something almost as loquacious.

"Fine, fine," Emore nodded and stood once more. "Well, Geoffrey of Trastaluche, it has been a pleasure, and I am... quite sure that we will meet again soon. I apologize that I must bid you farewell already, but there are certain urgent matters I must attend to. Be assured that if your… assistance is needed, we will know just where to find you. Take care, Bard, and remember my proposition to you. You seem like just the sort of person we could use on the Committee of Spectacles."

Geoffrey nodded his thanks and gave his goodbye, breathing a sigh of relief as the senior Member of the Committee of Social Order bowed to him and then swept out the door. No sooner had he exited, when a guard entered and informed Geoffrey that he was free to go, motioning at the bard to follow him to the exit. Geoffrey got up slowly, one hand placed discreetly behind his back so as to keep the book pressed into place, and thanked the guard in the same flattery-filled tone. Satisfied that the man in his care was going to follow without any trouble, the guard turned and started down the passageway, giving Geoffrey the precious seconds he needed to slide the book to his side, where he could keep it hidden and secure under his tightly pressed arm. "Almost there," he thought to himself. "Just don't get caught now, or it'll be the end of everything." His heart pounding, he followed the crimson-clad soldier down what now seemed to him to be the longest passageway in Trastaluche, until at last they passed through the looming bronze doors and out into the sunlight of early afternoon.

"Alright then, you're free to go," declared the guard, and took up his post outside the entrance again without a second glance at Geoffrey. Resisting the urge to break into a sprint, Geoffrey forced himself to bow toward the soldiers, knowing that anything short of a proper farewell might make them suspicious.

"My every thanks to you, sirs, for your aid to me in these matters. A very good and prosperous day to you all; I do hope I
shall have the honor of meeting you again."

Suddenly quite grateful that a proper Trastalucherian farewell
didn't involve any sort of gesturing with one's arms, Geoffrey turned
finally toward the open courtyard which lay before him, drawing in a
gulp of fresh air.

"Wait!"

The military-like command rang out from behind Geoffrey before
he had the chance to release the air in a massive sigh of relief. Adrenaline surging once more, he turned around slowly and saw that the
leader of the guards, the officer he had encountered earlier that morning, had followed him down the wide stone steps and was now striding
toward him, one hand on his sword belt. Geoffrey's blood froze, but he
did his best to fake nonchalance as he stood his ground and awaited the
soldier's approach, despite every fiber in his body screaming at him to
run. The captain of the guard pulled out a small leather pouch which
clinked as he tossed it at Geoffrey's feet.

"With compliments from Emore, senior Member of Social Order. He says to send thanks for your future cooperation and
hopes that this will benefit you and your endeavors."

Inwardly releasing his sigh of relief, Geoffrey smiled and thanked
the captain, bending over and trying to collect the pouch as naturally
as possible with his one free arm. However, it was only once he had left

the central courtyard of Spiraluche and blended in with the crowds of people bustling to and fro during their daily occupations that he finally exhaled externally, letting out the pent-up tension within him. Ducking quickly into a side alley, he removed the *Pontilux Poems* from under his tunic and continued on his way, concealing the book's faded title with his palm. As he wound his way out of the upper levels of Spiraluche, he smiled for the first time in hours, elated at his lucky escape from a place of so much bloodshed, and recognizing for the first time the peace that had driven his actions since encountering those lines of verse in a book which strangely enough seemed to him to be the herald of a new life, even in the midst of all the death connected to it.

And so it was that later that night, Geoffrey the bard found himself standing in the shadows of lower Spiraluche next to a certain brook, dressed in a dark tunic, trousers, and cloak, and carrying with him the forbidden *Pontilux Poems.* He waited expectantly, and not without a decent amount of nervousness, for a Patroller of Social Order whom he had never met to come by and inquire as to what he was seeking. Several hours passed as the night grew darker, but Geoffrey remained where he was, trusting that Trentius and Xavier would keep their word. Not long after moonhigh, a figure loomed out of the fog which had arisen from the creek bed and now drifted in whisps around Geoffrey's feet. The bard recognized the distinctive plumed helmet which the Patrollers of Social Order always wore, and he felt a surge of excitement course through him. The soldier noticed Geoffrey crouched in the shadows and moved toward him, his lantern raised to penetrate the mist.

"Oy! Who goes there? Name yourself, sir, and state your purpose! What in the name of all that is light are you doing lurking about in such darkness?? Come now, quickly, or I'll be forced to bring you in!"

Taking a deep breath, Geoffrey stepped out of the shadows and, spreading his palms in greeting, addressed the Patroller.

"A good evening to you, Sir, and may you have no cause for alarm. My name is Geoffrey of Trastaluche, and I come in search of Xavier."

Chapter VIII

The Explanation

It was dark once again in the life of Geoffrey the bard, but this was not the sort of dark which fills you with the terror of an unknown malice lurking in the shadows, or even the sort of dark which settles upon you, irresistibly, as your body draws its final, shuddering breath. Rather, this was a darkness of another sort: the type that stifles and confuses, that turns you round and round and obscures your way.

It was the darkness one finds when one is blindfolded and led, bumping and twisting, through an unknown tunnel, and it was in this darkness that Geoffrey found himself, being guided downward by the Patroller of the Committee of Social Order who was also secretly a friend of the traitor Xavier and his band. However, it was a darkness that quickly lifted when, upon emerging into the same underground craft-room which Geoffrey had visited the night before, the Patroller removed the bard's blindfold, and, with a word of farewell, disappeared quickly and quietly back into the passage to continue his rounds. Geoffrey thanked him as he went and then turned as a familiar voice called out.

"Geoffrey! So good to see you again!"

It was the scribe Trentius, who had been hard at work at his table in the center of the room before Geoffrey's entry, and now strode toward him, smiling. Geoffrey returned the greeting and the smile.

"And it is good to see you as well, Trentius. I've brought you a sort of gift, which I thought you might find useful…." He produced his copy of the forbidden *Pontilux Poems* from under his cloak, his smile spreading as the older scholar's eyes widened in shock.

"Is that…? But where on earth did you manage to find this? I've been searching everywhere for this text, and I truly thought I owned the only two copies which existed in this city…."

"Oh, it's nothing that special," answered Geoffrey, suddenly wondering how much about the morning's adventures he should recount. "It belonged to a teacher of mine, Eldrige of the Committee of Spectacles, who recently… passed away. I happened to come by when they were sorting through his books, and this was in amongst a stack of old ones which no one wanted. I recognized it from our conversation last night, and since no one else had laid claim to it, I… I thought it might be safe here. It's not as nice as yours, of course; I think it might have been a portable copy which Eldrige himself or maybe his mentor carried around in their younger days." ("I won't tell them about the close call this morning," he decided. "At least, not yet. After all, they might suspect I was in league with the Committee of Social Order, or that I'm too much of a risk for them to associate with, and then who knows what they might say or do. Best to keep it to myself, at least for a little longer.")

"Not as ornate, perhaps," answered Trentius, who was thumbing through the contents of his new treasure, his smile growing by the minute, "but it contains some pages which I'm afraid are quite damaged in my copy and almost impossible to read, and that alone makes it very valuable to me. My deepest thanks to you, Geoffrey; this really is a magnificent gift. But now, what can I do for you? I trust you've given more thought to the offer Xavier made you?"

"Yes," replied the bard. He took a deep breath and then said:

"I've thought quite a lot about, well, everything that has happened to me here, and although I'm still not quite sure what it all means and what it would entail, I'm ready to hear about that 'something more' Xavier mentioned. I... I don't know what the next step is to learning more about what it is you do and eventually joining all of you, but I want to begin it as soon as I can. Tonight, in fact, if that is possible."

"Tonight?" Trentius stroked his beard, looking Geoffrey over with a serious expression. "You must have come to some mighty sort of revelation if you've already reached that decision."

"You could say that," remarked Geoffrey, grinning ruefully. "It happened last night, in fact, when you told me that if I wanted to see you again to ask for Xavier..."

"Somebody say my name?" Xavier's question boomed across the busy confines of the storage chamber as he ambled toward Geoffrey and Trentius, a flour-stained apron covering his beige tunic which had become drenched with sweat from standing in front of the room's oven, where the leader had been busy preparing yet another batch of fresh bread to be distributed to the forgotten destitutes of Muckland.

"Geoffrey! It's good to see you! We hoped you'd come back, but I didn't expect myself to be the reason! Must be my impeccable sense of fashion, eh?" He gestured at his soiled outfit, chuckling at his own joke, and continued: "I jest of course, but I did hear you mention me. Did you have a question for me, then?

Geoffrey took another deep breath, this time to steady himself for the news which he both dreaded and yet desperately wanted to hear, the truth which had ruined his life when he had not known it and yet threatened to turn it upside down even more violently once he had heard it. But then he thought of the burning ruins of Xavier's home, the verses in the *Pontilux,* and the screams of the tortured Eldrige, and his resolve hardened.

"Yes, sir, I did, and please, I ask for your pardon in advance for any disturbance it may cause. You are Xavier of Trastaluche, correct?"

"Why, yes, of course, but I'm not sure what you are getting at by asking questions you already know the answers to."

Geoffrey ignored the response and concentrated on his next two questions, making sure they were phrased exactly how he wanted them to be. After he had left the Courtyard of Committees earlier that day, he'd made his way down to a series of dusty warehouses in the middle level of Spiraluche, which served as the Lesser Depository for the

Committee of Social Order. He had used the money Emore had given
him to bribe his way past the guards and into the stacks upon stacks of
scrolls, books, and parchments which contained the records of those
incidents the Committee had handled and were no longer being looked
into. There, after an hour or two of searching, he had located a small
number of parchments which addressed the raid on the home of the
Family Xavier and its consequences. He had studied the documents
thoroughly, reading them over and over again and racking his own
memory to re-familiarize himself with everything that had happened
leading up to and during that fateful night.

"Yes, yes, I'm sorry for that. What I meant was, are you Xavier
of Trastaluche, husband of Mariela and father of Vincente,
Elisheba, Raphael, and Helen, shop owner and seller of general
goods?"

Xavier's eyes darkened a little, and his face grew less carefree as he
responded.

"Yes, Bard, all of that is true as well, although I'm not entirely
sure how you are aware of it. And may I ask what the point of
all of this is? Why are you asking me these questions?"

Geoffrey gulped and, before he could stop himself, continued onward.

"My apologies again, good sir, but I have one last question if it
pleases you to answer. Are you in fact the Xavier who was accused by the Committee of Social Order of being an Enemy of
the highest level against Tratstaluche, whose house was subject

to a raid by Ministers of Social Order who were to carry out the execution and apprehension of you and your family, and whose home, by some strange magic, was completely destroyed? I'm sorry sir, but I must know: are you that Xavier of Trastaluche?"

The middle-aged man's face grew pale with shock for a moment, and even Trentius appeared unnerved. Then Xavier seemed to regain his wits, and looking straight at Geoffrey with eyes which burned with that strange intensity, he responded, speaking slowly and clearly.

"Yes, Geoffrey, I am that Xavier, although I am mystified as to how you might know it."

"I was there," blurted out Geoffrey, before realizing that at the moment he might look as if he were a spy for the Committee of Social Order or some other sort of undesirable presence. "Well, not there, exactly. I mean, I wasn't a part of the raid or the executions; I swear I wasn't! I was sent to write down what happened, only I didn't see what happened, not inside at least, and that's why they threw me out of the Committee of Spectacles and took away my bard's commission...."

Before anyone could stop him or accuse him of anything worse than the disgrace which he felt himself to be, Geoffrey launched into an explanation of his past: his achievements as a bard; how he came to be outside the house of the Family Xavier that night; what he had seen and hadn't seen; how the Committees, needing someone on whom to pin the blame, had cast him out; how he had sunk deeper and deeper until finally, one night, he had found himself face down in Muckland without a hope in the world, when he was saved by a group of shadows who

appeared and pulled him out of it. He didn't mention what had happened since, still feeling that it wasn't quite the right time, but from the
astonished faces of Xavier and Trentius, he guessed that his story was
not quite what they expected it to be.

"…And that's how I ended up where I was, but, you see, I didn't
put two and two together until last night, when Trentius mentioned your name for the first time, and I realized who you
were. How on earth did you get out alive? And not just you, but
your wife and Vincente and… are the rest of your children here
as well? How did you survive the executioners? I've seen how
they kill an Enemy of Trastaluche, and I don't see how anyone
struck with a death-blow of Lucherium could live. But yet, here
you are, with that scar on your neck and everything. Is this the
more you were talking about? Is that how you managed to overpower the Ministers?"

Xavier held up a hand to quiet Geoffrey's babbling. He looked the
bard over for a moment, as if sizing him up to determine whether or
not he was worthy- or ready- to hear the answers to his many questions.
Finally, he spoke to Geoffrey in a tone which bore a new respect but
also not a small amount of wariness.

"I'm ever more impressed at you, Geoffrey of Trastaluche, and
not just for figuring out who I am, although I must say that was
quite the feat. But even after knowing, you came back, a decision which I'm sure was not an easy one, based on what they
teach you about me and those like me. Now before I tell you

anything, you tell me: why did you choose to come here? Why not turn us in?"

Geoffrey opened his mouth to answer, but he found that he could not yet bring himself to talk about everything that had happened: about his suspicions of Xavier and his family, about his plan to sell them out and ensure his rise to prosperity again, and most of all about the death of an innocent Eldridge and the nightmare he had lived only that morning. He searched frantically for an excuse, but no sound came out. Xavier noticed his panic, however, and after a moment his eyes softened. Raising his hand once again, he waved away Geoffrey's pathetic attempts to speak.

"You don't have to answer that now, my friend. I can see from your eyes that whatever it was that guided your decisions, it has been a difficult load to bear. And yet here you are, and that alone is proof that you have borne it well. If you wish to know what really happened that night, we will tell you, but it is quite a long story, and there is much that needs to first be explained. Come and sit with Trentius and myself; I'll fetch us some cider, and he can begin. *But*," he added as he went, "I do expect an answer from you before I decide whether or not you can be admitted to our company."

Thanking Xavier for his understanding, Geoffrey followed the two men to the room's central table, where he and Trentius sat while the leader of the band excused himself to search for a barrel of cider and some mugs. Trentius pulled out the copy of the *Pontilux Poems* which Geoffrey had given him and began flipping through it. Geoffrey

thought that he had perhaps forgotten about Xavier's promise of starting the story without him, but as he opened his mouth to say something, the elderly scribe placed the book onto the table and turned to
look at Geoffrey.

"So, you wish to know the truth, do you? About what happened
that night?"

"Yes, please, and if it's not too much trouble," answered
Geoffrey, "about many other things, too. About what you do
here, about who you really are...."

"Patience, patience," replied Trentius, rocking back and
forth slightly in his chair. "What you ask for is no easy task,
both for the teller and for the listener. And I can guarantee that
what you hear tonight will not be easily forgotten, nor can it be
heard without effect. Are you positive that you want me to continue?"

Geoffrey wasn't sure what "cannot be heard without effect" meant,
but he had made it this far, and he had promised himself that he wasn't
leaving until he knew what was going on.

"Yes, I'm sure."

"Very well then." Trentius picked up the *Pontilux Poems*
from the table once again and leaned back in his chair. "The
truth of all of this starts very long ago, even before the creation
of this land, in fact. Yet most all of it is contained, in some way
or another, in the book which is in front of you. Did you read
any of this before you gave it to me?"

"A little," Geoffrey confessed. "Just whatever page it was opened to. Not this part," he said, gesturing to the page which Trenitus showed him.

"This 'part,' Sir Geoffrey, is the beginning of the *Pontilux*, and it recounts the tale of the beginning of the land that is now known to be Trastaluche, the beginning of the Era of Joaquin, and the beginning of Lucherium. And that, my dear bard, is where we must start if you are to truly understand what you wish to know. Now, I can tell you what it says, of course, but you know as well as I do that verses such as these contain much more than the words which form them. Together they have a life all of their own, a life which has rhythm, movement, and spirit and which can reveal to the reader much, much more than what it merely says. And so, if you don't mind, I'd rather read it to you, at least to start anyway."

Geoffrey nodded his assent, settling back in his own chair with nervous anticipation.

"This section, I'll have you know, is called, simply enough I suppose, *The Story*, and it speaks of the Author and of the coming to be of all that is. Ready yourself, bard."

> Before this Story, and before all stories,
> before the days of legends, quests, and tales,
> before man's life, his triumphs, and his glories,
> speaks Author, and the Story thus unveils:
> the Story of man's hopes, joys, fears and worries,
> before which other story fades and pales.
> The tale of Light, which Life does bring to form;

writes Author, then, the drama to perform.

Speaks Author so: Light all things shall sustain,
for Light gives sight, that Story may be viewed.
Thus Light to Life gives wisdom to explain,
and Life that welcomes Light sees power imbued.
Thus man who lives in Light all goods shall gain,
for Life in Light is Life in all renewed.
For Living is in Light and Light in Life,
and man who has not both is doomed to strife.

Life then, writes Author, shall give rise to all,
for Life is that which grants each being design.
From crying babe to towering mountain tall
so shapes each feature, Life, with sight divine.
Through Life, Light gains expression to enthrall;
through Life, the precious gem, shall Light then shine.
Thus mingle Life and Light in all and one,
and tale which tells not both cannot be spun.

So Author pens, that Story might reflect,
that Life and Light divided cannot be,
and so that man might not their bond reject
a Guide to him, the Author did decree,
in whom their marriage Light and Life perfect;
through whom man and man's mission shall agree.
A guide which teaches Life its Light to find
and man to live with brilliance on his mind.

Thus writes the Author, Light and Life extend
to play their parts as given by their end;
that Guided, man in beauty might ascend.

Silence followed, as the final verses which Trentius had recited faded into memory. And in this silence Geoffrey sat, not quite understanding what he had just heard, yet transfixed by its beauty all the same, and unwilling at first to break the stillness which to him seemed a part of the stanzas that preceded it.

"Well?" asked Trentius, turning from the *Pontilux* to face Geoffrey once again. "What do you have to say to all of that?"

"I… I'm really not quite sure," answered Geoffrey, struggling to piece together what he had just heard. "It's all very beautiful of course, but what does it have to do with Xavier and the Committees of Trastaluche and Lucherium and all that?"

"*What does it have to do??*" spluttered Trentius, more worked up with excitement than true exasperation. "Why, it has *everything* to do with it, because this, *this,* is how it all began, eras and eras ago. Do you not see?!"

"I'm sorry; I'm afraid not," apologized Geoffrey, "at least, not clearly, anyway. It's all just a bit too much to take in, I guess. What does all that talk about Life and Light and an Author *mean* anyway?"

"What does it *mean??*" Trentius started spluttering again, his face turning red with emotion, but then he caught himself and, calming down somewhat, let out a deep sigh.

"Yes, well, I suppose I ought to apologize too. After all, it's not as if you would have heard any of this before tonight. Let me start over from the beginning and see if I can't clear things up. Now, as the legend you just heard goes, before all of this- the world, humans, Trastaluche- existed, there was a Being of some sort which we call the Author. No one knows who the Author is or even His real name, of course, but we call whoever it was the Author, because He "wrote," or "fashioned," if you will, the story of, well, everything, including the land which we now call Trastaluche, although since its beginning until the fall of Joaquin it was known by its first name: Haczaluche, a name which I'm sure you've heard, although probably less and less these days. Are you following so far?"

Geoffrey nodded eagerly. "Yes, thank you, but what about the Life and Light the poem mentions so many times? What do they mean?"

"Ah, very good! You've hit upon a key point there. My dear bard, the Light and the Life are what forms *us*, or at least a great deal of us, and not just us, but everything else besides. Did you not listen to the verses? *Life then, writes Author, shall give rise to all/ For Life is that which grants each being design/ From crying babe to towering mountain tall/ So shapes each feature, Life, with sight divine.* Life, my good sir, is what we might now call all existence, but not so much in general as in every unique existing being. It does much mean any certain movement, such as swimming or breathing or thinking, as it does the existence of a particular object as itself. Your Life, of course, is different from mine, which is quite different from that of fox, or a bush, or even the "life" of a boulder. Life is thus universal, for if you exist, you have "life" in that sense, but it is also very much personal, for the way that you exist is unique to you. And as for Light, well there you see why we must go all the way back to the beginning of things to answer your questions. For Light, my dear Geoffrey, is Lucherium itself."

Trentius stopped for a moment, looking rather pleased at his explanation, and it was only when he noticed Geoffrey's blank look that he realized that the bard still lacked a decent notion of what on earth he was talking about.

"Don't tell me," he smiled; "you're about to ask what on earth Lucherium is. Dear me," he complained, when Geoffrey nodded apologetically, what *do* they teach you these days?"

Geoffrey, feeling a little defensive and wishing to prove that he knew something after all, spoke up.

"Oh no, I have heard of it actually. It's just so rare that few people speak of it; only the most advanced Members of certain Committees are able to wield it. But I saw it used that night, at Xavier's house. I'm not sure exactly what sort of magic it *is*, of course, but it appears to be very powerful...."

"No, no, no!" burst out Trentius. "Magic?! Why you literally could not be further from the truth of things! Lucherium isn't magic at all! Is that what those blasted idiots at the Committees want you to think they're performing?!"

Geoffrey sat up in shock, not so much due the scribe's outburst as to the ease with which he hurled insults at the highest power of Trastaluche. He started to apologize, but Trentius had already cooled off and waved away Geoffrey's attempts.

"No, no, my friend, it is I who need to be apologizing again. As you can see, I'm quite… enthusiastic about this topic, and it was wrong of me to direct my rantings in your direction. I do hope you weren't offended."

"Not at all," answered Geoffrey, who noted with some interest that the elderly scribe's remorse came not from his badmouthing the Committees, but from his concern for Geoffrey's own wellbeing. It was a novel concept to him, and he found that he quite liked it. "But please," he asked, "do continue, for I really have no idea what Lucherium is."

"Ah, yes. Now, I can't give you a simple definition for all that it is, but I can tell you this much: if Life is particular existence, as we said, you might think of Lucherium, or Light, as the *Pontilux* names it, as the energy which allows such existence to be. Lucherium is in one sense the fabric of reality itself, my good bard; it is the substance from which Life- or existence- rises, and it is what Life gives form to. It is a mystical energy which flows directly from the Author himself, just as Life is a mysterious "becoming" which has the same origin. Imagine, if you will, that each of us is a particular piece of clothing, made up of our own unique patterns and stiches. Well, that unique pattern is your "life," you might say, whereas the cloth from which we are all cut is our "Light," which we call Lucherium, and the tailor is the Author. Lucherium is thus our link to the Author, to His Being and to the Story which includes each one of us. It's more than that, of course, but trying to understand it all would be like trying to explain the Author Himself: a fruitless and arrogant effort on our part, doomed to failure. But, my good Geoffrey, it is most certainly *not* magic, for magic, as they normally call it, is something otherworldly, or unnatural. And Lucherium is supremely natural. Do you understand?"

"I think I'm beginning to," replied Geoffrey, "but there's a few things I'm still not sure on. First, if Lucherium is, as you call it, the Light of reality, then why can't everyone use it? And how come the Committees are able to harness it so well and with such power?"

"They don't harness it, not really anyway. They just want you to think they do." This time it was Xavier who responded, as he made his way back to the table with several mugs of steaming cider.

"What do you mean, the Committee Members don't harness Lucherium?" asked Geoffrey, perplexed. "What do you call what they did to your house, and what they use at the public executions?"

"Oh, they use it in a sense," replied Trentius, "but not in the way that you think. But we haven't quite reached the War of Liberation in our little tale, and as to why everyone can't use Lucherium.... Well the simple answer is that before the fall of the Lord Joaquin everyone *could*."

"They... what?!... but if that's the case, how did Trastivo and the Committees ever take power? And if everyone could use it, why can no one use it now?"

"Your questions, dear Geoffrey," broke in Xavier, "are excellent ones, and they do you credit. But perhaps let's save them for a little while longer; I do believe that Trentius was about to explain some of them."

"Oh yes, of course," apologized Geoffrey. "Do please continue."

"Quite all right," said Trentius, "and I promise I will answer them all in good time, but there's one more character we've yet to discuss: Joaquin, Lord and Guide of Hazaluche, of whom the *Pontilux* speaks when it declares: *A Guide which teaches Life its Light to find/ And man to live with brilliance on his mind.* Joaquin, my dear Geoffrey, really is the key to the whole story. For it is *in Him* that, as the poem goes, *their marriage Light and Life perfect,* and it is He who was sent by the Author to teach man how to see and to harness the power of Lucherium. Am I making sense so far?"

At Geoffrey's nod, Trentius continued.

"Good! Now listen: the Committees will tell you all sorts of lies about the reign of Joaquin. I believe they call it the Time of Oppression, do they not? And they claim that under Him each man and woman was tied to their lot in life, a lot they didn't choose and from which they could never advance?"

"Yes," replied Geoffrey, "that's more or less correct. And that he hid the true power of Lucherium from his subjects, which is what Trastivo and his followers discovered. At least that's how the story goes."

"Yes, and a great bit of hogwash it all is. The truth of the matter is that Trastivo and the first Committee Chiefs were mistaken as to the true nature and use of Lucherium. Now, if you remember, I told you just now that Lucherium and Existence, or Light and Life as our poem calls it, are "married" so to speak? That is, their "being" is quite intimately intertwined, because Lucherium is the fabric of reality, and existence is its 'expression' in 'real things,' you might call it. Well, all of that is really rather important, and it's what Trastivo didn't understand. You see, if Lucherium is so bound up in existence and reality, then it can only be harnessed *in service* of a reality which is already there, a reality which, may I remind you, is the Story of the Author and the guidance He provided through Joaquin. Are you still following?"

"I believe I am," answered Geoffrey with some hesitation, "although I'm not sure where this is all going yet or what it all quite means."

"Why, what it *means*," answered Trentius, "is that Lucherium isn't a magic that you harness to do strange and unnatural things; it's a deeper connection with reality, with life *itself*, and one that makes you *more real, more alive.* You can't just up and decide to harness Lucherium to fly, because you, good bard, can't fly in the first place. And you can't just up and decide to use it to make yourself rich, because humans can't spew gold out of their orifices, no matter how hard they try. 'It isn't natural,' is what people would say if that happened, and they are exactly right. The 'natural' way of things is what the OverLaw, as they call it, declared, and its contents are what occupies most of the *Pontilux*. However, it's not so much a series of restrictions as a description of how reality *is,* so that people might know how better to harness Lucherium. Now, the Committees twist this in every which direction, of course, in their silver-tongued waxing about the slavery of man under the Lord of Oppression, but all they're really saying is that under Joaquin, people *knew* who they were and what they were made for. And let me tell you, no one who has ever lived the life of a man would settle for that of a pig, even if he had the option to choose the latter, just like a pair of pants functions best doing what it was made to do: being a pair of pants. Use it as much else and not only will it not work nearly as well, but the fabric will wear out and tear much more quickly than usual. Now, when I told you that everyone could harness Lucherium before the fall of Joaquin, I was telling the truth. But the *way* one harnesses it and *what* one uses it for, if you can even say that, is to do *human* things, and to do them *moreso,* or better if you will -although that doesn't quite capture what I'm saying- than ever before. And when you did use Lucherium, not only did you become 'better' at whatever it was you were doing, but *you* became *more you* as well; more human, more beautiful, more intelligent...."

"Ahh, I think I'm starting to understand," answered Geoffrey. "So you, Trentius, might harness Lucherium in your work as a scribe and in doing so produce the most beautiful scrolls ever copied down. Is that correct?"

"Exactly! Now you're catching on quickly. And not only that, but *I* would become *more* of a scribe, *more* of a human, and *more* of myself too. And if flying would help me to do all that, then I could use Lucherium to fly as well! Not for its own sake, of course, but experienced wielders of Lucherium have been known to find a way to achieve any real goal, no matter how impossible it seems, provided it is in accord with the Story the Author has written. Before the fall of Joaquin, Lucherium could be harnessed this way by anyone who was 'being' *really human,* or really a mother, or a husband, or a blacksmith, or any sort of thing which *really was* to be."

"But..." said Geoffrey, "and forgive me for repeating myself, if that's the case, then how do people like Trastivo and the Ministers use Lucherium to kill prisoners or to raid the houses of the Enemies of Trastaluche? Is all of that "part of reality," too?"

"That's a rather damning question, isn't it? And lucky for you, we've finally arrived at the answer, so I don't need to beg Xavier to shut you up again," grinned Trentius. "But what he said earlier was right; they don't really harness Lucherium. You see, if you were to try to use Lucherium, to say, hold a bucket of water upside-down above your head, it wouldn't work and you'd end up soaked; levitating water just isn't a part of everyday reality and no amount of you wishing it was will make it so. You heard the same thing only a few minutes ago in the poem- *that Light and Life divided cannot be.* But if you, say, tried to use Lucherium to influence another person to fall prey to your deceit, or to break into a home and steal from or harm its inhabitants; why that's another thing altogether. Some actions just aren't a part of who we are and the Life we live in. Other things- such as the killing you described by the Ministers of Social Order- are totally against it. And trying to harness the fabric of reality to damage that very same reality goes just about as well as you'd expect: people have seriously injured or even killed themselves trying to do so. Now, as I said before, Trastivo and his followers believed that you could fashion Lucherium to do anything, even to change reality to be however you wished

it to be, and that Joaquin was hiding the true power of Lucherium from his subjects."

"Wait a moment," broke in Geoffrey, "but if what you're
saying is true, then when Trastivo and the Committee founders
tried to seize power, wouldn't they all die if they tried to use
Lucherium? Or at least be defeated by those who could use it?"
"And is death not a part of our reality, Geoffrey?"

Trentius' voice was suddenly horribly serious, and he stared at the bard
as if both their lives depended on his answer.

"Why... yes, I suppose it would be, in a sense at least," responded Geoffrey uncomfortably. Although he hated to admit
it to himself, he'd never really taken the time to contemplate
death and what might or might not exist beyond it. "But what
does that have to do with anything?"

"What if you wished to turn against it? What if, in your efforts to rupture reality, you strayed so far that you stepped beyond the realities of death and life?"

There was silence in the room, and Geoffrey was unsure of how to
answer. Finally, it was Xavier who spoke, motioning to Trentius that he
would continue now, and sliding the other man's untouched mug of
cider closer to him.

"Geoffrey, what Trastivo and his followers learned was not
a harnessing of Lucherium. They acquired the art of *voiding* it.
The power that you see them wield is not the use of any mystical
energy; rather, it is the destruction that occurs if you rip

everything – every scrap of life, every piece of existence, right down to almost, but not quite, the smallest bit of reality itself- from a place and watch the things around it collapse into the void you created. It is an anti-Lucherium, if you will, and although it is extremely powerful, its use comes at an incalculable cost. You've doubtless heard the rumors that Trastivo and a select few of his inner circle, those who can most fully harness this 'voided Lucherium,' are so powerful as to seem almost immortal? Well, the truth is far worse. They've stepped so far beyond the bounds of "the real" that they've passed beyond the boundary between life and death itself. To void the fabric of reality is to step into the void yourself, and the further you go, the less *real* you become. You might say that Trativo and his inner circle aren't alive enough to die. They aren't dead, of course, and they can never quite annihilate themselves and the world around them so completely as to entirely remove Light and Life, but they aren't quite alive either, and they definitely aren't human in the way we think of it. And it's worse than that, because the voids they create suck the life out of everything around them as well, keeping anyone who wanted to use Lucherium from being able to harness it, as if they had a lead curtain draped over the whole of Trastaluche and no Light could get in. It's a terrifying thought, isn't it? They've given themselves over to nothingness, and, in the end, that's why all they preach is Progress."

Geoffrey nodded in agreement, inwardly shuddering at the horror of such a state of existence. It was a terrifying state indeed, and, what was more, he now realized, it was the state which he had seen and felt while in the presence of Emore that very morning.

"And is that how Trastivo was able to destroy Joaquin, then?" Geoffrey asked. "by 'voiding' himself?"

"Now who said anything about destroying Joaquin? We only said that Trastivo and the Committee founders used the power they gained to overthrow Joaquin's reign, not Joaquin himself."

"But," Geoffrey protested, "they *did* destroy him, didn't they? It's like the tales say: Trastivo and his band combined their power and, in one unforgettable assault, toppled Joaquin from his throne and pinned him to the wall of his own great hall with a thousand spears before splitting open the earth itself to swallow his palace whole. That part of the story can't be false, can it? After all, the palace isn't here, and no one is using Lucherium these days. And anyway, if Joaquin were still around, wouldn't He be fighting back?"

"But He *is* fighting back, my dear Geoffrey," replied Trentius. "And as for no one using Lucherium these days, why, I don't know wherever you got that idea. You said it yourself only a few minutes ago: I harness Lucherium in my work as a scribe."
"You what?!"

"We all do, in fact," said Xavier, "in everything we do. Isn't it a little obvious? I mean, you can see for yourself the quality of every last piece of work in this room."

Geoffrey glanced around him, acknowledging once again the sheer beauty of the jars, chairs, rugs, and other objects which surrounded him. It made sense, he thought, but still...

"But I've *watched* you all work, and everything you do seems so, so..."

"Human? Real? But isn't that the point? Remember what I just told you about how harnessing Lucherium works," chuckled Trentius.

"But how do you access it with Joaquin, well... vanquished? And what exactly did you mean when you said He wasn't destroyed? You're not saying that He's alive?"

Xavier and Trentius exchanged glances, and there was a pause before the latter responded.

"Geoffrey, do you remember the verses in the *Pontilux* which speak of Joaquin? *A Guide to man, the Author did decree /In whom their marriage Light and Life perfect.* It is in Joaquin that both Light and Life, Lucherium and Existence, are *most,* or *fullest.* They are "married" within Joaquin, so to speak, because they are so perfectly intertwined and so perfectly *themselves.* Now, do you seriously think that anyone, even Trastivo and his followers, could completely destroy the perfection of Life and Light Himself? Disembody Him, maybe. Topple His reign in this land, most certainly, especially if, as was the case, many of His subjects succumbed to the lure of Progress and joined the ranks of Trastivo, and many more succumbed to laziness or fear and simply did not or could not defend themselves and their way of life. But destroy Him? That's like asking if you could completely annihilate reality and existence, and while you can get close, you can never quite get there, because if you did, you wouldn't be around to do it."

"So the Lord Joaquin *is* still alive then?" Geoffrey's head was spinning from this realization, and he felt overwhelmed by the life-altering reality which loomed in front of him.

"Well *of course* He's still very much alive! Haven't you been listening?! He's the perfection of Life and Light itself!" Trentius' voice was once again trembling, this time with enthusiasm, exasperation, and something else besides: an emotion which Geoffrey couldn't give a name to at that moment, but which seemed to be a mix of desire, hunger, and delight. "And to answer *how*," he continued, as if sensing Geoffrey's question, "well, if Trastivo and his followers are not *alive enough* to die, you might say that Joaquin is *too alive*, or too bound up with Light, Life, and even the Author Himself, to stay dead. In fact, if the goal of Trastivo's servants is to void themselves like him and to 'a-void' death in that way, you might say that the goal of the Followers of Joaquin- such as myself and Xavier- is to unite ourselves with the source of Light and Life so fully that when death comes, we too are able to move beyond it and into the *too alive* of the Author and His companion Joaquin. I'll bet they don't teach you *that* at Bard school these days, eh?"

Geoffrey, who had never given the idea of an afterlife any real amount of thought, was too stunned to process a question of such

magnitude. Instead, trying to steer the conversation in a more compre-
hendible direction, he asked:

"But… but He's still *gone,* isn't He? Like, He might still be
alive, but He isn't ruling Trastaluche anymore…."

"Oh, He's still very much present; even here. *That* I can
promise you," replied Xavier, "although not in the way that you
think. In fact, before you go any further, I think you ought to
meet Him. Would you like that?"

"Like that??" Geoffrey was dumbstruck at the question. He didn't
really know how to respond. On one hand, nothing sounded more terrifying. After all, this was the Lord of Hazcaluche they were speaking
of, and even if he was not the tyrant the Committees painted him to be,
he was still without doubt an incredibly dangerous being. And yet, on
the other hand, how could anyone say 'no' to such an opportunity?

"Why, yes, I suppose I would. You could arrange that?"

"This very morning," said Xavier; "in fact, we ought to be
heading that direction straightaway if we want it to occur. But
I have to warn you, Geoffrey: this encounter will not be what
you expect, and once you witness what you will see tonight,
there will be no going back to your former way of life. It will
also no doubt seem strange, and quite possibly terrible, to you.
Now, I tell you this not to drive you away but so that you might
come before him with courage in your heart."

"What… what exactly do you mean?" asked Geoffrey, dis-
concerted. "What sort of audience is this?"

"That you shall soon see for yourself," promised Trentius, "but what I will tell you now is this: when the forces of Trastivo assaulted the stronghold of Joaquin in this very city, and when they were on the point of triumphing, Joaquin, knowing some- how that this was all to pass, added one last section at the end of the *Pontilux*. This section contains the words whereby the Rite of Lucherium can be invoked, which is the way Joaquin arranged for those who were loyal to Him to harness the Au- thor's mystical energy, even in His absence. It is a way inacces- sible to Trastivo and the Committees, and it allows us not only to harness Lucherium, but to do so in a manner and in a meas- ure which has never been seen before. The Followers of Joaquin, or rather *we* and the others, are a small part of His sol- diers, the ones who chose to stay behind when He was over- thrown and the remnants of His army were driven across the eastern border and into the Volunaltus Mountains. We keep alive in this land the Way of Life which He taught, striving to follow it to the utmost, so that we might someday arrive at its conclusion of never-ending Light and Life in unity with their very source. And if, dear Geoffrey, you choose to pledge your allegiance to Joaquin, Lord of Hazcaluche, and to his Way of Lucherium, you shall be a part of that same mission as well. *That* is who we truly are and that is what we do."

Geoffrey sat electrified, listening to Xavier, who with his words had once again destroyed the very foundation of the bard's life, but this time had promised to rebuild it in a manner far grander and more luminous than before if the news he spoke was in fact true. And the most amazing thing for Geoffrey was that, despite the fact that only a week ago he would have dismissed all of this as sheer nonsense or even treason, he now found himself incomprehensibly and irresistibly attracted to the strength of the words that had been uttered. He was still not sure about it all, but he felt at the very least a sort of affection toward what was being said, and his mind hungered for much, much more. He could have sat there for hours ruminating over all he had heard, but then Trentius and Xavier stood.

"It is almost time to be off if you are resolved to come with us, Geoffrey. Have you any more questions for us?"

"Just one," answered Geoffrey. "At the house that night. You never told me what happened. How did you escape? I know what that scar you wear means; you were struck with the death-blow of the Committees."

"Ah yes," said Xavier. "My apologies, I had completely forgotten about your first question. Well, as you have just heard, Lucherium empowers a person to be in reality as perfectly as they can be, and the reality of it is that I am a husband and a father whose task it is to protect my family from harm. Harnessing Lucherium in such a dire situation can be very effective indeed and can grant the wielder almost unlimited powers to achieve his aims, powers which can include the ability to confront and overcome entire squadrons of enemies singlehandedly. Hence the annihilation of the house and the defeat of the Ministers within it, while my family and I were kept safe."

"That makes sense," acknowledged Geoffrey, "but I still don't understand how you escaped the killing blow of the Ministers so that you were alive to be able to do so. I mean, Lucherium didn't make you immortal, did it?"

"Not exactly," laughed Xavier, "at least not in that sense. But you are right; had I been hit with the full blast of such a blow, I would not be alive to tell you this story today. Thankfully though," he grinned, "I was not the only Lucherium user there. It was my wife who protected me; she was able to partially shield us in the few moments which we had before the Ministers moved in, and that is quite honestly what saved me and our children. It wasn't enough to completely deflect the death-blow, but it was enough to diminish its potency to the extent that I was able to overcome my injuries and fight back. The Committees completely ignored her, and yet she is more adept than I am at harnessing and wielding Lucherium. In fact, I may be the leader here in terms of organizing the nightly activities and directing them, but when it comes to what really matters, the one to follow is most definitely my wife. But come now, much work remains to be done tonight, and there is much more of us that you need to see."

Chapter IX

The Encounter

The tunnel through which Trentius and Xavier guided a once again blindfolded Geoffrey led in an entirely different direction than any he had taken before. Its many curves befuddled the bard so that he wasn't sure exactly where they were headed, but one thing had remained consistent during the entirety of their journey. They were climbing steeply uphill, which meant they were moving toward the center of the city and the Courtyard of Committees. Geoffrey felt a growing sense of confusion as this became ever more apparent. He had no desire to set foot anywhere near the Courtyard again, even if he was underneath it, and he seriously doubted that anything that went on remotely close to it could happen without the knowledge of the ever-watchful Committees of Progress and Social Order. And yet they continued onward, ascending ever higher, until at last the bard's blindfold was removed as they arrived in a roomy chamber, which Geoffrey thought looked like a natural cave, probably discovered by chance when the followers of Joaquin were first beginning to expand their tunnel complex. It was lit only by a few torches which dotted the wall nearest to Geoffrey, revealing several other dark, gaping holes which no doubt led to other hideaways.

"Is this the place?" he whispered. He felt rather disappointed at the general lack of grandness around him. It really was nothing but a simple cavern, smaller and less spectacular than even the craft-room they had come from.

"This?! Hardly. Patience, by dear bard," answered Xavier from somewhere ahead of Geoffrey. "Follow my voice; don't worry, the floor is level and there is nothing to run into."

Geoffrey stepped forward into the blackness of the room and inched his way blindly across it, guided by the occasional calls of Xavier ahead of him and Trentius behind, until he felt the elder's hand grab his own and steady him.

"Just ahead now. Prepare yourself."

And with that, Xavier reached out to push open a massive oaken door which stood only inches from Geoffrey's face, cloaked in the darkness of the antechamber. Geoffrey stepped out into a different sort of place altogether, a place which he recognized instantly from drawings and paintings and poems: it was the Great Hall of the Lord Joaquin, which the earth had indeed swallowed but not destroyed.

His eyes widened as they adjusted to the soft golden light of pre-dawn which filled the room, filtering down in dozens of tiny beams streaming through hidden shafts in the tall, pointed ceiling which was held up by graceful, sweeping arches perched upon rows of stately columns. The hall was massive, almost the size of the Courtyard below which it lay and was swathed in a shadow that Geoffrey had to strain to pierce. From the little he could see, the walls appeared ornately paneled and inlaid with images of trees and scrolls and fair figures with swords and bows, and the floor was tiled with an obsidian of deep, clear black, streaked with veins of gold and silver and red. The ceiling, in contrast, was covered with gold, and it gleamed dully in the morning twilight, helping to illuminate the fact that the hall was empty and bare save for two things. The first was the presence of several large bronze vessels which were dotted here and there throughout the chamber, and the second was a raised dais at its far end, upon which sat an old, weathered stone table which contained a single book, and behind it a glorious throne, splintered and cracked down the middle. Above the dais and the table Geoffrey could just make out a looming, undefined shape which jutted out from where the rear wall met the ceiling of the Great Hall, and from which protruded a multitude of thin, spine-like somethings.

"Sit here and wait a bit," Trentius beckoned to a small stone bench which was nestled up against the foot of one of the rear columns. "Xavier and I have to depart to prepare for the Meeting, but we will return shortly. Until then, keep your wits and your courage about you."

And with that they were gone, exiting out of the door which Geoffrey now saw was one of three dominating the lower regions of the near wall. He sat on the stone bench and waited for something to happen, his breath seeming loud and out of place against the immense silence of the hall.

The sun was beginning to rise, and the angled beams of light began to brighten and shift their illuminating gaze from the grand hall's center to its far end. Quite suddenly all three sets of doors at the entrance of the chamber swung open, revealing rows upon rows of hooded figures, clad in robes of silvery grey, many carrying torches and goblets. They processed silently into the chamber, in columns as smooth and straight as the one below which Geoffrey was seated, until they reached the foot of the table and the throne. Then, they filed off to either side of

the central pathway, forming ranks upon ranks which faced the dais
and the jumbled, spiked mass looming above it. Whether it was the uniform dress of the participants or some other trick Geoffrey did not
know, but his eyes seemed cloaked in a sort of mist, as if he couldn't
quite glimpse what was really going on in front of him. A voice rang
out from somewhere around Geoffrey, shattering the stillness, and then
another joined it, and another, until the hall was filled with song,
strange and sweet and sad, which at one moment seemed like the most
beautiful piece of music in the world, and the next moment seemed to
not quite fit within Geoffrey's mind no matter how hard he tried, as if
a certain chord or harmony was somehow off. The lyrics affected him
the same way too; Geoffrey could understand every word which was
being chanted, but try as he might, he couldn't make heads nor tails of
it. As the music swelled, several hooded figures plunged their torches
into the large bronze vessels arrayed about the hall, and which Geoffrey
now realized must hold some sort of incense, for upon receiving the
flames, towering pillars of smoke began to curl up toward the ceiling,
filling the room with a sweet, piercing odor. The shafts of morning
light, now dancing through the columns of smoke, had reached the foot
of the dais and illuminated the book which sat upon the ancient table
and the shattered throne behind it. As the last of the darkly garbed figures took their places, the music swelled once more, and, out of the
most central doorway, there emerged a dozen more attendees, each one
holding an exquisitely carved goblet of their own and dressed in brilliant robes of white. Their heads were bare, and as they passed him
Geoffrey saw that among them were Xavier, Mariela, and Trentius.
They were the Elders of the Followers of Joaquin, Geoffrey could tell,
and he was amazed how their eyes seemed to shine almost as brightly
as their robes, despite the shadows that lay around them. Two-by-two

they entered, almost gliding above the tiled floor as they crossed the length of the hall and ascended the steps leading up to the dais, where they encircled the table and the book.

As suddenly as it had begun, the music died away, and the hall was deathly silent. One of the Elders stepped forward and took up the book, and Geoffrey recognized Trentius' voice, ringing out clearly throughout the hall as he recited from what Geoffrey now realized was the other copy of the *Pontilux*, this one much larger and more ornate than any he had yet seen.

> By Author Life and Light were formed,
> in Guide were Light and Life infused,
> that both for glory might be used
> by man and union not abused;
> that Story may be well performed
> and man throughout might be transformed.
>
> Yet now book burns and scroll is torn,
> and Guide is cast out from his throne.
> No Life is lived, no Light is shone,
> but man in darkness bleeds alone;
> for Darkness Life from Light has shorn,
> and Darkness rules o'ertop the morn.
>
> But still writes Author in the night,
> that Guide in wisdom shall foresee:
> that Light and Life, though dimmed may be,
> yet in their falling, rise shall He
> and come victorious from the fight;
> that in Him, might rest Life and Light.
>
> So come now, man, to fallen Guide,

within whom Life and Light yet hide,
that power new He might provide.

The words reverberated throughout the hall, the echo of each verse building upon the one that came before it, until the entire chamber was filled with the voice of Trentius. As the final lines rang out, the light from the rising sun rose up past the dais and its white-robed occupants and finally illuminated the bulking mass of spikes which protruded from the wall and ceiling above it. Geoffrey stared, struck dumb in awe and confusion, as he beheld for the first time what could only be the skeleton of the Lord Joaquin, still impaled above his own throne by the dozens of iron spears which had ended his life.

But that was not what rendered Geoffrey unable to speak.

As the first full rays of the day touched the corpse of Joaquin and the final words of Trentius faded into nothingness, a writhing movement of what at first appeared to be a swarm of tiny insects seemed to envelop the skeleton, twisting this way and that and so covering it that many of its own kind were flung out into space where they plummeted to the ground below. And yet, as Geoffrey looked more closely, he realized that it was not a horde of insects or vermin. Rather, it was *blood*.

And not old, dried blood, but fresh blood, which came pulsing out of the corpse of Joaquin as if he were bleeding out all over again and began cascading in streams off of the tips of the spears which held him in place and down toward the crowd of Elders still standing on the dais, who held up their goblets to catch the falling drops and, once they had done so, raised them to their lips and drank deeply. Geoffrey was so shocked at what he was seeing that he forgot to be disgusted, and just continued to gawk in disbelief at the scene unfolding before him, a scene which was growing more grotesque and yet more fantastic by the moment. For as the Elders of the Followers of Joaquin slaked their thirst for the blood which was still pouring from the corpse of their former leader, their bodies seemed to shimmer to the point of almost glowing, as if they were filled with a mysterious energy that penetrated their very beings. So intense was the power which emanated from them that Geoffrey could scarcely bear to look upon it, and yet he also could not tear his gaze away. Radiating their newfound light, the Elders filled their cups again and began to share them with the dark-hooded members of the company, passing amongst and through and even above their brethren as if they were made of light themselves. The singing began again, this time more beautiful and yet more discordant than before, as the white-clad Elders passed cup after cup of blood to the people below. Then, quite suddenly, when everyone had drunk of a goblet, the flow of blood, the luminous bodies, and the music all faded away, and a silent darkness once more reigned as the Followers of Joaquin, led by their leaders, processed outward as quietly as they had come in.

Within moments everyone was gone, and the Great Hall was as silent as before. Geoffrey remained on his bench, frozen in horrified wonder at what he had just witnessed, and he probably would have stayed that way for the better part of the morning had not Trentius, who had removed his white robe to reveal his simple grey tunic and trousers beneath, come back to guide him to a more familiar place. As the two of them wound their way down from the upper city, Geoffrey wasn't sure whether he ought to vomit, fall to his knees in homage of the sheer power he had just seen, or get away as fast as he could and tell it all to Emore or another Committee member. He felt sick, and his mind was spinning from everything he had just witnessed. "Drinking blood?!" And so the accusations of the Committees were correct, he realized, or almost. He hadn't seen any sacrifices, of course, but they were right about the blood rituals and the cannibalism and all of that. And yet… what marvels that blood had worked! The revival of Joaquin, the light, the levitation, all of that…. He had witnessed it with his own eyes, and he had no doubt that he had just seen the harnessing of Lucherium and in a highly exalted form too. "But… but blood?!" Try as he might, Geoffrey was revolted at the idea of drinking human blood, even if it came from a corpse which was decades old and whose blood flowed magically whenever his name was invoked. Or perhaps, especially in that case.

He was so engrossed in his thoughts that he didn't realize they had left the tunnel, emerging this time into the wine chamber where Geoffrey had first shared bread with Xavier and his band. When Trentius undid his blindfold, Geoffrey was staggered at the sudden brightness which assaulted him. He made his way shakily over to the wooden table, unable to look directly at Trentius. The elder man seemed to sense Geoffrey's state of mind. Going to a fresh cask, he poured two tankards of ale, handing one to Geoffrey, who downed it in a single draught. The warm tingling of the alcohol helped to steady his nerves and gave him the courage to look Trentius in the face once again, a face which smiled at him from behind the flowing, greying beard, and whose teeth and lips somehow showed no sign of the ghastly fluid they had just consumed. And yet, Geoffrey realized, there was something different about him. Or not quite different, but it was almost as if there was *more* of him there. His face was nobler, his beard and hair richer, his muscles more defined, and his eyes even brighter than before. It was as if this were the real Trentius, and the other Trentius had been but an image in the mirror, and Emore and the Committee Members were nothing but shadows and wraiths, mere figments of existence.

"Not at all what you expected, was it?" Trentius spoke gently as he walked back to the cask, pouring Geoffrey another pint. "The first time I ever saw what you witnessed tonight, I was so shocked it took me hours to make heads or tails of what I had seen. Now, as hard as it might be to believe it, it's the moment in my life I look forward to the most. To the outsider it appears supremely grotesque, I'll admit, but I promise you that partaking in it is an experience unlike any you've ever had, and not in a bad way either. And all perceptions aside, that is the manner in which the Followers of Joaquin are able to harness Lucherium. And not just harness Lucherium, but harness it in the way that Joaquin did, as if we were sharing in His very life."

"But what...? How...? Why his blood??"

Trentius spread his hands outward, shrugging. "Truthfully, we don't know exactly how it all works. We know that the words of the Rite of Lucherium at the end of the *Pontilux* allow us to access the light and life of Joaquin (which is of course the Luchierum within Himself) whenever they are read before the body of Joaquin, and that, as you heard already, Joaquin could never be fully destroyed, nor fully severed from Light and Life. We also know that He somehow knew what was coming to pass and wrote the very words which allow all this to happen. Beyond that, I'm afraid there just isn't much I can explain. But it happens, without fail, each time one trained in the art of the Rite invokes it before part of his corpse. He ordained it thus, and so it is. As for why His blood, well, I supposed because it *had* to be that, in a sense, or at least it was most fitting that way. After all, as the Guide, Joaquin's purpose was to teach man to harness Lucherium. After His defeat, reality was so damaged that mankind was all but unable to reach the mystical energy, but within Joaquin, within His own Life, or lifeblood if you wish to be poetic, it remains. It is from Him, and at least for now only from Him, that we are able to access it by taking a part of Him into ourselves."

Geoffrey reflected on Trentius' explanation as he sipped his second pint of ale. It made sense, he realized; even if it all seemed horribly disgusting to him, it did make sense and, more than that, he had seen it happen and knew that it was so. But the thought of partaking in such a ritual still scared him, and he became even more unsure about ever fully becoming a Follower of Joaquin. It was a worry that gnawed at him as he finished his ale and as Trentius, who had wisely decided not to pursue the topic further, offered to lead him back up to the surface of Spiraluche, and it was a thought which would continue to bother him throughout the upcoming months, although to what extent he was not yet to know.

As the two of them emerged into the shadows under the wall which arched its way over the creek- moving much more cautiously than normal, as by now it was midmorning- Trentius grasped Geoffrey by both shoulders and stared at him with those luminous eyes which Geoffrey now realized betrayed the hidden power of Lucherium within the man before him.

"What you saw tonight is hard to understand, and even harder to want, Geoffrey, so let me offer you some advice. Don't make a decision about it yet. Keep meeting with us at night, learn who we really are, and help us in what we do. But don't pledge loyalty one way or

another until you truly know what and to whom you
are pledging it to... and against whom as well. Best of
luck, Geoffrey, and until tomorrow night."

And then Geoffrey was alone in the bright morning sun of Trastaluche, his world once again shattered and his mind whirling such that
he thought it would never stop. On one hand the bard wanted no part
in what he had just seen, in the ghastly carnality of it all. And yet, on
the other hand... he thought of Eldrige, and of the executions and the
torture which he had seen carried out at the hands of the Committees,
and he was forced to admit that he had seen the same bloodlust there,
too, and with only awful consequences. Furthermore, if the bread-giv-
ing and exquisite crafting had shown him anything, it was that at least
some good did in fact come out of the blood-drinking of the Followers
of Joaquin. So Geoffrey decided to follow Trentius' advice, at least for
the time being.

He chose not to choose.

And so began a period in his life which he would later consider to
be one of the most important. Almost every other night he would meet
with a member of the Followers of Joaquin in some obscure part of the
city, who would then conduct him, still blindfolded, to one of the many
underground meeting rooms of those who sought to embrace the Way
of Lucherium. Here Geoffrey would enter into the life of the Hazcalucherians, and soon he began to do so with an energy and a gusto which
he had not felt within himself for a long while. Given his skill with a
quill and paper, he spent most of his nights working with Trentius at
the laborious task of copying the contents of ancient parchments, passing the time asking questions about Lucherium, about the Era of Lord
Joaquin, and about the passages they were recreating, the less

controversial of which would be compiled into books and sold in the city along with many of the other goods which were being produced in the underground craft rooms. The reason for all of this production was, in the words of Xavier, "to fund the other more important activities of the Followers of Joaquin," which Geoffrey now understood to be preparations for an uprising against the Committees of Trastaluche and the return of the "Era of Lucherium," as Trentius was fond of calling it. On other evenings he would help with the bread-baking or the loom-weaving, although he had to admit that he was quite bad at the latter. In fact, he noticed with some frustration that no matter how hard he tried, he was far worse than the others at almost every task he set himself to do. One day, in a discouraged state, he complained to Mariela about this fact. She simply smiled at him and asked,

"And are you harnessing Lucherium when you do these tasks?"

Taken aback, Geoffrey shook his head and reminded her that he didn't yet know how. Her response surprised and encouraged him.

"Then don't be so downhearted about your mistakes. In time they shall pass away. Embrace this as an era of preparation, so that when your moment to harness Lucherium does arrive, you are prepared to do so in harmony with all reality."

Geoffrey took her words to heart, although not without some difficulty, and soon found that the principal cause of his errors had in fact been the distraction of comparing his work to others. His results were still not perfect, of course, and they were nowhere near as beautiful or accomplished as those of Trentius and the rest, but he was much happier with them, and he more and more frequently began to view his mistakes as motivations to do better. And of course almost every night finished with the inevitable trip to Muckland, or to some other unofficial sector of the city, where he and his companions tended those who were down on their luck in some fashion or another, an activity which Geoffrey at first quite detested in spite of his efforts not to, but which little by little became more tolerable. When he asked Ayila, who he discovered was in fact almost as proficient and respected as Mariela in the art of harnessing of Lucherium, about the reason for such excursions- as to him they seemed to have no visible benefits which could be harnessed to help one make ready for war- she assured him that, in fact, they were some of the most vital acts of preparation they could undertake.

"You see," she explained, "using Lucherium these days in Trastaluche is like trying to light a match underwater. Unless you have some special way to do it- which we do, but as you know it is still very much secret and hidden- it is nigh impossible. So we like to think of our work in Muckland, and in other places too, as hauling the water away, a bucket at a time, so that matches can be lit wherever and whenever they are needed. After all, the old and the sick- our fathers and mothers and grandmothers- abandoned and dying alone is not at all what the Author wove into the fabric of reality. The more we work to eradicate such "voids" in Life, the more hospitable Trastaluche is to the use of Lucherium overall."

And so passed the better part of two months, with the nights spent laboring under the guiding eyes of Trentius, Mariela, and Xavier, and the days spent composing ballads about the wonderful adventures he had- which he then promptly burned lest a Minister of Social Order search his room and find them- and sleeping in a small room near the back of a run-down inn in lower Spiraluche where Xavier had kindly lodged him. He had also provided Geoffrey with sufficient funds for meals and any essentials he might need as payment for the work he was doing, "lest you end up back in Muckland and we have to pull you out again," Xavier explained with a smile.

Having a place to rest his head, a full belly, and a little bit extra to spend on himself was a welcome change for Geoffrey. As the weeks passed, he realized that he was beginning to enjoy his new occupation and the companions with which he worked to the point where he almost looked forward to his blindfolded journeys into the underground world of Trastaluche. However, he was not yet a full member of the Followers of Joaquin, and he found that, if he was being honest with himself, he was not quite sure that he wanted to be. He was comfortable working with them, no doubt, but baking bread and transcribing books was one matter, while taking an oath of loyalty to a fallen Lord, drinking his blood, and swearing to serve as his soldier in what would probably be a long and most likely disastrous fight against Trastivo and the Committees was another thing entirely, and not something which he thought he would be particularly good at, at any rate.

Thoughts such as these were most common after especially long nights, such as a particularly unpleasant one during which Geoffrey knocked over his inkwell on the parchments both he and Trentius were working on, erasing a week's worth of progress, and afterwards had to tend to a sickly woman in Muckland whose breath smelled overwhelmingly like rotting onions. When morning finally came, Geoffrey found himself, much more tired than usual, trudging his way wearily back up to the inn where he was staying. He was feeling rather disheartened, and as was such he did not notice the group of men in long, crimson-colored cloaks who lingered suspiciously near the doorsteps, or the figure who was easily recognizable as a sergeant of the Patrollers of Social Order conversing with the innkeeper. Dragging himself up the narrow, leaning stairs, he reached his room and turned the knob wearily, looking forward to hours of well-earned sleep. The door stuck on its frame, and cursing with irritation, Geoffrey forced his shoulder against it, shoving it open in a sudden, awkward motion.

Immediately, his tiredness drained away, replaced by a paralyzing rush of shock and terror. For sitting in the one simple chair which the room contained, flanked by two soldiers of Trastaluche, was Emore, senior Minister of Social Order.

Chapter X
The Conversion

"Ah, Geoffrey, come in," smiled Emore, and it was the smile of a snake, a smile which matched the dark, soulless pits which were his eyes. "I hope you don't mind my paying a visit to your abode unannounced, but you and I have much to talk about."

Geoffrey felt a pit inside him begin to grow as he fought to stop his breathing from accelerating to match his heart. He had no idea how Emore had found him, but then he recalled the Minister's words about keeping an eye on him and cursed inwardly, realizing with a sinking feeling that the Committee of Social Order could have been watching him all along.

"If they know where I am," he worried, "then perhaps they know where I've been traveling to each night, or perhaps they don't know and they're here because they want to know. They might even know who I've been dealing with…."

Forcing himself to smile halfheartedly, he spread his palms in greeting to the Minister, who remained completely impassive, the serpentine grin still planted on his face, neither acknowledging nor returning the greeting. "A bad sign, a very, very bad sign," thought Geoffrey. Doing his best to feign surprise, he responded to Emore.

"Minister Emore, a prosperous morning to you, sir. Your presence is always welcome, but I must apologize for my ignorance and forgetfulness; about what things did we need to discuss?"

The Minister's smile widened, and his tongue shot out, licking his lips with anticipation.

"Why, your future, of course. I must say, Geoffrey, that we've been a little worried about you, ever since that unfortunate incident where you lost your bard's commission. It can be… difficult to obtain work after such a misfortune, I know, but you… you seem to be doing rather well. How can you afford a place like this, and night after night too?"

Geoffrey gulped, realizing that even if Emore knew nothing of his nighttime activities, it did seem rather suspicious that a disgraced bard was able to so easily afford lodging.

"Well then, I must thank you for your concern," he replied, "but as you can see, I am doing well-enough. I've been working as a laborer in the Lower City, in the markets and such, doing odd jobs. It doesn't pay much, but it's just enough to cover this room with a little left over for bread."

"A laborer, eh? Well, I must say, you don't look much the worse for wear for it; in fact, you look better than the last time we met. Much better, especially for someone undertaking such a hard occupation for the first time…."

"Yes, all the manual work has been rather good for me," laughed Geoffrey nervously. "I didn't expect I would enjoy it this much, but I can go for hours and hours on end."

"Very good! Just the sort of spirit that Trastaluche needs in its men. But tell me, Geoffrey, what market vendors have you been working for?"

"Oh, too many to count," he answered. "The fish sellers, the lumber yards, the fruit-haulers, even the sheepshearers once or twice…."

"I see, I see. And do they all require your services at night?"

"Why… I'm not sure what you mean," responded Geoffrey, the knot of dread within him growing.

"Well, your innkeeper downstairs told my man that you're always out late into the night, and that you don't return to bed until the morning hours. Now what sort of sheepshearers would need you at those times, eh?"

Emore's eyes bored dangerously into Geoffrey, and he felt himself trapped, being sucked into them as if they were pools of black tar, threatening to mire him ever deeper into the web of his own fears and lies.

"No… not the sheepshearers, of course, but some of the others…."

He was mid-sentence when Emore suddenly launched himself out of the chair in which he had been coiled and bounded across the cramped room, grabbing Geoffrey by the collar and shoving him against the wall. His face, although still smiling, was a mask of barely concealed contempt, but his voice showed no change in emotion as he addressed the terrified bard.

"Geoffrey, Geoffrey, come now. You've no need to lie to us. We may not know exactly where you've been and who you've been with, but we know it wasn't any market seller."

He stepped back from Geoffrey and, without loosening his grip on the bard's collar, half-yanked him over to the chair and forced him to sit.

"But you see, Geoffrey, we're not here to arrest you or even to question you; don't worry. We're here because, as I told you before, you're just the type of person the Committees can use, and we'd like to offer you a new occupation with us."

"Occupation?" rasped Geoffrey, still trying to catch the wind which had been knocked out of him. "What would the Committee of Social Order want me for?"

"Why, it's almost nothing, really. You see, we believe you're the sort of fellow who can be trusted as a loyal member of Trastaluche, and we want to reward that. Keep your eyes and ears open for us, and we'll make sure you're well-compensated, as I promised before. Better lodging, extra funds, and a bard's commission are just the beginning, my friend."

"I... I'm sorry," stuttered Geoffrey, "but I'm sure that I don't know anything that would be worth reporting, and I don't even know if I would know what to look out for."

"Ah, but with your incredible skills of remembering and telling, you don't have to know. In fact, you don't have to do anything different at all. For now, keep going about your work at the... market... and tell us everything you see and hear. It's quite an easy occupation, I assure you."

"I do apologize, but I'm just not sure I'm worthy for the task," answered Geoffrey, trying to look calm as the wave of panic within him threatened to spill out and flood his senses.

"Are you quite sure? Because I, for one, advise you to consider the proposition a little more closely. We really do think you'd be ideal for us, but if you're positive that you can't contribute, we might be able to find something else for you, such as a position up in the yard of the Chamber of Social Order. We just transferred a different bard there, actually. Eldrige, was it? Yes, he's quite enjoying his new occupation...."

Geoffrey's blood went cold as he realized what Emore was implying.

"No... no, I would be even worse at that sort of position, I'm sure. I think...."

"Oh, I think you'd do quite nicely," smirked Emore, "but since you insist, I'll let you consider your options and choose between the two. I'll be waiting for you here in, let's say, two days' time? Yes, that should be ideal."

Emore motioned to his henchmen that the meeting was over and turned to go, the smile still frozen to his face. As he was headed out the door, he glanced back toward Geoffrey once more.

"Think about my offer, Geoffrey of Trastaluche, and choose well. We can make everything go back to the way it was before

if you decide to work with us. Wouldn't that be nice, eh? A
prosperous day to you."

The door slammed, and Emore was gone. Geoffrey held his breath
as he waited for the footsteps to recede down the hallway, then collapsed onto the floor and let out a choked sob. The fear within him finally swept away the last of his strength. He was in shock about what
had just happened, and he was utterly lost as to what to do.

He was afraid, terribly afraid, he realized, of facing the wrath of the
Committees, of ending up like Eldrige, and yet he was almost as afraid
of seeing Emore daily, of telling him what he knew about Xavier and
Mariela and Ayila and the others. He felt repulsed at the idea of even
being near Emore, or any Committee Member like him again, and yet
he knew that if they took him, if they dragged him into that yard and
threatened to slice his tongue out, that he would cave, that he would tell
them everything. The promise of something greater after death didn't
help his confidence either, as he doubted that the Lord Joaquin would
take kindly to someone whose loyalty didn't extend to situations of torture. And he hated himself for his weakness almost as much as he hated
the thought of what might happen to him if he didn't turn his back on
the Way of Lucherium.

"I'm no follower of Joaquin," he realized. "I'm just a wretch
who has been leeching off the good graces of Xavier and his
band, leading them on, when at the first sign of pain, I'd sell
them all out!"

He felt miserably low, even more than when he had lain that night
covered in muck in Muckland, and he cursed himself again, cursed his

bad luck and all he had been through, wishing everything could go back to how it used to be. Emore had promised him that life again, he knew, but he also knew that it was all a lie. He had seen what happened to Eldrige, and he had heard the stories told by Xavier and Mariela of loved ones lost to the Committees who had met their demises in ways even more sinister.

"I just want to be away from it all," he realized, "to go back to when I was happy and prosperous and progressing as a bard, when I hadn't a care in the world and when all of *this* was nothing but rumor and shadow and would always stay that way."

He was walking now, although he couldn't remember getting to his feet, his mind as clouded as it was with the mists of confusion and horror. All he knew was that he needed to get away from it all, and he found that his strides were taking him, almost of their own accord, to the middle levels of Spiraluche, to the streets he had walked and the inns and taverns where he had performed with his friends as a newly commissioned bard. He could almost hear the cheers of the crowd- the rowdy "hurrahs" of the older men and the shriller, more pleasing "hoorays" of the ladies and the children- as they laughed and tapped along with the music and the verse, some dancing and singing, others merely swaying, lost in the mysterious land of beauty to which only music can take you.

He wandered, lost in thought, outside of time so it seemed to him, up and down the cobbled streets of the city he had grown up in; with its wide, central lanes lined with oak trees whose branches stretched so far that they intertwined with those reaching out from the other side; with its heavy, stone walls and mighty towers which rose in three circles around each section of the city, bright banners waving from the parapets and stout, wooden doorways protecting what lay within; with its graceful yet simple houses built of grey stone and red tile roofs which matched the crimson uniforms of the Patrollers who kept order in the streets and watch along the ramparts; and, more recently, with its looming granite monoliths which towered above the upper city: six small giants and one massive one. He thought of the hope he had once placed in the Committees and their motto of "Progress Before All," the ambition he had shared with many of his fellow bards, and the harsh, bitter disillusionment which had come when he realized the untruth of it all. He thought of the Followers of Joaquin in their underground world and marveled that they would dare to stand up against such a mighty force as Trastivo and the Committees. He thought of their traditions and their occupations, which even now seemed utterly strange to him while at the same time making more sense than anything he had ever encountered. He berated himself for being too much of a coward to be one of them, and he wished, above all, that he could forget about all of it and go back to a simpler, an easier, time.

He remained in his tormented yet nostalgic trance for hours, until finally hunger, fatigue, and the initial dimming of the sun alerted him to the fact that he had spent almost the entire day at his musings. Realizing that he needed food and a new, unknown place to stay, he turned toward a nearby inn and dining-hall in the middle city, *The Flashing Peacock*, which he remembered from his younger days as a popular haunt for bards. He bartered with the innkeeper for an out-of-the-way room, dinner included, until they reached an agreement, and, securing a pint of ale and the bartender's promise to "keep them coming," he sat down with a plate of boiled sausages, potatoes, and carrots to listen to the evening's music, hoping to forget his misfortunes for at least a couple of hours.

The inn was packed for the entertainment which was scheduled to start at sundown, now only a few moments away. There was movement at the far end of the room where a few tables had been shoved together into a makeshift stage, and a young, dark-haired jongleur emerged, a mandolin strung over one shoulder and a set of reeds in his hand. He flashed a smile at the crowd and bowed so low that the feathered cap which he wore tickled the heads of the spectators nearest to him. The crowd roared their approval, stamping their feet and calling for a song, a request which the youthful bard wasted no time in obliging. Setting his cap at the edge of the stage where it expectantly awaited the coins which were to fill it throughout the night, he bowed once again and blew a playful stream of notes from his reeds, which rippled and danced throughout the room, at once quieting the crowd and creating a sense of theatre and excitement.

"He's good, very good," thought Geoffrey, sipping his ale and preparing himself for as enjoyable a night as could be expected given his situation. The young bard cleared his throat and then, introducing himself in proper Trastalucherian fashion, launched into a tune about a barmaid who fell in love with a duke who was really a magical pig, a song whose details Geoffrey could only describe as bawdy at best or downright repulsive at worst. Taken aback by the lyrics, which left out no detail in describing not only the romantic trysts which the barmaid had with her pig-duke, but also the grotesque child which came of their affair, Geoffrey was shocked not only by the content of the ballad but also by the crowd's reaction. They loved it, and they gleefully howled for more of the same.

"What rubbish," he snorted. "Why, these young bards don't know any of the really good pieces. I was just as much a crowd-pleaser in my day, and yet our ballads were sophisticated; real pieces of art, not garbage like…."

Before he could finish deriding the performance, which he thought was in horribly poor taste, there was a commotion near the bar, and a string of curses was shouted at the young bard, who had just begun to tune his mandolin for the next piece. Turning around in his chair, Geoffrey was startled at the sight of the innkeeper striding angrily toward his nightly entertainment, hurling abuses at him as he approached. Geoffrey couldn't understand why at first, but then as the crowd of people parted to let the enraged owner past, Geoffrey saw that he was being followed by a second bard, much closer to his own age, whose face was crimson in rage, and at whose heels trailed two small girls, quite obviously the man's daughters, clutching each other's hands and looking fearfully at the crowd of people which towered around them.

"Why, I know that bard!" realized Geoffrey. "Unless my eyes deceive me, that's Lursio! We used to perform together in this very inn, although he was always the favorite of the innkeeper and the regular patrons. I didn't realize he'd been married; those must be his daughters, and they look just like him too!"

Suddenly Geoffrey realized what had happened. Lursio was in all probability *still* the favorite of the innkeeper, and he had most likely been hired in advance to be the entertainer for the night when this young jongleur had swooped in, looking to steal his spot and win the favor of the crowd before the innkeeper knew what had happened. Filled with indignation for his former companion, Geoffrey joined the older patrons, Lursio, and the innkeeper in verbally driving the younger bard from the stage, yelling and stomping to drown out his music until he was forced to sulk off into the audience, where he quickly disappeared from view.

> "At last," sighed Geoffrey, "we'll hear some *real* music, perhaps an epic of the War of Liberation, or maybe one of the venerable tales of the dragon-hunters."

He settled back into his chair as Lursio began strumming his own small guitar and whistling a jaunty tune, while his daughters perched on the edge of the stage, humming along. The crowd didn't seem to mind that their first entertainer had been kicked out in disgrace, and they cheered just as heartily for Lursio, who was obviously a familiar face around these parts. But to Geoffrey's disgust, the music was, if anything, worse than what came before; Lursio began with the tale of an idiot innkeeper who, in the midst of a drought and finding himself to be out of water, felt the urge to lick the boots of everyone who came in, "lest covered in loam/ they ruin my home," until, upon encountering a village girl who had just arrived, dusty and tired, to visit her long-lost family in the city, decided that "dirt in all places she hath/ thus I shall give her a bath." The audience reveled in the tale, singing loudly to the chorus led by none other than Lursio's own two little girls.

Geoffrey, indignant, couldn't believe what he was hearing at first, but he suddenly found himself humming, almost involuntarily, a clever harmony which fit perfectly with the piece. Then he realized that he had performed this very ballad with Lursio dozens of times before, never stopping to realize just how repulsive it was.

He wondered about this change in himself, and perhaps he would have shouted for something 'better,' something more 'old-fashioned,' when at that moment there was a rupture in the crowd, and the young bard bounded up onto the stage again, his eyes dark with the fury of being humiliated. Geoffrey scarcely had time to realize what was happening before the younger performer was on top of his elder, grabbing his hair and yanking his head back. A knife blade flashed, people screamed, and blood spurted everywhere, covering the stage, the onlookers, and the little girls who sat petrified with horror, soaked in their own father's blood, suddenly orphans. With a flash, the murderer dashed across the rear of the stage and slipped out an open window against which it butted. He disappeared into the blackness, never to be heard of again, until, dressed in different clothes and under a different name, he would arrive some few nights later at the very same inn, inquiring about whether or not they needed a new jongleur.

Around Geoffrey, some people were in hysterics, others were crying, and still others were cheering for what they considered to be the spectacle of the season. Above all of the turmoil he could hear the cries of Lursio's daughters, who were hugging their father's body, begging him to be ok, while the innkeeper's wife tried in vain to comfort them. Geoffrey sat in total shock as the last vestiges of a world he had sought to return to crumbled around him, a golden age which he realized had never been golden but had been made up of false memories of companions, culture, and perfection, an age which had been filled with as much vileness, betrayal, and violent ambition as the most lawless members of Muckland.

The shouting of orders and the flash of crimson uniforms jolted Geoffrey back to reality, and he realized that the Patrollers of Social Order had arrived to see about the commotion and to keep the peace. He didn't think any of them would recognize who he was, and anyway he doubted that he was officially on the Committee's list of wanted citizens at the moment, but he couldn't risk taking the chance of being discovered, especially after his conversation with Emore this morning. Ducking down, he made his way quietly along the wall, out of sight of the Patrollers who had just entered the inn and were trying to restore order, until he reached a side doorway and slipped silently into the darkness, leaving behind him the life of Geoffrey, bard of Trastaluche.

Not that there was actually a life to go back to, he realized. His experiences of the past seasons had opened his eyes to exactly what he had been doing and who he had been during that time of his life, a time when he was ambitious enough to hurt to get what he wanted without caring about the aftermath. It wasn't a golden era he longed to return to, but a blind one, and he had seen far too much to go back to being blind. That sort of life wasn't enough anymore, he reflected, and then, in a moment of revelation, he realized that what he really wanted was *more,* and for once, he knew where to find it. And in the darkness outside of *The Flashing Peacock,* Geoffrey made another of the most important decisions of his life: to forget that he wasn't enough, that he wasn't brave enough or prosperous enough or intelligent enough to be a full Follower of Joaquin, and to choose to be a Follower *because* he, his life, his past, wasn't enough. Because he desperately needed *more.*

The garden where he'd first bid farewell to Xavier and Mariela was quieter and more overgrown than ever, and the ancient ash in its center seemed to have lost more of its branches to the rot of old age. Geoffrey sat on the old stone bench beneath it and waited. He hadn't arranged to meet with anyone tonight, and he wasn't sure if or when anyone would happen to come by to retrieve him, since he still didn't know where the entrances to the tunnels which led to the underground levels of Spiraluche were located. The garden seemed like the best location to wait because it was sheltered and less public than many of the other spots he'd used. He figured that someone would emerge sooner or later and find him sitting here, someone who could lead him to see Xavier and Trentius and the others. Time seemed to pass by quickly for once, and his mind was uncannily empty as he sat motionless in the garden, removed from the noise of the city; hovering, so it seemed to him, in a limbo between worlds. It must have been almost moonhigh when he detected the familiar grinding sound of rock on rock, followed by the soft footfalls of someone approaching, and within moments the graceful figure of Ayila appeared in the clearing, clad from head to toe in black, with a covered lantern in one hand and a bulky satchel under her cloak. She jumped when she saw Geoffrey and reached for the dagger she also wore, but relaxed when she realized who it was.

"Geoffrey! You scared the life out of me! What on earth are you doing here?! You hadn't arranged to meet anyone tonight...."

"Ayila, I'm sorry, I know, it's just... I've come to a decision, and I need to speak to Xavier right away. I want to pledge my allegiance to Joaquin and become a full Follower of the Way of Lucherium."

Chapter XI

The Immersion

Ayila stared at him for a moment with her star-filled eyes, and Geoffrey saw that she didn't seem surprised at all; rather, it was as if she was contemplating whether or not he truly meant what he had just said. After a moment, she nodded in assent, and turning back the way she had come, she beckoned to him to follow without a word. Geoffrey did so, and after winding for some time through the thickest sections of the garden, they arrived at an ivy-covered wall, upon which Ayila began knocking until she found a section which echoed less dully than the rest. She lifted up the green, leafy curtain and, reaching into a space left by a brick which had fallen out of place, grasped a small, latched handle which had been fashioned so that it lay hidden in the shadow of the hole, pushing until a section of the wall swung inward, revealing a door which, for those who didn't know exactly where to look, would have been impossible to spot. She uncovered her lantern to reveal the long, winding passageway that lay before them and gestured again at Geoffrey to follow. It was only once they had been walking for some time in the twisting confines of the tunnel that Geoffrey realized that he was, for the first time, not blindfolded while entering the world of the Hazcalucherians. His eyes, therefore, had time to adjust to the pinprick of light which appeared in front of him and grew steadily larger as they approached the journey's end, which came when he and Ayila stepped out into the dimly lit wine chamber that Geoffrey had visited many times before, and that, according to Xavier, served as a local assembly hall from which missions and tasks could be organized and assigned to a large number of people at a time. The lengthy room was deserted except for the presence of a few men and women who were manning the stove at its far end, and Geoffrey guessed that most of the group had, like Ayila, already departed for their nightly tasks.

"Wait here," said Ayila, and jogged over to one of the men who was kneading a fresh batch of dough. The two of them conversed for a few moments. Then the man nodded and, gesturing for another baker to take his spot, took Ayila's bag from her, shouldered past Geoffrey, and headed back up the tunnel from which they had just emerged. Ayila, meanwhile, turned back to Geoffrey.

"He has promised to make sure my tasks are completed to-night," she reported. "You and I will see to finding Xavier and the Elders."

Geoffrey thanked her and then, struck by an impulse, said,

"Ayila, may I ask you something?"

"Yes, of course."

"It's just… I know what must be done, but it all seems so… ghastly, to put it lightly. How do you… you know, drink it? Do you like it?"

Ayila looked at him and smiled. "Geoffrey, let me ask you something. Do you truly think that Joaquin *had* to be overthrown?"

"Well, no, not really… I mean, I don't know. That part doesn't make much sense to me actually. From what I've heard, no matter how powerful Trastivo was, Joaquin should have been far more so."

"And so He was," nodded Ayila, "so wise and so powerful that He *chose* to triumph precisely in his defeat. He chose to no longer be with us so that He could be *in* us. He could have abandoned us and fled east with the remnants of His army. Or He could have fought with Trastivo and won, and their battle would have been of such epic proportions that when it ended there would have been no Hazcaluche left to rule, and all those who were blinded by their ambition or greed and had followed Trastivo into his void of blackness, of non-being, would have perished without the chance to really see true Light and Life. But He chose neither, and because He chose to be overthrown, we now possess the power to protect ourselves, and not only that, but to defeat Trastivo and his followers and to liberate Hazcaluche without causing its destruction. And, most importantly, we can harness Lucherium in its fullest sense, which is what the mission of Joaquin has always been. Although He isn't 'with us' in the normal sense now, because of His loyalty... no, His *love*, for there's really not a better way to explain His actions... for us, we have the chance to enter fully into Light and Life someday, and to be with Him again in a manner and a place which are far, far greater than here and now."

Geoffrey was stunned. No one had explained the fall of Joaquin to him in this way before, and he wasn't quite sure how to respond. Before he had a chance, however, Ayila went on.

"So do I like receiving Him? Geoffrey, I love it. I love being filled with Him, being full of Him, and being *more* of me all the while. It's a reality unlike anything you've ever known, and one that you do not need to be afraid of joining. You've made a truly wonderful decision today, and one which many people would not have had the courage to make. I tell you this so that you might have the heart to follow through."

And with that she embraced Geoffrey fondly, and after a moment of surprise, he hugged her back, finding his eyes filling with tears of gratitude for this woman who, with so few words, had consoled him and strengthened him like no one else could.

The two ducked into a small side passage which led from the wine room to another of the many underground chambers where they met Vincente, hard at work sharpening a collection of exquisitely crafted swords and daggers. Upon hearing the news, he leapt away from the whetstone, sword still in hand, and wrapped his massive arms around Geoffrey so enthusiastically that the bard would have been stabbed in the back had Ayila not intervened and removed the sword from Vincente's grip. Apologizing, he set aside his leather apron and gloves and led the two of them through yet another set of tunnels and into a room which Geoffrey had not seen before. It looked to him as if it could have been another storeroom, like the one they had just left, but it was oval in shape and its walls were now stacked with books from floor to ceiling, the only exceptions being around the entrances to half a dozen tunnels, all of which seemed to intersect here. In the center of the room, which was brightly lit by a chandelier of candles hanging from its ceiling, there was a large, rounded table, and at the table sat a handful of mostly elderly men and women, amongst them Xavier, Trentius, and

Mariela, as well as several others who Geoffrey had not yet met but who he recognized as some of the white-clad Elders from the Rite, this time dressed in the same simple grey and brown garb that everyone normally wore. They were going through scrolls and poring over several detailed maps which were rolled out in front of them, but they stopped when Ayila, Vincente, and Geoffrey entered the room.

Vincente and Ayila bowed to the Elders, and Geoffrey, after hesitating a moment, did the same. Xavier looked confused, but he smiled at the three of them and, his palms spread in welcome, strode toward them.

"Well, my friends, this is an unexpected surprise indeed, especially to see you, Geoffrey, and without a blindfold.... What is going on? Why are the three of you here?"

Geoffrey glanced at Ayila and Vincente, who smiled at him encouragingly, and then took a deep breath and answered.

"It is good to see you too, Xavier, Mariela, and Trentius, as well as the rest of you, whose names I have not had the honor of hearing and whose acquaintances I have not had the pleasure of making.... I have come to request that I be permitted to swear my full allegiance to Joaquin, Lord of Hazcaluche, and to become a full member of the Lucherians...."

And, unable to keep it within himself any longer, Geoffrey began to tell the true story, the full story, of his journey from a young, ambitious bard of Trastaluche, to the broken, bitter creature they had found in Muckland, to the person who stood before them today, in many ways more broken than he had ever been, and yet more whole as well, and more sure of the decision which he was making now than he had been of anything else in his entire life. He re-told the story of the night outside the house of the Family Xavier and revealed, not without a bit of shame, his deliberations about the true identity of Grey-eyes and about his intention to report what he had seen to the Committee of Social Order. He recounted the tale of Eldrige, his encounters with Emore, and finally the violence of the past evening which had made him understand that he was no longer a part of the world of Trastaluche- the world of Committees, of ambition, and of Progress Before All- and of his decision to choose *more*, precisely because he saw himself as less.

He later figured that he must have spent the better part of two hours seated around the oval table with the Elders of Hazcaluche, pouring his life out before them and answering their questions, before finally, when Xavier, Trentius, and the others were satisfied with his account, he was asked to withdraw while the Elders deliberated about his petition. After what seemed like an eternity of moments to Geoffrey, although in reality it was only a few minutes later, Mariela, speaking on behalf of the Elders, called him to rejoin them.

"Welcome, Geoffrey," she smiled, and then she embraced him with all the warmth and tenderness of a mother. "We are overjoyed to accept your request to swear allegiance to Joaquin and join us as a full member of the kingdom of Hazcaluche and a wielder of Lucherium. Xavier and I, and indeed many others, have hoped since we first met you that this day would come, and we are so, so happy that it has."

And then there were applauses and embraces and hearty claps on the back and all manner of congratulations from Xavier and Trentius and all of the Elders, but Geoffrey barely took notice of it. He was quite suddenly entranced with a bliss which filled every fiber of his being, the likes of which he had never really felt before, and he was much less afraid of the decision he had just made, even if, as a part of him still expected, it was a decision which in all likelihood would lead him to his death. Ale and wine were called for, and several happy hours were spent in celebration of Geoffrey and his imminent admittance into the Followers of Joaquin. As the dawn drew nearer, the Elders excused themselves for their own preparations for the Rite, and Geoffrey was escorted by Ayila and Vincente back to the wine chamber and into the second, smaller room where he had once spent the night. Once there, Vincente handed him a silvery-grey robe.

"Here," he said. "This is what you'll wear to the ceremony. Ayila and I have other preparations to attend to, but we will come and fetch you when it is time to depart for the Great Hall. The next few hours are for you to be alone. Try to sleep, if you can."

Geoffrey bade them goodbye and made his way over to the cot, where he lay down, staring up at the moonlight which filtered in through the tiny windows high up on the wall. Sleep was elusive in his nervous state, and after a while he grew tired of trying. Sliding off the cot's edge, he ambled over to where Vincente had left the silver-colored robe and slipped it over his own tunic and trousers. It was surprisingly cool, and it seem to shimmer as he moved around, as if it were one with the moonlight which reflected dimly off its surface. He started to pace, and as he did so he tried to recall what had happened when he had last

witnessed the Rite of Lucherium several months before. He remembered the music, sweet and strange, the silent processions in and out,
and the booming words of Trentius. He cringed in spite of himself as
he recalled the cascades of blood streaming from the skeleton of
Joaquin and the delight with which his followers drank it in, and he felt
his sense of awe returning as he replayed the glorious moments which
followed. However, he couldn't remember anyone reciting any sort of
oath, and despite being comforted by the Elders' acceptance of his request, he still felt very much out of his depth.

He tried to keep down the tightness in his throat and the fluttering
in his stomach. He still wasn't sure what to make of the idea that partially resurrecting a dead corpse and drinking its blood would grant you
access to a mystical energy, but he had made his decision to swear loyalty to Joaquin, and it was one which he was resolved to carry out, even
if it meant agreeing to partake in a blood Rite. He'd spent years swearing loyalty to Trastaluche and the ideal of Progress, after all, only to find
that all it led to was violence and bloodshed of the most malevolent
kind. Now he was preparing to pledge his life to a group which openly
acknowledged their identity as partakers in the life-blood of their fallen
Lord. "Perhaps," he thought, "they might just turn out to be as magnificent as the Committees are vile."

He tried to recall what Ayila had said, about love and courage and
not fearing what was about to befall him, and it was these words he
clung to when Vincente returned to fetch him in the last hours before
the dawn, and which he repeated to himself as he followed him, once
again without a blindfold, up the sloping passageways which led to the
Great Hall of Joaquin. The two ascended without speaking until they
arrived at the natural cave which formed the antechamber to the Hall.

Here, Vincente pulled Geoffrey aside to give him some last-minute instructions.

> "You are to come in last among the company of Followers, right
> before the Elders, do you understand? Don't worry, you're not
> the only one. A woman is pledging allegiance tonight too… I
> don't think you've met her yet, and there isn't time now, but
> her name is Lucia. You'll walk beside her and right behind me,
> so just follow me and do as I do, alright? When the time comes
> for you to swear allegiance, they'll call the two of you forward
> and tell you what to do." He grasped Geoffrey's arm. "Courage,
> brother; you're almost there."

He led Geoffrey through the shadows of the antechamber, this time
more brightly lit by additional torches and full of people donning robes
and hoods and getting in line, until they reached a corner of the cave
further away from the doors. The procession started and the music began again, every bit as beautiful and yet infuriatingly incomprehensible
as it had been the last time Geoffrey had heard it. As the ranks of silver-
hooded figures filed through the archway and into the Great Hall, Vincente guided Geoffrey to the rear of the line where he took up his spot
behind the fair-headed man and across from a beautiful young woman
who Geoffrey assumed to be Lucia. She was dressed in the same robe as
the others, but like Geoffrey, her head was still unhooded. She had ol-
ive-toned skin, dark, silky hair and massive hazel eyes which betrayed
the same fear which Geoffrey felt as she glanced at him and raised her
trembling chin to bravely smile a greeting. Geoffrey had but a moment
to smile back, and then they were scrambling to catch up with Vincente
and Ayila, who glided forward in front of them.

The massive pillars, the shadowed walls, the golden roof with its shafts of pre-dawn light, the gleaming tiled floors, and the towering columns of incense loomed before Geoffrey once again, and he felt just as small and insignificant as he had the last time he had been here. The Great Hall was much fuller this time, he realized, and as he snuck a glance backward at the Elders who were processing in behind him, he saw that there were well over twenty who had arrived to witness the oaths of loyalty of Geoffrey and Lucia. He felt weak in the knees and found himself repeating the words of Ayila under his breath: "Courage and Love." Hooded faces, torches, and vessels of incense all swept past, and then the procession had ended. Geoffrey was standing in the front row, not ten paces from the dais, the Elders, the book, and the throne. And above him loomed the black, spiked mass which he knew hid the corpse of Joaquin, but try as he might, his eyes still refused to fully take in what was before him. One of the Elders whom Geoffrey had not yet met stepped forward and gave some sort of greeting to the masses assembled below, and then another began to read from the *Pontilux*; not its final lines just yet, but from an earlier section Geoffrey was not familiar with. Another Elder did the same, but Geoffrey was too nervous to listen to what they were saying. Then suddenly his name was being called along with Lucia's, and the two of them were nudged forward until they stood in the central pathway, directly in front of the dais and the table as Mariela stepped forward to announce them. She smiled at them both warmly, and Geoffrey felt just a little of his anxiety melt. "Courage and Love," he murmured.

"Friends and Followers of the Way of Lucherium, witness here the acts of Geoffrey and Lucia as they pledge their loyalty to the

Lord Joaquin, and share with us for their first time in the Rite of Lucherium, the Rite of the Life and Light of Joaquin."

Lucia was called forward first, and she climbed the stairs leading up to the dais confidently, betraying none of the queasiness which Geoffrey knew she must feel.

"Lucia of Hazcaluche," spoke Xavier, "is it your true and resolved intention to swear loyalty to the Lord Joaquin, to become his Follower in the Way of Lucherium, and a full citizen of Hazcaluche?"
     "It is."

Lucia's voice rang out clearly, without any tremors, and Geoffrey was amazed at how calm she looked.

"Then place both hands upon the *Pontilux* and read the words which lie before you."

> To Joaquin my life I give,
> to Him my loyalty declare,
> that in His Light I now may live,
> His mission now as mine to bear;
> this oath eternal now I swear.

Then Lucia was crying, and Xavier and Mariela embraced her, and although the solemness of the Rite was not broken by cheers of any sort, Geoffrey could sense a wave of acceptance and affection rumble over him from the Followers behind him, directed toward the newest member of their company. And then she was walking back toward him, a radiant smile on her face, and quite suddenly his own name was being called.

"Geoffrey of Hazcaluche, is it your true and resolved intention to swear loyalty to the Lord Joaquin, to become his Follower in the Way of Lucherium and a full citizen of Hazcaluche?"

A deep breath. The words "Courage and Love" flashing through his mind. A clear resolve which had been growing in strength and fullness ever since this choice had been made many hours ago. And then two infinitely significant words.

"It is."

"Then place both hands upon the *Pontilux* and read the words which lie before you."

His oath was not as beautiful or inspiring as Lucia's, but he had never meant anything as much as those five lines of verse.

And then, the release of fear and the unstoppable onslaught of tears which were born out of peace and joy. The hugs, the wave of affection, the walk back, and Geoffrey was standing again next to Lucia, with a smile on his own face that could rival hers.

Xavier was speaking now, reciting the words of the Rite of Lucherium, and Geoffrey caught his breath as the first rays of morning touched the body of Joaquin, and the dry, dry bones burst forth in their own rays of luminous blood. Now the Elders were catching and drinking, and their bodies were shining as if one with the robes they were wearing and the Light they were consuming, and Vincente was guiding Geoffrey forward, and Ayila, Lucia, and a moment later a goblet was pressed into the bard's hand, filled to the brim with the life-giving red liquid.

He drank.

And almost choked. But not from revulsion; rather, his reaction was one of surprise and awe. For while the sight of the cup's viscous contents seemed repulsive in every form to him, the taste was a different matter altogether. It was unlike anything Geoffrey had ever consumed, and yet at the same time its flavor seemed to ring a thousand bells in the bard's mind, bringing back fond memories of half-forgotten banquets and dinners filled with Geoffrey's favorite foods and dearest friends. The actual flavor of the blood was sweet, yet tangy at the same time, and it seemed to both warm Geoffrey like the spiciest mug of mulled cider, and yet at the same time send chills throughout his body as if it had been drawn directly from the purest, iciest mountain stream in Trastaluche. It was smooth and refreshing, and yet it burned as it coursed down Geoffrey's throat and into his churning stomach as if it were made of living fire, filling him with the sensation of a thousand dancing sparks. As he finished his first sip, it seemed as if he were full to the brim, as if the smallest amount of this mystical liquid was all he needed for sustenance.... But at the same time, he found that he wanted more of the blood of Joaquin, more of His Life and Light, and his desire was so strong that he thought it could never be satisfied in a dozen lifetimes, let alone with the contents of a single cup.

"Courage and Love." And he drank it all.

And yet, as he drained the final drops from his goblet and the wonderful sensation of the drink faded away... he suddenly felt nothing. Nothing different, anyway. He certainly wasn't levitating or anything like that.

He made his way back to his spot, not sure if he'd done something wrong, if for some reason he hadn't made the oath correctly or perhaps hadn't meant it enough. "Is that all there is?" he wanted to ask, even though he knew that he shouldn't. He closed his eyes to ward off the hecticness of the moment and to gather his thoughts, searching back to see if somehow he had made a mistake. But he couldn't think of anything. He was almost disappointed, but he wasn't sure if it was disappointment in himself or in all of this. He stayed where he was, unsure of what to do next, humming along to the music which rose and fell around him and joining in the chorus, trying to blend in while he frantically searched for an answer as to what had – or had not – happened.

> At feast in song we raise
> our voices now in praise,
> for He whose Life we take,
> until he shall awake,
> His kingdom new to make.

He smiled, appreciating the beauty of the lyrics and the masterfully crafted harmonies in spite of his despondence. And then stopped in shock, his jaw dropping with wonder.

He could understand the music.

The harmonies, which before had seemed to him so discordant and out of place, now flowed about him sublimely. The words, which before had no rhyme or reason, now fit within him as if they had been written for his mind.

The oath had not been for nothing, nor the cup. For now he understood what before he could not.

He opened his eyes with wonder, and it was as if the entire hall was now filled with the splendor of a noonday sun where before there had been shadow and mist. The walls, floor, and roof seemed to shimmer and dance with a hidden fire, and Geoffrey's companions shone even more intensely than before, illuminated not only from within but from above....

Geoffrey raised his eyes to the jumbled mass of spikes that enveloped Joaquin's body and gasped once again. For where all had been darkness and death now all was Light and Life.

The skeleton pinned to the wall by countless spears was still there, but it was both illuminated and eclipsed by a new, greater reality. In place of a lifeless corpse pinned to a wall, Geoffrey's eyes met with those of a man and yet more than a man, who was very much alive and yet more than alive: the Lord Joaquin. He was clothed in flesh and radiant glory. The spears that had impaled him now flashed as if they were shafts of luminous blood bursting forth from his body in every direction, while the walls and ceiling that before had served as his perch now appeared to branch out from him as if he were their source.

And the Lord Joaquin looked upon Geoffrey and smiled, and in that instant Geoffrey was himself and yet more than himself.

And as the Rite drew to a close, and as the Elders processed out, and as Geoffrey and Lucia, now clad with hoods and full Followers of the Way of Lucherium, led the silver-clad members of the Company through the Great Hall and out its triple doors, Geoffrey sang. And he did so better and more fully than he ever had before.

And he understood.

And when they had taken off their robes and descended once again into the wine chamber, where the Elders, Vincente, Ayila, Geoffrey, Lucia, and many others joined in celebration over a great feast of suckling pig, roasted apples, wine and ale, and, of course freshly-baked bread, Geoffrey slipped away for a moment and, ducking down a short tunnel, emerged into the craft room where he had spent almost every night for the past two months working. Before him sat his quill and parchment, onto which he had been copying a section of Hazcalucherian love songs from a book which was so old that its pages had completely separated from its binding, and which Trentius insisted must be preserved "for future lovers." Sitting down, he dipped his quill and began to copy the next poem on the page.

> My love, what boon you bring my wearied heart;
> what joy your fairness is to tired eyes!
> What wisdom to my mind you do impart,
> and with you, toil does lose harsh duty's guise.
>
> Yet broken shall my love for you still grow,
> and wounded shall I sing your praises whole;
> for fractured you reveal what is below,
> and then shines forth true beauty from your soul.

Geoffrey stopped and looked over his handiwork, and it was flawless: the lines and margins perfectly straight, the letters bold and swooping and beautifully formed in a font which flowed easily from the page. He was sure in his writing, fast in his execution, and confident in the style he had chosen. It was a result which was more perfect than any he had ever produced And he understood that he, Geoffrey of Hazcaluche, was harnessing Lucherium, and, in fact, he had been since the moment he drank from the cup. And at that moment a wave of joy and peace flooded over him, and a new, unquenchable desire awoke within him: the desire to drink of the blood of Joaquin as often as he could, and the desire to partake in the Lord's Life and Light every second of Geoffrey's existence.

"It's incredible, isn't it? That experience?"

Trentius stood leaning against the tunnel doorway, watching Geof-frey. The bard nodded enthusiastically and showed the older man what he had written. Trentius looked it over and whistled with appreciation.

"This is superb work, Geoffrey, even for someone who can har-ness Lucherium. Keep this up and you'll be replacing me before the season is out! But come; now is no time for work, but a time to be joyful and to celebrate, and there is at least one cask of ale with your name on it, I can tell you that. Now, if you'll please lead the way? I suspect that even with the blindfold on, your eyes were still better than mine in the blasted darkness of these tunnels."

The two of them laughed, and Geoffrey of Hazcaluche led Trentius back to the wine chamber, back to the company of good food and good companions, to a place where Lucherium was harnessed, as it is in every action by a true Hazcalucherian, to tell jokes and share tales and to truly live as a member of the Followers of Lord Joaquin.

Chapter XII

The Preparation

It was dark, but not the sort of dark that resides beneath the waters of a deep, fast-moving river whose currents threaten to suck you under. Nor was it the sort of dark which you might find in the depths of an ancient wood even in the daytime, the gnarled branches of trees as old as the earth itself blocking out every last bit of sunlight from the forest floor. Rather, this was a sudden, painful sort of dark, with bursts of red and flashes of gold and white.

It was the sort of dark you experience when someone smacks you upside the head with a stout wooden staff, and it was a sensation which was becoming all-too-familiar to Geoffrey the bard.

"Ow!"

Geoffrey dropped his quarterstaff and grabbed the rapidly swelling lump on the back of his head, glaring indignantly at Vincente, who grinned apologetically as he stepped back, twirling his own staff with practiced skill.

"Focus, Geoffrey! And never, *ever* drop your weapon. Most enemies aren't as kind as Vincente is."

It was Ayila who shouted at him from the far side of the room, while she sent shaft after shaft from a deadly-looking recurve bow into a stuffed straw target with an almost contemptuous ease.

"Why do I have to learn this, anyway?" Geoffrey whined for possibly the tenth time that day. It had been almost a season since he had pledged allegiance to Joaquin and first drank of the Cup of Life and Light, and his life had changed forever. One season of striving to harness Lucherium in everything he did, in trying to unite his goals and actions with the reality of Light and Life, failing at times and greatly succeeding at others. One season of working primarily with Trentius as a scribe, but also with Mariela at the loom, with Vincente in the kitchen, and with Ayila, Xavier, and many others in Muckland. One season of study and questions and learning all he could about the Way of Lucherium and the mysteries it contained. One season of growing closer to the Company of the Followers of Joaquin and to their dead yet ever-living Lord and of hearing about the lives and stories of those around him: of Mariela and Xavier, whose parents had been Followers and whose children were raised in the Way; of Trentius, who had joined after attaining the position of senior Member of the Committee of Ways and Means and then realizing that such a life was not enough; of Ayila, who had been orphaned and abandoned in Muckland and rescued and brought up by the Elders; and of many other Followers, each with a story at once unique and yet common in its encounter with the beauty and truth of the Way of Lucherium. One season of being more of a scribe, more of a bard, and more of a person than ever before. He was more fulfilled than he had been in a very long time, and each week he looked forward with ever-greater anticipation to the Rite of Lucherium, to its terribly grotesque yet mystically sublime moment of unity with the Light and Life of Joaquin. It was a unity brought about by drinking of a cup that held blood and yet more than blood, and which allowed you to live a life that was your own and yet more than your own, and more *of* your own all at the same time.

And one season of training in the art of battlefare, a practice in which, Geoffrey had found, he was absolutely awful.

"You know very well why, my friend. How do you expect to harness Lucherium in a battle if you don't know how to battle in the first place?"

Vincente's voiced brought Geoffrey back to reality, and he nodded reluctantly in understanding. This lesson was one of the first which he had been taught after becoming a full Follower of Joaquin: in order to perfect your reality, you didn't just need proper orientation and intention (although that was important), you had to actually have a reality to perfect. Geoffrey couldn't expect to harness Lucherium to be a great warrior unless he had first mastered the art of battlefare, at least in its rudimentary forms, because, as Trentius had explained to him, Lucherium didn't replace what you had or didn't have; rather, it made you more of yourself. Thus, if you were no fighter in the first place, that wouldn't change just because you could harness Lucherium. By the same token, Geoffrey was very adept at harnessing Lucherium in his writing and composing, because he had already been quite good at those things before. "More implies something there to begin with, and perfection means something was there to be made perfect," Trentius had said to Geoffrey on more than one occasion. "So, practice, practice, practice! Someday you will most certainly need it."

Geoffrey knew the scholar was right, but as he bent over to pick up his staff, his muscles screaming in agony, he wondered how much more practice he could take. He hadn't even landed a blow on Vincente in the weeks the two had spent training together, and as for harnessing Lucherium... well, he could hardly remember to hold to his weapon, much less infuse his actions with mystical energy.

"Come now," encouraged Vincente, "you're doing much better than yesterday, even if you don't see it. Now remember: your staff always stays in front of you, no matter what. Move it and you leave yourself open to attack. Swing out too far and you'll either lose your grip or hit yourself with the other end. Let's try it again, shall we? And one! Two! Three! Four!"

Vincente came at Geoffrey like lightning, and this time the bard was able to block half a dozen of his strikes before the fair-headed man broke through his defenses and delivered a swift blow to the back of Geoffrey's knee, causing him to lose his balance and tumble to the floor. He kept hold of his staff, however, and Ayila, who had finished her archery and ambled over to watch the lopsided exchange, nodded in approval.

"Much better, but you're too focused on your own survival. You'll end up killing yourself at that rate."

"But... isn't that the point?"

"Sometimes, yes, but not now. The point is mastering the art of the fight as best as you can, and, of course, to triumph over your opponent. Winning only comes at the risk of losing. Here, hand me your staff and watch the two of us."

Geoffrey did so, and scrambled out of the way to let Vincente and Ayila spar. Neither were experts with quarterstaffs: Ayila preferred archery and Vincente was exceptional with the traditional Hazcalucherian short sword. However, both had received extensive training with the current Lucherian weapons of choice: the staff and the dagger. Xavier had explained to Geoffrey that these were the easiest to master at short notice, as well as the easiest to carry in all situations without arousing suspicion; thus, every member of the Company, even bards, were to be trained to use them well, and Ayila and Vincente were no exceptions. Geoffrey watched as they circled each other, each waiting for an opening in the other's defenses; then there was a sudden whirlwind of movement and the hearty "thwack thwack thwack!" of oak on oak, and the two broke apart again, having exchanged over a dozen blows in the space of a few seconds. Geoffrey was astounded by their speed and precision, both of which, he knew, were highly augmented by the Lucherium each warrior commanded, such that they were able to perceive their enemy and react accordingly in almost superhuman time. They engaged again, and then spilt apart, and then engaged again, until at last, Vincente, leaping impossibly high above Ayila, twisted in midair and, coming down behind her, struck her staff with such force that it split it two.

Geoffrey clapped for the two of them, and Ayila, after congratulating her opponent, made her way over the barrel where the training staves were kept and tossed Geoffrey another.

"Try it again, and remember: the goal is not survival but art and triumph, and art and triumph come only through Lucherium."

Geoffrey grasped his staff and breathed deeply as he and Vincente circled, trying to let go of his nervousness at the lightning onslaught he knew he was about to face and instead focusing on any weak points he could find in his competition's defensive stance. Then suddenly Vincente lunged, swinging his weapon downward at Geoffrey's head then following up with two quick rotating strikes at his thighs. Geoffrey sidestepped the first blow and parried the others, giving ground before the ferocity of the attacks. He narrowly escaped a sweeping cut at his legs, jumping at the last minute, a necessary reaction which left him off balance for a follow-up jab which he just barely managed to deflect. His breath was coming in ragged gasps now, and he fought off discouragement, straining to concentrate on the fight before him, realizing that if he wanted to win against the bigger and stronger Vincente, he would have to do it before he was completely worn down.

Then suddenly his senses cleared, and he saw his opening. Whenever Vincente pushed forward, he was slow in bringing his staff back in front of him for defense. It was almost as if he was expecting his foe to fall back, thus giving him time to always make the next move. If Geoffrey were to step inward instead of giving ground, well... the idea seemed ridiculous, but the bard had no better option. He narrowed his gaze as the two of them circled and waited for the moment when Vincente would next attack.

Even though he was prepared for it, Vincente's movements were wickedly fast, and as he lunged forward, his staff screaming through the air at Geoffrey's side, it was all the bard could do not to follow his first instinct and shrink away from the danger in front of him. But he pushed it down and, as he parried, used the force of the blow to propel himself toward his opponent instead of away from him. He saw Vincente's eyes widen in shock, and a split-second later Geoffrey found himself inside the deadly arc of his opponent's staff with nothing in the way. He swung his own weapon toward Vincente's exposed right side and felt the satisfying impact of wood on flesh as he landed a blow for the first time in his training. He saw Vincente grimace in pain and was able to enjoy a feeling of elation for all of a half-second before the fair-headed man shoulder-shoved him into the ground and disarmed him with a backhand swipe. Still, he had *done* it. He had broken through.

"Well done!"

Ayila's voice rang out approvingly, and Vincente smiled at Geoffrey as well, offering his hand to help him up and gingerly touching the welt which Geoffrey had left on his side.

"That was a fine bit of staff-work, if I do say so myself. We'll make a warrior out of you yet, Geoffrey of Hazcaluche. Now, what do you say we go once more?"

Geoffrey didn't win the next bout against Vincente, or any bout that day, but from then on, he improved steadily, his blows becoming quicker and surer with each hour spent practicing. His use of Lucher-ium to analyze his enemy's weaknesses and to react almost instantane-ously and with incredible force became more and more consistent. His body began to change as well, his muscles hardening, his senses sharp-ening, and the staff and the dagger becoming more and more like ex-tensions of himself than the heavy, awkward tools they had once seemed to be.

Geoffrey always credited that bout when he first landed a blow on Vincente as the moment he really began to understand how to consciously allow the Light of Joaquin to illuminate everything that he did with true success. For, as Trentius had explained, that was in fact the true nature of the Lucherium which dwelt within each person. From then on, whenever Geoffrey was assigned a task he was unfamiliar with or just plain awful at, he would make the effort to remind himself what the *real* purpose of his toils were and *why* he was undertaking them, a reality and a reason which were ultimately, as Ayila reminded him daily, a part of the Story of the Author and the Way of Lucherium. He quickly found that doing so made it much easier to harness the mystical energy he sought, allowing him not only to produce better results, but to become better and better at the arts of learning and practice themselves, and he began to look forward to his training in combat as much as he did his work as a scribe with Trentius.

Then, one day, when he had bested Vincente three times in a row, the final time by vaulting off the nearby wall and hurling himself upon the fair-headed man with such force that he shattered his opponent's staff, Vincente declared that he was satisfied with the bard's skills.

"Already?" Geoffrey was surprised. "But most days you pound me four out of every five times we spar. I'm still nowhere near the level you're at."

"And neither will you be for more several seasons and countless hours of practice," Vincente smiled. "But you've more than proved yourself capable of standing up to me in a fight, and I believe you will find it to be a rare occurrence that you meet anyone- even a soldier of Trastaluche- who can match you blow to blow. Remember, most of them aren't harnessing Lucherium. Outside of the Company of Followers and, of course, the elite Guards of Trastivo and the Committees, you'd have no trouble besting anyone you came up against."

"But what if I *do* come up against one of the Elites, as you call them? I mean, isn't being able to overcome them kind of the point of our training?"

"If you do, then it will make little difference whether or not you even *have* a staff and dagger, much less that you know how to use them. But I'm glad you asked that" -it was Ayila who re- sponded- "because that brings us to another step in your train- ing." She stepped into the sandy rink which was used for spar- ring and turned to face Geoffrey, weaponless. "Here. Attack me."

Geoffrey was confused, but he reluctantly did as he was asked, lung- ing forward and taking a half-hearted swing at Ayila's side.

He never got the chance to touch her.

She shouted, and Geoffrey's staff suddenly stopped in midair as a shimmering sphere of light seemed to surround Ayila with the strength of a stone wall. Then Ayila thrust her hand forward, and Geoffrey felt as if the wall had come to life and decided to trample him underfoot, as the sphere expanded outward with incredible force, throwing Geoffrey to the floor and pinning him there. Ayila drew near and gazed down at him, a hint of a smile on her face.

"I should hope if you ever find yourself in battle with an enemy who is a woman, you'll treat her with a little more respect than that. I could have dumped you on the ground even without Lu- cherium."

She helped an astonished Geoffrey to his feet and held up a hand to forestall the flood of questions which she could see were about to burst out of him.

"Patience, my dear friend, and in time all shall be explained to you. What you just saw and felt was an example of an ancient art, which was once known by the name of Lucherian battlefare and was practiced and perfected by all the defenders of the Way of Lucherium. You remember how you mentioned to us just a few days ago that your weapons had ceased to become clumsy objects you waved around and now seemed to be extensions of yourself? Well, Lucherium is what allows such a unity of wielder and object to happen, making your reality almost one with the reality of the staff, the dagger, the bow, or whatever else you are wielding. This unity, along with the strength and speed infused within you through Lucherium, are what make a Follower of Joaquin- or, on the other side, a wielder of the Void and a follower of Trastivo- so especially deadly on the battle-field. But," she paused and removed Geoffrey's dagger from its sheath, placing it on a table in the corner of the room, "what if you were in a situation where you had no weapons? Or what if, instead of harnessing Lucherium to make a weapon an exten-sion of yourself, the unity you perfected was that of yourself with the Light of Joaquin and the Author, of yourself with Lu-cherium?"

"But… but I thought that one could only use Lucherium to more perfectly do the things which one could already do in the first place…," Geoffrey responded. "Like, I can't use it to turn stones into gold because that's impossible, but I can use it to become a great scribe or a better bowman."

"All of that is true," replied Ayila, "but remember: how and why do you fight, or write, or train in the first place?"

"By the Light and Life of Joaquin, and For the Way of Lucherium," answered Geoffrey, faithfully reciting the phrase which Ayila had drilled into his head.

"Precisely! And I believe that Xavier and Trentius have both told you that doing so can sometimes mean being able to perform acts which by normal standards are beyond your ability. Not contrary to it, mind you, but beyond it."

"Like Xavier's defense the night his house was invaded?"

"Just like. Now listen; there are two keys to mastering the art of Lucherian battlefare. The first is knowing *precisely* what it is you are doing, what you are seeking to do, and why you are doing it. As you know, that's essential for harnessing Lucherium fully in any circumstance, but especially in this case. For, you see, to wield such a concentrated and powerful amount of Lucherium involves a very intimate link with reality. In theory you already know how to do it, of course, since you've drunk of the Cup of Life and Light and been trained in the art of battlefare; that is, you've got all the pieces. But in practice it can be very difficult to focus in on what exactly you're wanting to do without distractions or just general misdirection. The second key, and this is just as important, is to strive to allow the Light and Life of Joaquin and of the Author to work within and through you and your actions. For that, of course, is what Lucherium really is. This second element is very closely related to the first; if you know the reality of things and the Way of

Lucherium, you'll already be open to living the life of Joaquin. Still, it's important enough that it's worth mentioning. To make it easier to master both of these elements, I'm going to teach you some phrases which you can utter to help you understand and express the precise nature of what it is you are trying to do. You don't have to say them, of course, and those of us who are practiced in this art often don't, especially in the heat of a battle, but it is an indispensable help when you're just getting started. Now, are you ready?"

Geoffrey nodded enthusiastically, excited at the prospect of learning such a mysterious and powerful art.

"Good! Now, we're going to start with the simplest and most essential act: forming a shield. You've seen the Conexios before, correct? Well, this is a sort of personal version which can be summoned as an incredibly potent form of protection, and it's composed of the same combination of willpower and Lucherium. It'll stop almost any weapon, even up to a catapult if its wielder has any sort of experience. And, more importantly, it is the only defense against the Voided Lucherium harnessed by Trastivo and the Committee Elites. Now repeat after me, and bear in mind that this may not work perfectly, or at all, for the first several times you try it. But down here, where Lucherium runs freely, is the best place to learn."

Ayila closed her eyes and exhaled slowly, calming herself. Then she thrust her arms outward and chanted, *"Light within, your shield begin!"* At once there appeared around her the same crackling orb of energy which had flattened Geoffrey a moment ago, but this time it remained in its place. Then just as suddenly it was gone, leaving no trace except in Ayila's eyes, which flashed as if she had just drunk of the Cup of Life and Light. Nervous but eager, Geoffrey breathed deeply to clear his own mind and, closing his eyes, repeated after Ayila. His face fell, however, when after opening them again apprehensively, he saw nothing. Ayila noticed his disappointment and smiled encouragingly.

"It's quite alright. Very few people get it on the first try. You were nervous about what was going to happen, weren't you? Yes? Well, there's part of the problem. Try it again and focus on what it is you're trying to do and why. Remember, the power by which you construct your shield is not only your own, but it is the Light of Joaquin. It is His work, which is also your fulfill-ment, that is to be carried out through your actions."

"Yes, yes, I know; all things are done by the Light and Life of Joaquin and For the Way of Lucherium," Geoffrey answered back. He closed his eyes again, and this time tried to rid himself of any negative thoughts as he chanted the double verse. Upon opening them, he gasped; for just a moment he saw something flickering and shimmer-ing, as if he had stepped into the center of a bolt of lightning, whose tendrils of energy coursed and snaked around him, forming a barrier of light. The moment passed in less than the blink of an eye, but Geof-frey was sure it had happened. Eager to see more, he closed his eyes and began to recite the phrase again, pouring his energy into this one act as part of the Way of Lucherium and his service to the Lord Joaquin. The brilliance he saw lasted the space of several heartbeats this time before his concentration wavered, and Ayila and Vincente nodded in approval.

"Well done! Very well done!" Vincente bounded over to Geoffrey and clapped him on the back once the moment had passed. "Why, it took me perhaps a week of practice before I could sustain a Lucherian shield for that long."

Ayila said nothing, but the proud look on the face of the woman who Geoffrey knew was widely regarded as the one of the most powerful wielders of Lucherium was worth more than an entire ballad of accolades to the bard.

After several more weeks of practice, Geoffrey could fashion a Lucherian shield as long as he wanted and whenever he wanted, provided that he was given time to clear his mind, to concentrate, and to recite the verses he'd been taught. Doing so in the midst of a sparring match or while he was occupied with something else was still quite difficult for him, as he was prone to distraction and the fear that something would go wrong -which then of course it always did. But he kept at it doggedly and was heartened to see improvement come slowly but surely. He learned other tactics as well, such as how to expand one's shield rapidly to flatten unsuspecting opponents, as Ayila had done to him, and he even began to work on mastering the much more difficult act of funneling Lucherium into a focused blast which could then be hurled with destructive force, although he managed to accomplish the latter with only limited success. While Ayila and Vincente were quite satisfied with his improvements, they warned him not to get too confident in his abilities. It was one thing, Vincente had said, to harness Lucherium within its strongest haven, but it was an entirely different matter to do so when one stepped out of the underground world of Hazcaluche and into the "Leaden Curtain" of the reign of Trastivo. It was not impossible for one who had drunk of the Cup and was properly trained, but the sheer weight of the Void which the Committees had created made it like swimming upwards against a swift current.

"That's why it's imperative that you train, and train intensely," said Vincente one day, as he, Geoffrey, and Ayila took a short break from an exercise which involved the both of them attacking an unarmed Geoffrey with staves, while the bard did his best to fend them off using only Lucherium. "One false step, one hesitation out there can get you killed. You need to live and breathe your unity with the Light and Life of Joaquin in everything you do- be it battle, toil, or leisure- if you want it to keep *you* alive and breathing. Now, let's try that last situation again, but this time, Ayila, let's give you a bow...."

"Are you trying to impale my bard?" Xavier's voice boomed out from the tunnel as he made his entrance, smiling and offering greeting to the three younger people. "Ayila, Geoffrey, Son, it's good to see all of you hard at work. Unfortunately, you'll have to set the training aside for a while now. For you see, the time has come to put it to use. I've come to fetch you, *all* of you," he glanced pointedly in Geoffrey's direction, "to council with the Elders. We've just received news that our efforts have paid off. Our preparations are aligned, and the time has come to act."

"To act? What do you mean?" Geoffrey wasn't quite sure at first what Xavier was trying to say, but even as he asked he felt a thrill of realization course through him, and the answer of the older man did not surprise him.

"Why, to go to war. The time is right for the retaking of Hazcaluche. Now, all of you, follow me. We have much to discuss.

Chapter XIII

The Design

Geoffrey followed Xavier, Ayila, and Vincente through the series of cramped tunnels and dimly-lit rooms which led from the training area to the oval-shaped chamber which served as the meeting place for the Elders of the Followers of Joaquin. His mind was still ablaze with the news he had just heard: the time had come for the Hazcalucherian forces to go to war against the armies of Trastivo and the Committees, and he, Geoffrey, was specifically to be involved. That last part both frightened and confused him; although his battlefare skills had greatly improved since he had begun training with Vincente and Ayila, they were still sorely lacking in comparison to the others, and on top of that, Geoffrey, who had never been in a true battle before in his life, wasn't sure if he would have the courage to put them to use if the time came to do so. Still, if he had learned anything over the past season, it was that Xavier usually had a very good reason for anything he did or asked Geoffrey to do, so he quelled the questions and protestations welling up within him and took his seat along with the others at the large, rounded table that dominated the center of the council room.

Glancing around at those assembled, Geoffrey recognized the faces of Xavier, Trentius, and Mariela, as well as the Elders Asvoria and Alberic, a married couple with faces so ancient and hair so silver that Geoffrey thought they looked as if they had been alive before the War of Liberation. He had met them once or twice before, during which he had learned that they *had* in fact witnessed the War and the time of the fall of Joaquin when they themselves were very young. Besides himself,

Ayila, and Vincente, there were two other non-Elders present, neither of whom Geoffrey had met previously. The first was a tall, red-haired man, with almost frighteningly pale skin, green eyes, and long, boney fingers who introduced himself as Julius, a fellow scribe and scholar, and in charge of keeping the records of the Company of Follower's many market transactions in the northern city of Covern. The second was a short, bulky man with equally short brown hair and muscles which rivaled those of Vincente. His name was Carlos, he said, and from the long kiss which he and Ayila shared upon seeing each other, Geoffrey suspected that they were at the very least promised to each other, if not already married. It was only when Carlos turned to greet the bard that Geoffrey noticed he was missing his right arm entirely; yet his smile and the flames in his eyes were such that he seemed to possess the life of a dozen men, despite not quite being whole himself. Xavier waited while warm greetings and introductions were made all around before rapping lightly on the table with his knuckles to call the meeting to order.

> "Thank you, friends, for being here at this hour which is so grave and yet so hopeful. As all of you know already, the Elders and I have called you here because each of you is to play an essential role in the maneuvers of the Company of Followers over the next few days. Alberic, if you would do the honors of explaining just what is going on?"
>
> "With pleasure, Xavier." The elderly man stood slowly, his hands pressed firmly onto the wood of the table to support himself. "I ask for your patience and attention, fellow citizens of Hazcaluche, for there is much to be told and little time to tell

it." Hesitating for a moment, he turned to Xavier and asked: "Where shall I begin?"

"How about with the defeat of Joaquin and the dispersion of his armies, if you please?"

"Very good. Now, as I'm sure you have all learned, with the fall of Joaquin's reign and the rise of the Committees, the forces of Hazcaluche were scattered. Many were hunted down and slain by the armies of Trasitvo, but a small number, led by Mikhail, one of the chief lieutenants of Joaquin, fled eastward where they disappeared into the furthest reaches of the Volunaltus Mountains. I was just a boy at the time of their defeat, and at first we cursed them bitterly, thinking that they had abandoned us just when our need was greatest and had allowed Trastivo and his servants to lay siege to the city and overthrow Joaquin. However, in the first days of the new reign of Trastivo, not long after the Elders of the Company had discovered the existence of the Great Hall and the skeleton of Lord Joaquin, a man named Jeremy appeared, claiming to bring a message from Mikhail. He was the first to bring us news about the foreknowledge of Joaquin regarding his own demise and of the design which he had set in motion regarding the care of his Followers thereafter. According to Jeremy, it was Joaquin himself who, knowing what was to befall him, sent Mikhail away with the remnants of His army and their families, so that living on in exile they could, through their own offspring and those they recruited, continue to exist in preparation for the day when the Followers of Joaquin would need them once again for the battle to retake the land of Hazcaluche. And there in the Volunaltus Mountains have the forces of Joaquin remained, ever watchful, ever growing in number, awaiting the day when word is sent to them by the Elders of the Company to assemble and lay siege to Trastaluche's easternmost city of Astraia, the primary defense against any threat which might arise from the mountains."

He paused for a moment, his quavering voice feeling the strain of the discourse, and drank from a cup of water his wife handed to him before continuing.

"Scarcely a week ago we sent them that word," he said, "and now they are amassing in the foothills which surround Astraia, preparing for an assault on the city. We did so because, for the first time since the fall of Joaquin, an opportunity has arisen which maybe, just maybe, could allow for their re-entry and the beginning of the war to re-capture Hazcaluche...."

His voice faltered again, and he broke off into a spasm of coughing. His wife stood and, helping him back into his chair, handed him his cup once more. Then she turned to face the group seated around the table.

"Perhaps I should take over for a little while," she said, her voice soft and sweet as a chuckling mountain stream, but strong and clear all the same, despite her advanced age. Xavier nodded at her gratefully, and she continued.

"Now, as many of you might have guessed, the defenses of Trastivo and the forces of Trastaluche are not merely those of spear and sword. Around each of the seven central cities has been woven a dark sort of shield, similar to a Conexio, but of course not fashioned out of Lucherium. Together, these form part of a greater shield which encompasses not only the cities but the entire land of Trastaluche. We call it the Leaden Curtain, and its presence is in large part what stifles the harnessing of Lucherium by anyone who has not drunk of the Cup of Light and Life. In fact, even for us it can be very difficult to access the Light of Joaquin within those places which are held most strongly by Trastivo and the Committees. This curtain is especially hard to penetrate because it is composed of the collective will of the senior Members of all seven Committees. It is this shield which has been keeping the forces of Dantius, the son of Mikhail and now leader of the armies of Joaquin, out of Trastaluche; not only are they unable to enter, but even if they could, they would be quickly annihilated by the enemy, as the presence of Trastivo's dark power would keep them from harnessing Lucherium. It is toward the penetration of this shield that the Company of Followers has been working all these years, and we have just recently received word that our efforts have been rewarded."

Geoffrey leaned forward, almost holding his breath, riveted to every word uttered by Asvoria, and around the table he could see that each of the non-Elders was doing the same.

"Ever since we realized the true nature of the Leaden Curtain, we have been directing the bulk of our efforts to finding a way to penetrate it. Over the past several decades, Followers of Joaquin have been secretly infiltrating or influencing each of the seven central Committees with the goal of either sitting as a senior Committee Member themselves or ensuring that one current member is at least sympathetic toward the plight of the Company of Followers. It has been a long and dangerous path, with far too many deaths, but several seasons ago we finally established our people- or friends of them- in positions of power in six of the seven Committees. Six of the Curtain's layers, therefore, while still intact, are weakened sufficiently that one skilled in the art of Lucherium could penetrate them. The only one we have been unable to infiltrate has been the Committee of Progress. However, less than a season ago, this changed."

She turned toward Geoffrey as she continued.

"On the night you pledged your allegiance, Geoffrey, there was another young woman who joined our Company as well, do you remember?"

"Yes, I do...," answered Geoffrey. "Lucia was her name, correct?"

"Your memory serves you well, bard. What you may not know, however, is that Lucia is in fact the wife of none other than Eligesh, who was recently selected to be a senior member of the Committee of Progress. So recently, in fact, that he has not yet been corrupted by dabbling in the Void. He and his wife reside in the Upper City, and just yesterday she sent us word that he is close, very close, to showing enough sympathy toward our cause to weaken the final layer of the Curtain. This caused us great excitement, of course, and we immediately notified the armies of Dantius to begin their assembly and to advance on the city of Astraia. Lucia contacted us again just yesterday and told us that the Committees are aware of the massing of Dantius' forces. They have decided to send none other than her husband to oversee the defense of Astraia, and, of course, she is to accompany him on the journey. The Committees are confident- too confident, in fact- that their defenses are more than secure. However, mark my word, as soon as they are given time to think as to why Dantius, surely knowing of the existence of the Leaden Curtain, has chosen this time to attack, they will begin to suspect some of their own of turning. Our sympathizers are well-hidden, but we cannot hope that all of them would survive such an intense inquiry unscathed. So we must move now."

She turned to Xavier, who sat in the chair to her right. "I believe that it is your task to explain what exactly their mission is?"

"Quite right, thank you, Asvoria." Xavier stayed seated in his chair and unfurled a rolled-up parchment which had been lying in front of him, and which, Geoffrey now saw, contained a detailed map of Trastaluche. It was the type which not only included its seven central cities and the roads that connected them: Hilio and Lamagria in the west, engulfed by broad swaths of forest; Platus and Alora in the south, bordering the Sea of Lakyam; Astraia in the east, nestled in the foothills of the Voluntaltus Mountains; Covern in the north, guarding the pass which existed between the final peaks of the Voluntaltus Range and the wild, barren moors and highlands of the Northern Regions; and finally, Spiraluche in the center; but also a great many of the forts, villages, rivers, streams, hills, valleys, and forests of that land.

"Now," said Xavier, "in order to give ourselves the best chance at breaking through the Leaden Curtain and allowing the Hazcalucherian forces to enter the country, we have decided to send small groups to every one of the seven central cities, each of which acts as a separate tether, or source, of the Leaden Curtain. In each place, they will attempt to penetrate it using Lucherium. We are not entirely sure of its strength, but we think that such a coordinated attack will be our best option for unraveling its weakest threads in a manner such that they cannot be immediately rewoven. I myself, of course, and most of the other Elders, will remain here in Spiraluche, where, gathered for the Rite directly under the Courtyard of Committees and the dwelling place of Trastivo, we will do our best to break through the Curtain at its strongest point. The five of you" -He gestured at the companions at the table- "are to travel to the city of second-most importance: Astraia, where the situation is perhaps the most complicated. You see, apart from the impending attack of Dantius, which of course has caused the Committees to pour their efforts into strengthening the city's defenses, of all of the seven cities, Astraia is the only one where we have no well-founded company. Perhaps because of its proximity to the mountains, Astraia has always remained, apart from Spiraluche of course, the place most under the power of Trastivo and the Committees. Apart from Lucia, who will meet you there, you can expect no outside help unless you succeed in your mission and the forces of Dantius are able to enter the city. Your task, therefore, is three-fold. First, you are to infiltrate Astraia and, when the moment is right, you are to harness Lucherium to expose and break through the Leaden Curtain, thereby giving the forces of Hazcaluche the opportunity to assault the city directly. Second, you are to assist Lucia in any way possible in the conversion of her husband. He is close, she tells us, to at least sympathizing with our way of life, but he has not quite swayed far enough in his loyalties to weaken his link in the Curtain, and as of yet he does not know of his wife's oath to Joaquin or of her involvement with the Company of his Followers. If she fails in at least opening his mind to the Way of Lucherium, then all of our efforts in every city will be for naught. However, if he is turned, then all seven of the Curtains layers ought to be vulnerable to our attack. Finally," continued Xavier, "you must understand that even if all of our designs succeed and the Curtain is torn through, we shall have only penetrated it slightly. It will in no way be destroyed, and even if weakened, it will still render the use of Lucherium nearly impossible to any who have not drunk of the Cup of Life and Light. And among this number are included the soldiers of Dantius, who are able to harness Lucherium readily enough in their mountain strongholds but have had no way to partake in the Rite or drink of the Cup. As a result, their access to Lucherium will be severely stifled once they come in contact with the shadow which Trastivo has cast over this part of the land. Thus, at the very least in Astraia, the Curtain must be not only torn but partially lifted, or the forces of Dantius will surely be destroyed even if they manage to enter the city. This last fact is the cause of the overconfidence of Trastivo and the Committees. They believe that even if we were to put a tear in their shield, our forces would be demolished before they advanced even five leagues into Trastaluche. Therefore, we are sending this with you, to be kept in the care of Vincente and used when the time is right."

Walking over to one of the many bookshelves which lined the room, he removed a section of books, revealing behind it a small, hidden cupboard which was locked three times. Fishing a set of keys out of his pocket, he opened the heavy iron door of the cupboard and took out a small box, ornately carved and covered in what appeared to be gold.

"I will not open this here, and nor should any of you until the moment arrives, but know that within this box lie the bones of a finger of the Lord Joaquin. It is one of several which we dared to remove many years ago in case we ever needed to invoke the Rite of Lucherium outside of the Great Hall. One has been given to each of the Companies of Followers which exist in the other central cities of Trastaluche, so that they too might invoke and partake in the Rite and the Cup. They shall each invoke the Rite in the sacred places of their cities, as we shall here in Spiraluche, but no such space exists in Astraia, and no such band exists to invoke the Rite. You shall be the first to give Light and Life to that city, and in doing so you will begin to lift its Curtain so that the forces of Dantius, albeit with great difficulty, might be able to harness Lucherium in their fight against the armies of Trastivo and, upon reaching you, drink from the Cup and enter into the Life and Light of their fallen Lord."

He handed the box solemnly to Vincente, who, his hands shaking slightly at the realization of what he was holding, placed it reverently and gingerly in his satchel. "It shall not leave my sight or my person while I yet live," he promised.

"Nor ours," added Ayila quickly, and Carlos, Julius, and Geoffrey did the same.

"Excellent. That is how it must be. If the Committees were to get their hands on it, I shudder to think what devilry they could wreak with it, or what destruction to our land they might unwittingly cause in trying to wield it. That is in fact why we have never taken down the rest of the body of Joaquin from the ceiling of the Great Hall, and why the few pieces we have removed and their places of hiding are guarded with such secrecy and care. Now," he continued, "as to the specifics of the mission; the first issue is travel to Astraia."

Using a sharpened piece of soft, grey rock which served as a sort of marker, he outlined the proposed journey on the map unfurled before him as he spoke.

"You shall exit the city tomorrow under the cover of the darkest part of the night using the tunnel which delves under the eastern wall. From there you will make your way across the countryside until you have crossed the first set of hills and are out of sight of the city walls. That is where you shall set up camp. Stay silent and unseen throughout the day; it is a wild, untrekked area, but you cannot afford to be seen or heard by anyone, lest our designs be revealed and destroyed by the Committees. From there you shall once again travel by night to the house of a farmer who is loyal to our cause. He shall provide you with horses, provisions, and clothing for the rest of the journey, which from then on can be made in daylight along the main road. Now, once you draw near to the city, one of you must enter before the others and make contact with Lucia. She has devised a way to get you all not only into the city but within the walls of the centermost courtyard as well, just outside of the keep. Geoffrey," he said, turning to the bard who sat up straight, surprised at the sound of his name, "you shall be the one who makes contact with Lucia. In fact, your presence is essential to carrying out this plan. You see, Lucia has arranged to throw a grand banquet for the officers, the Committee Members, and the distinguished citizens of Astraia, in celebration of her husband's visit and the imminent defeat of the forces of Dantius, and she shall see to it that Geoffrey is hired to provide the music and entertainment for the evening, and that the rest of you are hired as laborers to help with its preparations. This banquet will take place within the courtyard directly outside the Keep, and it will empty the building of its normal inhabitants, allowing Vincente, Carlos, Ayila, and Julius to overpower any guards who remain and infiltrate it. On the upper floor of the Keep you will find the meeting chamber for the chief Committee Members of Astraia. There, the Leaden Curtain and the city's own defenses have been crafted, and it is there that the Rite, if it is to fully weaken their power, must take place. The Rite, of course, can be invoked as soon as you have made your way into the Keep. However, the Curtain will have to wait until Eligesh, the husband of Lucia, has been swayed. If he has not already wavered in his loyalty to Trastivo, then some point during the night Lucia will call him away on some pretext and make her final appeal. If her efforts are in vain then it is possible, Julius and Geoffrey, that your way with words may be needed as a last resort. Once he has departed from their side, the penetration should take only a matter of minutes, as the integrity of each layer will already be compromised. The rest of the details I will leave to you to work out, as they will depend greatly on the situation you encounter once you arrive. In the event that disputes among you arise as to what the best course of action should be, Carlos shall decide. He is not only a city planner who is familiar with the streets of Astraia, but he is also perhaps our best strategist. In matters relating to negotiation, Julius shall be listened to; in battlefare, it shall be Vincente; and in Lucherium, Ayila. Do all of you understand what it is you are being asked to do, and do you accept to carry this mission out for the glory and the growth of the realm of Joaquin?"

The other four nodded, and after a moment, Geoffrey joined in. He felt very unprepared for such a mission, even if his role only consisted in providing a distraction for the others, and it was hard for him to keep down the already growing sense of dread as to what might happen if they were to fail. But he was a Follower of the Way of Lucherium. He had drunk of the Cup and had pledged his loyalty to Joaquin, and that was reason and inspiration enough to strengthen his resolve.

The rest of the night and the next day were a blur for Geoffrey as preparations were made, messages were sent, and farewells were said. There was little time for sleep with so much to put in order, but Geoffrey didn't mind; he doubted he could have slept any amount anyway. His mind and body were caught up in the nervous excitement of the mission which loomed ahead of them. Each traveler was to carry with them their staff and dagger, a rucksack filled with enough provisions to last for two-days' travel, herbs and other medicines, and whatever other personal items each chose to take: for Ayila her quiver of arrows and a short, compactly fashioned crossbow which could be concealed more easily than her normal weapon of choice; for Geoffrey his quills, ink, and parchments, as well as his own mandolin; for Julius, a set of stamps, seals, and letters used for forging papers and making documents look important and official, as well as a long, two-handed broadsword which was the northern warrior's weapon of choice; for Carlos a set of plans for the city of Astraia and a special single-grip saber which suited his fighting style; and for Vincente his short, bluesteel sword and the golden box which contained within it a finger of the body of Joaquin, source of the Company's power and the key to their success.

The next morning dawned clear and calm, and everyone but Julius, who excused himself regrettably to ensure that their forged documents of travel would be ready in time for that night, paused in their feverish preparations for a moment and gathered with the Elders and those members of the Company of Followers who knew of their upcoming departure to invoke the Rite of Lucherium and drink of the Cup of Life and Light once more before departing. It was an especially solemn affair, for despite their hope for success and the dawning of a new Era of Hazcaluche, few believed that they would pass through these next couple of days unscathed. For his part, Geoffrey struggled with the images of Eldrige which flashed through his mind with every greater frequency as the hour to depart drew nearer. He still doubted his ability to undergo such horror for the sake of the Lord to whom he had sworn his allegiance. Geoffrey's longing to drink of the Cup had never been so great, nor had the Light and Life of Joaquin ever seemed so necessary to him to carry out the task which lay ahead. And when the moment came, it was as if Geoffrey were saying goodbye to the dearest of friends, and yet at the same time losing himself in the immensity of Joaquin and taking his Lord into himself, to accompany and sustain him on the journey ahead. Although the Rite had no effect on his turbulent emotions and his uncertainty about his own capabilities, it strengthened his resolve to embark on the mission at hand and to see it through, not only for the sake of himself and his friends, but for the sake of the Way of Lucherium and for the Lord Joaquin Himself.

Food and drink were brought forth as the sun began to set, and the five travelers sloughed their way through a farewell banquet of roast chicken, fresh greens, mashed corn, and candied fruits, the likes of which would have been savored tremendously and remembered for weeks had their stomachs not been churning at the thought of the journey which now lay just hours ahead. As the night grew blacker and the streets above them more silent, Vincente emerged from the quiet corner of the hall where he, Xavier, and Mariela had been sharing the precious moments of heartfelt murmurs and long embraces of the goodbye between parents and a child with whom they are especially close. After hugging his mother tightly once more, the fair-headed man strode back towards the table where his four companions had been conversing with Trentius while finishing the last of the ale.

"It's time we're off."

His words seemed to fill Geoffrey with a thousand bolts of lightning and a leaden weight at the same time. He was finally and fully struck with the realization of what lay before him. Mariela, Xavier and Trentius embraced each of the Followers, murmuring words of farewell and encouragement. As Trentius came to Geoffrey, he whispered, "Pay no heed to the fears and the darkness, friend. Rejoice! Rejoice even when you feel it not, and live the Life and Way of Joaquin with every fiber of your being. For you are now part of a ballad which bards shall sing for generations to come. And therein lies the wonder of it all, eh?" Geoffrey nodded his thanks and hugged the older man tightly, wondering not for the first time if he would see him again. Trentius was not to remain in Spiraluche, he knew. As one of the younger elders, he was traveling to the coastal city of Platus, perhaps the third most powerful in terms of its connection to Trastivo and the Void, to attempt to sever the threads of the Curtain there.

Finally, the goodbyes, which always take too long to say and yet also seem too short, were finished. As the group headed toward the entrance of the tunnel which would lead them under the walls of Spiraluche and into the night beyond, Xavier called out after them in one last word of encouragement:

"I shall keep you no longer, friends, but as a parting word, remember this: the time which is even now upon us is not an easy
one, but it is a glorious one, and it is the chapter of the Story
into which we have been forever written. I hope that I shall have
many years yet to look upon your faces and to tell and retell the
tales which we are just now stepping into, but if that is not the
case, take heart and recall that there are times when it is death
which must first befall you before Life and Light break
through."

And then torches were lit, and Geoffrey, Ayila, Julius, Carlos, and Vincente entered the tunnel, and the voice of Xavier and the light of the wine chamber were left behind as they wound into the darkness.

Chapter XIV

The Journey

Vincente, Ayila, Geoffrey, Carlos, and Julius continued silently down the passage in single file for perhaps half of an hour, their way well-lit by the touches they carried, until they came to a small room, which was really no more than a place where the tunnel widened, and Vincente motioned for them to stop.

"From here on we can no longer use the torches," he explained. "The tunnel we are about to enter delves much deeper into the ground in order to travel beneath the foundations of the city wall, and unlike the rest of our network of passages, there are no ventilation shafts. Torches would suck away the little air which naturally exists there faster than it could be replaced. And anyway, we might as well get rid of them now, for we shan't be able to use them once we emerge on the other side; there is too much risk of being seen from the wall. But don't worry; there is only one pathway, and you cannot get lost. Stay close to the person in front of you and stay alert, and you'll be just fine. I'll go first and warn you when our descent begins."

He shoved his torch into the dirt floor, the others following suit after a moment, and the passageway was plunged into darkness.

"Alright then, follow me, and stay close."

Vincente's voice floated out of the blackness just ahead of Geoffrey, and doing his best not to trip over Ayila, who walked in front of him, he bumped and felt his way along the tunnel, one hand on the wall for support, another stretched out before him to sense changes in direction or speed. They had traveled only perhaps a hundred paces when Vincente spoke again.

> "We've nearly reached the edge of the city walls. From here the tunnel will slope downward much more steeply, and our going will be slow. In fact, I think it might be best for us to get down on our hands and knees now. Keep feeling in front of you until you come to the point where the passage drops off. Don't worry about the incline; there are rungs fastened into the floor, and you can descend it just like a ladder. I will warn you though; it's quite a climb, and it can get very stuffy and hot down there. Once you've reached the bottom, it's around fifty paces forward to clear the foundations and the moat; then the tunnel will start to rise upward. If you get turned around or stuck, just yell. Ready then? Alright, off we go."

Geoffrey crawled forward apprehensively, moving at what seemed to him to be a snail's pace and dreading the possibility that he might put a hand out into open space, lose his balance, and tumble down the shaft that lay in front of him, slamming into Ayila and Vincente and causing them to fall, too. His breathing began to quicken, and he felt almost frozen to the spot.

> "I've reached the edge, Geoffrey; just a few paces further."

Ayila's voice rang out reassuringly just ahead of him, and Geoffrey inched his way forward again until he felt the ground before him began to slope and the hard, cold metal of the uppermost rung against his palm. Twisting himself around, he began to descend feet first for what seemed like ages. The air around him felt thicker and thinner all at the same time, and his rapid breaths seemed to be of no avail. Sweat dripped from his brow and oozed from his hands, making them slippery and awakening the fear of falling once again in Geoffrey's mind. Nonetheless, he kept climbing, focusing on his journey rung by rung, trying not to succumb to the panic which flared in his chest. Finally, when he felt he couldn't go any deeper without bursting into flame due to the heat, his foot slammed awkwardly into the hard rock floor of the tunnel once again. Dismounting the ladder, he turned and began to grope his way along the passageway, trying to count his steps as he went.

"Twenty-three, twenty-four, twenty-five, Halfway there...."

He was sweating more now, and the tunnel seem to constrict around him as his body screamed against the lack of air.

"Forty-seven, forty-eight, forty-nine, fifty, fifty-one, fifty-two...."

Geoffrey was beginning to worry that somehow he had lost his way or stumbled down some other passageway which Vincente did not know about. In his fear, he surged forward... and then slammed into the sharp upward incline and identical metal rungs which marked the beginning of the journey to the surface, realizing as he did that

Vincente's longer stride meant that his paces were not equal to Geoffrey's. Desperate to escape, he began climbing upward as fast as his shaking limbs would allow. Soon the air began to cool and clear, and then, quite suddenly, there were no more rungs and Geoffrey burst out into the midst of a small grove of trees which grew on the edge of one of the many winding creeks dotting the Trastalucherian landscape. After pulling himself out with the help of Vincente, he collapsed on the ground, gratefully taking in massive gasps of the crisp night air. A moment later Carlos emerged awkwardly, his one arm making this part of the journey especially hard, and after him, Julius, each drenched in sweat and panting as well. The company sat in silence for a long moment, savoring their freedom from the cramped confines of the tunnel before Vincente stood once again and began helping them to their feet.

> "On to the next bit," he said. "From here it's just a few hours'
> walk to where we will camp for the day, but we must be there
> and out of sight before dawn begins to break."

And so they set off once more, following ancient trails which Vincente and Carlos seemed to know by heart, their link to Lucherium enhancing their eyesight such that no light was needed even when clouds blanketed the sky and blocked out the moon. This part of the journey was much more pleasant, and Geoffrey, who had always loved walks in the countryside and had taken them whenever he could, almost began to enjoy their trek through the long grasses which blanketed the low, rolling hills to the east of Spiraluche. Behind them the city loomed above the landscape, each level dominating the one below, culminating in the jutting towers of the fortress of Trastivo which rose almost as high again as the entire city beneath it. They had been walking for about three hours, and the darkness was just beginning to lessen, when after cresting a particularly large hill and descending partway down its other side, Vincente pointed toward a dense thicket of small, twisted trees and bushes scarcely a stone's throw ahead.

"That's where we'll set up camp for the daytime. It's well-covered and very much out of the way, and no one can spot us here, either from the main road or the city walls. In fact, as long as we use only dry wood, I expect we'd be fine for a fire."

Upon reaching the thicket, the five travelers struggled through its outermost tangle of branches and into the empty sanctuary which lay hidden within the web of brambles and spiked bushes. There, Geoffrey and Julius set about gathering dry, dead bits of wood for a fire, Ayila and Carlos rolled out bedding and laid down food, and Vincente, loaded down with everyone's waterskins, scouted the area for the brook which he knew would be trickling further down the hill and for any signs of life nearby. He returned a few minutes later, his search for water having been successful, and gratefully accepted the bread, apples, and cheese which Carlos had set aside for him. He handed out the drinking skins and sank wearily to the ground around the fire which Geoffrey had arranged and which Ayila had started.

"It looks as if we're the first people to set foot in this valley for at least a season, so we shouldn't encounter any sort of trouble unless the livestock decide to attack us. Still, just in case, we'll set a watch. I can go first, and then Carlos, then Ayila, then Geoffrey, and Julius, if you don't mind finishing us off?"

The red-headed man nodded his assent, and Vincente continued.

"We'll be laying pretty low here for the rest of the night and all of tomorrow. Once it's dark enough to move we'll set off for the farm which Xavier told you about. From there the journey should get easier, although we'll have to be more careful to avoid prying eyes of any sort since we'll be traveling on the main road."

"Shouldn't be too much of a problem," broke in Julius. He pulled out an ornately written piece of parchment stamped with what appeared to be the official seal of the Committee of Ways and Means. "I've taken the liberty of throwing this together; it says we have official authorization from the Committee of Ways and Means to be traveling to Astaria to see about its defenses. Everyone knows there's a battle brewing there, so no one should think to look twice."

"Excellent," said Vincente. "Now eat up, friends, and try to get some rest. The farmer ought to replenish our food, so don't worry about saving any past tomorrow."

The other four needed no urging and set about demolishing what was left of the provisions which had been laid out for the night. Once each had eaten and drunk their fill, all of them but Vincente, who crawled to the edge of the thicket to keep watch, settled down lazily around the small fire. The sun was beginning to rise, illuminating the path which lay ahead of them, and although they were wearied from their journey, none yet felt the urge to sleep. Julius pulled out a long, curved pipe from his rucksack and lit it, its fragrant smoke curling through the air and mingling with that of the fire. Geoffrey, meanwhile, strummed idly at his mandolin and stared at the wavering flames before him and then across to the other side of the fire where Ayila had reclined back into the lap of Carlos, who sat cross-legged, stroking her hair with his remaining hand. Geoffrey was reminded that they were in love, and he wondered what their story was, particularly that of Carlos, who he had not yet gotten to know well. Ayila noticed his musings and smiled across the fire at him.

"I suppose you're wondering about us, but too polite to ask, eh?"

Geoffrey laughed and nodded. "Or at least too tired. And anyway, I wasn't sure how exactly to bring it up. But since you did, what *is* the story with you two? And, Julius, if you don't mind, of you as well?"

"Not at all, bard, but suppose you start," grinned Julius.

And so the next several hours were occupied with the telling of stories. Geoffrey told about his time as a bard, his night at the house of the Family Xavier, his encounter in Muckland, and everything which had happened since. Then Carlos recounted his time as a city-planner, during which he had discovered and joined the Way of Lucherium and, in the midst of a particularly dangerous mission gone-wrong, had been captured and tortured by the Ministers of Social Order.

"Ayila led the band which saved me, or at least most of me," he chucked, and Ayila laughed along with him, before jumping in to tell the story of their friendship which had grown into a courtship which had grown into something more, and of their intention to marry as soon as they returned from this mission.

"We wanted to wait until the new Era of Hazcaluche had begun and Trastivo was overthrown, but then we realized that we didn't want to face the hard road it would take to get there alone," she explained, smiling at the romance in her own words. Her eyes shone not only with Lucherium, but with something else as well. "And Julius, what is your story? I don't believe I've ever seen you before two nights ago...."

"Ah yes; well, there might be a few reasons for that. The first is that I hail from the city of Covern, in the north, and this was in fact my first visit to Spiraluche. My entry into the Company of Followers and all of my time spent with them has been in the north, and it was the Elders of Covern who, after hearing of Lucia and the situation in Astraia, recommended that I travel to Spiraluche and offer my services to Xavier and the others for this mission, for there was no need of me in Covern. The other reason might be my occupation; you see, I have progressed quite a long way in my work, which is keeper of books and numbers, and only a few seasons ago became a senior Member of the local Committee of Wealth in Covern. Since then, my involvement with the Followers of Joaquin has had to be sparse and secret, lest I be discovered...."

"Well, I had no idea we had such an accomplished citizen of Trastaluche amongst us!" Vincente's voice betrayed his jesting as he made his way back to the fire, the first watch having ended. He helped Carlos to his feet who, after sharing a quick kiss with Ayila, belted his sword around his waist and went out to take the second watch.

"It seems that I've missed all the interesting tales while I've been away," grinned Vincente. "Although I must say, Julius, I'm glad I caught yours as I returned, for it was the only one I hadn't yet heard. I trust you've all gotten to know each other a bit better?" "Everyone but you," replied Geoffrey. "Actually, if you don't mind, Vincente, I've had a question about your story for some time now."

"Regarding my lapsed loyalty to the Way?" Vincente's frankness at his own failure caught Geoffrey a bit by surprise.

"Why... yes. How and when did you, you know... 'fall away' at first? And what brought you back, if you don't mind my asking?"

"Not at all," replied Vincente. "In answer to your first question, there wasn't any 'one' moment in which I chose to turn my back on Joaquin and the Way of Lucherium. It was a series of little things, really. One day my training was no longer about doing well so that I might serve the Lord Joaquin the best I could but to impress the other members of my class. Then I was wishing that my family was held in more esteem, so that the other boys I played with in the streets of Spiraluche would treat me with more respect. Then I admired the honors and the glories which the soldiers of Trastaluche received and wanted to be recognized in the same way. Until finally, one day, I found that I had lost interest in partaking in the Rite of Lucherium, and I came up with some pathetic lie as an excuse to get out of it that week. After that, I slid deeper and deeper with each passing hour; one moment I was slipping off to attend a meeting of the Committee of Progress, and the next I was seriously considering an act as drastic as running away and joining the other side. The funny thing is, I knew exactly what I was doing each time and that I was drifting further away, but I kept allowing myself to drift, if you understand what I mean."

Geoffrey, thinking back on his life and his own questionable decisions in the season after the night at Xavier's home, nodded. "I believe I do… but what brought you back?"

"The same moment that brought you to join us eventually, my dear Geoffrey. That night at the house, once I realized what had happened, I was horrified. I loved my family, you see, and I never meant for anything to hurt them. That night was as much of a shock for me as it was for you, I think. And I'm grateful to admit that my father, mother, and the others bore me no ill will for my mistakes. 'Everyone falls in some way or another,' they told me. I was given extra training and extra guidance for a long while after, but even that seemed to be more of a gift than a punishment."

The two sat in silence for quite a while, as Geoffrey reflected on Vincente's story, which in many ways was similar to his own. Around them, Julius and Ayila had both crawled into their bedding rolls and were fast asleep. As he replayed his own history along with Vincente's, a final thought occurred to him.

"My apologies for badgering you with questions, but do you mind if I ask one more?"

"Not at all. What is on your mind?"

"Well... do you ever feel... as if, when a moment came in which your strength and courage were really tested, that even with Lucherium, you wouldn't be enough? For example..."

And Geoffrey told him the story of Eldrige again, doing his best to convey what was on his mind.

"...It's just, I honestly can't be certain that if I were in that situation, I would be loyal enough to stand firm and not give in, to die in service to Lord Joaquin and for the Way of Lucherium. And I know that if I were loyal to the end, what came after would be well worth the pain and suffering, but that hardly seems, well, 'real' enough to sustain someone in the midst of torture. Do you ever have these sorts of thoughts?"

Vincente stared into the fire for a long moment before answering.

"You know, I used to, especially in the seasons following the raid on my family's house. But then I realized two things. The first was that if it was small decisions which had caused me to almost leave the Way of Lucherium in the first place, then all I could hope for was that in choosing to prove my loyalty to Joaquin in every little moment, I would be prepared to do so if a big one ever arose. The second was that you don't die for something, or *someone,* whom you don't know and love. That is, true sacrifice and true loyalty in the midst of pain are born out of love for the one you sacrifice for, and for us that means love not only for our friends and family, but for the Way of Lucherium and the Lord Joaquin Himself. It's a bit of a weird concept, I grant; I mean, how could one love a being who is both so filled with Life and Light as to be divine, and yet whose outwardly inert body hangs ever before your eyes? Still, the more I learned about who Joaquin was and about the Way of Lucherium He left for us, and the more I began to dedicate the undertakings of my day to Him before all else, the more I began to desire Him for His sake alone, and not for anything He could give me. And if that's how you view Him, then death under any form doesn't seem so bad, as it becomes the gateway to a new life; a life overflowing with the perfection of Life and Light Himself. It is a perfection which is as real and concrete to me as you are, thanks to the Rite and the Cup which He left for us to partake in, by which we are already joined to Him as closely as we are to our families and loved ones. And if an eternity of that type of unity, that type of *love*, isn't worth dying for, then nothing is or ever will be. It's not about the reward you see, but about the person, a person who has showed us what true love in Light and Life looks like, even in the darkest of hours." He stopped for a moment, breathless from his discourse, and looked over to Geoffrey uncertainly. "Does any of that make sense to you? I don't think there's any other way to be ready for situations such as the one you described, and once I realized that, I stopped worrying about them. I'm not sure if that's what you wanted to hear, but it is what has worked for me in the past."

"No, no, I appreciate any words of wisdom you can give me," answered Geoffrey. "Truthfully, I'm not sure that I know what I wanted to hear. Just that others felt like I did: that they weren't enough."

"You can be sure we all think that," laughed Vincente. "But that's the beauty of the Way of Lucherium, isn't it? You become more of what you are by the Light and Life within you, and that is what makes you enough. Now before you think of another question, I'm going try to catch some sleep, and I suggest you do the same. We have a long walk ahead of us when night falls."

Geoffrey thanked Vincente and made his way over to his own roll of bedding, where he wrapped himself up against the morning chill and closed his eyes to block out the ever-brightening rays of the sun. As he drifted off to sleep, the words of Vincente, Ayila, Xavier, and Trentius floated across his mind and blurred together, comforting and calming him. The last thing he remembered was the sun filtering through the dense undergrowth of the thicket, and the thought of how odd it was that when peace and rest finally came, the world was no longer dark but was filled with light.

Chapter XV

The Mission

Geoffrey the bard yawned and stretched, his muscles sore and knotted from three nights of sleeping on the cold, bumpy ground with nothing but a bedroll between him and the multitude of small sticks and rocks which he swore waited until he was almost asleep before worming their way back under him from the piles into which he had swept them before retiring for the night. He ignored his protesting body and got slowly to his feet, pausing to snatch a quick drink from his waterskin before making his way to the edge of the grove of trees which crowned the top of the hill on which they had spent their final night of journeying. He squinted against the first rays of the dawn as he peered out into the labyrinth of foothills which rose and fell in front of him before they seemed to melt seamlessly into the grey, jagged slopes and cloud-shrouded peaks of the Volunaltus Mountains. He paused, enjoying the warmth that came with the morning and the sheer beauty of the scene which lay before him, before turning his gaze downward and focusing on a small patch of land not a two hour's walk from their campsite. There, amongst the rocky foothills and icy mountain streams, arose a bleak-looking city, made of stone and ringed in stone, its towers and ramparts almost blending into the jagged landscape which surrounded them.

It was the fortress-city of Astraia, the easternmost stronghold of Trastaluche, and it was at war.

Well, half of it anyway. Behind it, on its eastern side, Geoffrey could see sheets of black, billowing smoke where outer defenses had been assaulted and burned, and his eye occasionally caught the glint of armor against the rising sun as he realized that the dark bands behind the city which he had at first thought to be rivers were not part of the landscape at all, but were battalion upon battalion of men, their motions so seamless that they appeared to be a surging flood which threatened the city and the valleys beyond it. However, they were held back from Astraia itself as if unable to breach some unknown dam, and Geoffrey realized that the Leaden Curtain was doing its work well, keeping the armies of Dantius from encircling the city and cutting off its supplies. Directly below him, on the main road which led from the interior of Trastaluche to Astraia, he could see columns of soldiers marching in the direction of the battle; they were just a few of the many squadrons the five Followers had passed along their way to Astraia, spurred on by their own sense of urgency and able to travel much faster than even the groups of mounted infantry on account of their own lack of armor and heavy weapons. They had finished the first leg of their mission almost without incident, and in less than an hour Geoffrey would be departing to find Lucia and bring her to their camp, where she would be able to brief them on the situation within. The wind shifted, and the first cold breezes which came sliding off of the mountaintops brought with them the smell of war: a smell of burning, of metal, of sweat, of flesh, and of some other odor which Geoffrey at first could not identify. Then he remembered the mission which loomed ahead of him and smelled it on himself: the odor of fear.

"It's quite something, isn't it?"

Carlos had come up on Geoffrey's side and now stood next to him, gazing over the beautiful- yet terrible- scene which stretched out before them. Geoffrey nodded his agreement and accepted the bread and coffee Carlos offered him with thanks. The one-armed man had been assigned the final watch of the night, and he had taken advantage of it to fix an early breakfast.

"It really is unlike anything I've ever seen before," said Geoffrey after a moment of silence. "It makes you realize how little those epic ballads of war really say about the grandeur and the seriousness of it all. And here we haven't even gotten close to it, so that's not even taking into account the bloodshed or the screaming or any of that sort of thing...." He turned to Carlos. "But you've been in battles before, correct? What does it seem like to you?"

Carlos gave a short bark of laughter. "Battles, yes, and I can tell you that they're no party. But this," he gestured outwards at the swarms of men which were assembled below them, "this is no battle. This is full, organized war, Geoffrey, the likes of which has not been seen for almost a hundred years. I don't expect I shall ever get used to the fighting which our missions sometimes require of us, but this is something else altogether. I don't think you could ever be prepared for what you will find in fields below us."

"Oy! Quit scaring Geoffrey!" Ayila's voice rang out behind them, her tone cheerful despite the somberness of the scene which stretched out below. "Remember, he has to be the first to go down there."

"As you wish, my love," grinned Carlos, greeting her with a kiss on her forehead. "But anyway, Geoffrey doesn't have to go into all of that. He'll be entering on the western side and staying well away from the fighting."

"Maybe, but that doesn't mean I want to get any closer to it," protested Geoffrey, joining in the teasing and smiling himself in spite of the knot in his stomach. "Got anything to go with that bread you gave me? An awfully poor last meal, that was."

The three of them chuckled, as Ayila, who had come to fetch them at Vincente's bidding, led them back into the clump of trees which had served as their final campground. The others were awake and murmured words of good morning as Ayila, Geoffrey, and Carlos rejoined them. Julius was cooking sausages, which he had somehow procured during his rounds with the other travelers the day before, in which he had listened to the rumors of the groups headed toward Astraia and the stories of those leaving it. He handed a plate to Geoffrey, who sat down on a moss-covered log to enjoy them. As the company finished breakfast, Vincente pulled out a map and began to go over the morning's activities, which were almost entirely Geoffrey's on this particular day.

"Right, well, here we are…." He marked an X overtop the hill where they had decided to bed for the night. "Geoffrey, I'd say if you start off in the next half-hour, you should have no trouble reaching the city gates well before noon. And then you know what to do once you arrive?"

Geoffrey nodded and replied: "Once I'm within sight of the gates, dismount and send my horse back to the camp. When I arrive, flash my papers at the guards, who should be busy with the incoming squadrons of soldiers, and slip through as best as I can. Then, head for the large fountain in the central market and begin playing for the crowds. Lucia should find me there, and I'll bring her back to you all. Once I'm with her I shouldn't have any trouble; she's the wife of the highest-ranking Committee Member in the city, so the guards will give her and anyone with her a wide berth."

"Precisely. And the rest of us will hope it all goes as smoothly as your recitation of it. Now, we'd best strike the camp and prepare for your departure, as well as our own. For better or worse, we won't be coming back."

The next half hour was spent rolling up bedrolls, scattering ashes, and returning everything to its original state. The others would stay hidden there, Geoffrey knew, until he returned with Lucia, but Vincente wanted all to be ready for his arrival and their imminent departure, whenever it might come. Quick farewells were said, and then quite suddenly, or at least so it seemed to Geoffrey, he was sauntering away on horseback down the backside of the hill, and then around to where the main road passed beneath it. He waited in the shadows of a clump of trees until he saw no one coming, then quickly made his way onto the tightly fitted flagstones. In front of him, in a valley in the foothills carved ages before by a river which had since sunk back into the ground, rose the city of Astraia, its pale grey stone now starkly illuminated by the black smoke of war which billowed up behind it. Trying not to think about what was happening on the other side of the city, Geoffrey rode forward until he reached the final bend in the highway. There, following his instructions, he left the road for a small clearing and, out of sight from curious eyes, dismounted, sending his horse back the way he had come with a slap on the rump. It would find its way without any trouble, he knew, since all of its friends were still congregated on the hilltop from which it had come. Then, setting out on foot, he traversed the final stretch of the road, jostled this way and that by columns of soldiers coming and streams of citizens going, until he finally stood at the grim-looking portcullis and the heavy oak gates which at the moment stood open. The way into the Astraia was barred only by a half dozen city guards in their bright crimson uniforms, brandishing spears and checking papers.

Remembering the advice Julius and Vincente had given him, Geoffrey made sure that his mandolin was clearly visible and strode forward confidently, waving an ornate piece of paper which was covered with writing so extravagant it was almost impossible to read, and which bore an expertly done copy of the official seal of the Committee of Spectacles stamped at its base.

"A prosperous morning to you," he announced in a tone which was brisk and official, but nonetheless friendly. "My name is Geoffrey of Trastaluche, official bard of the Committee of Spectacles, and twice honored for my service to Trastaluche and its citizens. I've come at the bidding of the Lady Lucia, wife of Eligesh, senior Member of the Committee of Progress, to offer my services at the grand banquet to be held this very evening within the central courtyard of Astraia."

Geoffrey's flowery words, combined with his demeanor and the weight of the names he tossed around, were indeed enough to sway the guard, and he waved the bard through after only a rudimentary glance at the papers which Julius had so cleverly forged. Geoffrey thanked the soldier and, struck by a sudden thought, slipped him a few coins, a custom he had learned in his younger days and which often granted him the sympathy of the guardsmen and an easy way out if trouble arose. He doubted it was necessary in this case, but he figured it didn't hurt to be cautious. The guard grunted his thanks and waved Geoffrey through the thick, arched doorway and into the crowded streets of Astraia, where he wasted no time beginning to wind his way through the clumps of wary-eyed citizens, grim-faced soldiers, and haughty-looking officials toward the central square.

He was surprised, as he always was since he had drunk of the Cup of Life and Light, how different the world looked when one gazed at it through the lens of Lucherium. The hard stone edges of the shops and homes seemed to stand out even more sharply than before, and the odors of bread and fish and roasted mutton seemed to be more pungent and more prominent than he had ever smelled. The mountains behind the city seemed taller and more majestic, and the whispering pines and meadows filled with strange wildflowers seemed to be more vibrant than he had ever noticed. On the other hand, the people around him - those who had no connection with Lucherium- seemed to be duller, slower, and less *there* than he had ever remembered them. Most just seemed as if they were walking in a daze, but here and there, Geoffrey would both see and sense an official of the city or a captain of Trastaluche who seemed to be engulfed in a sort of darkness which caused chills to run up the bard's spine; these were users of the Void, he knew, or at least those who were very familiar with it. Few would be so deeply involved as Trastivo and his inner circle, but even choosing to associate with them could suck the Light and Life out of you. Doing his best to avoid such shadows, he slid almost unnoticed through the crowds until he reached his destination: the fountain which occupied the center of the city, its carved statues spouting clear, sparkling water that was carried in by pipes from one of the many mountain springs running in the regions above Astraia.

Seating himself on the slick, weathered stones which ringed its lowermost pool, Geoffrey pulled out his mandolin and began to play the melody of a lonely, haunting wanderer's song, the melancholic chords and his own clear voice almost lost in the bustle of the crowd.

> I hail from towering mountain tall,
> from glen untouched by human pall,
> beside the misty waterfall
> and rivers tinged with foam.
>
> Yet comes the fire and comes the rain,
> and glen untouched is rent with stain;
> to stay my efforts are in vain,
> doomed now am I to roam.
>
> To sing of mountaintop afar,
> of deep black nights bejeweled with star,
> of lands sublime with nary'a scar,
> where I might find a home.

As he sang, a small crowd of passersby stopped to listen, a few even tossing coins into the hat which Geoffrey had laid out. Geoffrey nodded his thanks as he continued to perform, his gaze constantly scanning the crowd for the olive skin and hazel eyes of Lucia. When at last he saw her, it took him the space of several heartbeats to realize that he was looking at her. She had caught his eye right away, not because of her identity but because of the regal beauty she radiated. She was dressed according to her state, as a lady of the Upper City, in a long, swooping dress of vibrant green and silver. Her hair was done up and held in place by a bronze pin with a polished green stone at its end, and around her neck gleamed a row of similar gems, set in gold and worth more than Geoffrey could expect to earn in a year. She was followed by several female attendants and two armed guards, whose garish crimson tunics seemed only to accentuate the refreshing style of the woman they served. She had obviously been making a pretext of shopping at the many different market stalls dotted around the square, and she stopped before Geoffrey, seemingly entranced with his music and bursting into applause along with the townspeople as he finished singing.

"Oh, how beautiful!" She gushed. "Why, I must have you for the grand banquet tonight. Everyone important will be there, and they will absolutely adore your music! Tell me, young bard, what is your name?"

Geoffrey gave her his most charming smile and bowed low, playing along.

"At your service, madam, and a prosperous morning to you. I am Geoffrey of Trastaluche, official bard of the Committee of Spectacles, and twice honored for my service to Trastaluche, and more than willing to perform for you and your guests tonight. May I ask where this banquet is to be held? For I am but a lowly traveling bard and have never before set foot in this fair city."

"Why, of course! Follow me right this way, Sir Geoffrey, and I will show you where it is you need to go."

Lucia grabbed Geoffrey by the arm and steered him in the direction of the Keep, which really was no more than an especially large, rectangular tower in the center of the easternmost wall. She walked quickly, and for a moment, she and Geoffrey were out of earshot of her attendants. Taking advantage of the situation, she leaned in close to him and whispered in an urgent tone.

"I'm so glad you made it safely, and it is lovely to see you again, Geoffrey of Hazcaluche. We haven't much time, so I shall talk fast. I shan't be able to go with you outside the city to meet with the others. Eligesh has insisted, under new orders from someone in the Committee of Social Order concerning travel in areas of conflict, that I keep my ladies and my guards with me at all times with the battle going on so close, and if I try to break away from them it will raise suspicion for sure. You'll have to be the one to bring them to the courtyard. I've arranged everything for you already. You are to present yourself to the steward or any one of the other servants and soldiers at the main entrance of the Keep; he knows you are to be playing so there shouldn't be any trouble. The others should go around to the side entrance, where I've arranged it so that they'll be hired to help with preparations for the evening. They'll also be allowed to stay inside during the banquet to assist with the serving and the cleaning which comes after, as long as they stay out of sight, so they should have no trouble accessing the Keep."

She raised her voice suddenly as her attendants drew near and laughed gaily. "Why, you're so full of marvelous stories, Sir Geoffrey! But do tell me more!"

Geoffrey laughed along with her, and then, as they passed in front of an old man wheeling a cart full of fresh potatoes and cabbages which he claimed were "two for the price of one," he asked the question the whole company had been burning to know the answer to.

"And what of Eligesh? Has his loyalty been swayed?"

Lucia's eyes filled were filled with worry and hope as she answered him.

"Not yet, but, oh Geoffrey, he is so, so close. I'll talk to him once more during the banquet tonight. He has been shaken by all the killing he's seen in the last few days. I think one more nudge will be enough." She squeezed Geoffrey's arm quite suddenly. "Courage and Love, my friend," she breathed, her voice almost inaudible.

And then suddenly she was the Lady Lucia again, prattling on about the banquet she was hosting, and telling Geoffrey just which streets he ought to use to get there and when he ought to arrive and what songs he ought to play. After handing him a sizable pouch of coins 'for his troubles, she excused herself and flitted away in the direction of the Keep, her ladies-in-waiting and men-at-arms struggling to keep up with her seemingly boundless energy.

Geoffrey made his way back through the streets of Astraia and out its western gates onto the main road, where he began to walk briskly toward the hilltop where he knew Vincente, Ayila, Carlos, and Julius lay in wait. It would be a longer trip this time since he had no horse, and it was imperative that he get back as soon as possible to explain the situation to the others. The fact that Lucia was not coming with him made him uneasy. They had counted on her presence as the key for getting them past the guards and into the city without too much trouble. One bard could slip in and out easily enough, Geoffrey knew, but he doubted five people would be as unnoticed as one, and anyway their excuse of being laborers for the Committee of Ways and Means was a much harder one to sustain under any real sort of scrutiny than his identity as a bard, which of course he actually was.

"We'll never make it as a group without Lucia. We'll need to split up and try to enter one by one."

Julius' face was grave as he spoke, and his voice betrayed the same uneasiness which Geoffrey felt and which the faces of the other three showed as well. Geoffrey had made it back to the hilltop without any trouble and had related to his companions what he had seen himself and heard from Lucia. They were heartened by the news of how close Eligesh was to swaying in his loyalties, but each one agreed with Geoffrey that the absence of Lucia at the gates might cause a problem.

"With all respect, Julius, I disagree," Carlos said. "It makes no difference whether we try to get in together or on our own; we will either make it or we won't. And anyway, not everyone knows where to meet up in the city. We'll just have to risk going together and hope that nothing goes wrong. Splitting up just increases the variables we have to juggle and our chances of being discovered."

"I agree," spoke up Ayila. "It's a bump in the road, and an unwelcome one, no doubt, but it's nowhere near the biggest obstacle we have faced, or will have faced, before the day is out. I say we start out at once and trust in the power of Joaquin that all will be well."

"Easier said than done," muttered Julius, "but you're right about leaving now. If this doesn't work, we won't have much time to figure out something else, and in that case we'll most certainly have to split up, since our group will already be known to the guards."

The next step decided, belts were tightened, daggers girded, horses released and sent on their way back to the farmer who had lent them, swords were hidden, and staves were grasped. After a cold lunch of bread and hard cheese which everyone had the sense to eat but no one had the stomach to enjoy, the company set off, dodging squadrons of infantry and more than the usual mix of merchants, farmers, and day-laborers going both to and from the city. After nearly a two hour's trek they reached the eastern gates of Astraia, where Julius, with much fan-fare, presented his impressive-looking set of papers to one of the guards, which presumably said something about himself, Ayila, Vin-cente, and Carlos being master-laborers sent by the Committee of Ways and Means to see to the defenses of the city. Geoffrey, meanwhile, re-mained behind, as his own identity was already established.

"Hark there, guard," Julius declared in a haughty tone. "Here, have a look at these and let us through; we've little time to waste with the enemy so close to the city."

Geoffrey's hopes fell and his pulse quickened with worry as the guard, who seemed more annoyed than impressed at Julius' efforts to seem overimportant and imposing, sauntered aimlessly toward the tall, red-haired man and proceeded to make a show of looking through the papers as slowly as he possibly could, even waving another guard over to do the same for good measure.

"If he looks too long at them, he'll know they are false," Geoffrey thought, his mind racing. Focusing on the Way of Lucherium and on the mission at hand, he stepped forward, pulling out his own papers as he did so and ignoring Julius' furious glance at his interference.

"Excuse me, good sirs. A prosperous morning to both of you. I was wondering if I might trouble you to allow me through? You see, I must be at the central courtyard in an hour's time to prepare for my performance in honor of the triumph of the armies of Trastaluche and the visit of Senior Committee Member Eligesh and his splendid wife Lucia...."

"You'll wait your turn, Bard!" barked the first watchman, clearly still peeved at Julius for putting on airs. "We'll see to you just as soon as we've finished examining these folks' papers."

"Now hold on a moment."

It was the voice of the second guard, and on seeing who it was Geoffrey's heart soared, for he realized it that was the same decent-looking fellow he had passed a few coins to earlier in the day. "This fellow's alright, Persus. He showed me his papers earlier today. A very prosperous morning to you as well, bard, and best of luck in your performance this evening."

"Why thank you good sir," replied Geoffrey, bowing deeply to show his gratitude and to hide the nervousness in his eyes. "Your memory is as noteworthy as your courtesy." As he rightened himself, he dug into his purse once again and, pulling out twice as many coins as the time before, passed half to each guard. "And if it would be at all helpful to you, I traveled part of the way with these four individuals"- he gestured at Julius, Vincente, Carlos, and Ayila- "and I can vouch that they are indeed who they say they are. A little rough on the outside, to be sure," he said, leaning in toward the guards and making a face while he gestured in Julius' direction, "but not at all dangerous in any way."

"We see what you mean," chuckled the second guard, while the first one grunted appreciatively as he pocketed the money. Rolling up the papers he had been scrutinizing, he tossed them back to Julius and waved all five of the Company through.

"You're authorized to enter, but stay out of trouble! And remember, here in Astraia we curb our speech and keep our discourse courteous!"

This last part was said with an eye on Julius, while Geoffrey, thanking the guards on behalf of both groups, ushered everyone through the gates and into the city itself. Only once they had melted into the crowds and were well beyond earshot of the soldiers stationed near the walls did he let out a massive sigh of relief and pent-up anxiety.

"That was marvelous, Geoffrey!"

Ayila's eyes were dancing even more than normal as she smiled proudly in his direction, and Vincente, Carlos, and even Julius nodded their approval as well.

"You truly do have a way with words," added Vincente. "And that was a first-rate use of Lucherium if I ever saw it."

"Thank you, but it wasn't near as impressive as it seems," said Geoffrey, squirming a little at what seemed to him to be unfounded praise. He explained about his earlier encounter with the guard and the "insurance" he had paid him, and the other four laughed.

"So it really was more luck than anything else," he said sheepishly, but Ayila shook her head emphatically.

"In the story of the Author, that guard was meant to be there both times," she declared. "It was your own good judgement, your quick thinking, and your cooperation with the power of Lucherium which allowed us to get through."

"Ayila is right," chimed in Carlos, "but as much as I'd like to stand here composing accolades to Geoffrey all day, I believe that we have somewhere to be...? It's already mid-afternoon, and we need to arrive early enough that they still legitimately need helpers for the preparation of the evening banquet."

Sobered by the reminder of the mission that lay before them, the company began moving eastward again, directed by Carlos' knowledge of the streets of Astraia and what Geoffrey had learned from Lucia earlier that day. As they wound their way through side streets and past war machines being wheeled toward the eastern walls, where they might bombard the enemy forces while remaining untouchable themselves, Vincente and Carlos outlined the plan for the upcoming evening.

"Now, Geoffrey, once we arrive, you'll go around to the front entrance of the courtyard and go right in. You shouldn't have any trouble; they should all know you're coming, and anyway no one would refuse an additional bard for a grand banquet such as this. The rest of us will go around to the side gate and hire ourselves out as servants of some sort for the event. Once you're in, busy yourself by mingling with the servants and guards and preparing for your performance. The banquet is set to begin around three hours before sunset. You've been to more of these things than we have, so just act natural and throw your whole self into it. The better you are, the more guards and officers you'll draw out to listen to you. Once you've begun to perform, your part in the mission should be done, unless for some reason Lucia should need you and Julius to convince Eligesh, but from what you've said that seems unlikely. Keep playing until you see the Curtain severed and Dantius' forces begin their assault on the city proper, then get out and find some place to stay out of sight. We'll regroup in the Keep sometime the next day if we are able. Got all that?"

Geoffrey nodded, noting morbidly that they would not need to establish an alternate meeting place; if they were not successful and the Keep did not fall, very few of them could expect to escape alive.

"Very good. Now Julius, you're to stay in the courtyard during the ceremony. Mingle and keep an eye on Lucia. If she needs you, she'll signal you, and you are to help her convince Eligesh. Otherwise, don't stay too long in one place and alert us if anything seems wrong. You'll be in charge of making sure our presence in the Keep stays undetected. Clear?"

"No trouble at all," replied Julius. "It should be quite the exciting evening."

"That's one word you could use for it," said Vincente, smiling grimly. "Now, Carlos; you, Ayila and I will be responsible for the rest. We'll wait until the banquet is in full swing before we act; hopefully by then Lucia will have swayed her husband's loyalties. Then we'll make our way around to the far side of the Keep, which is where we'll enter. Once we're inside, we'll head for the central meeting chamber of the Committees, lock ourselves in, and begin the Rite and, once we have confirmation from Lucia if we don't already, the penetration of the Leaden Curtain. We'll keep it quiet, we'll move fast, and we won't make any mistakes. Understood?"

Carlos and Ayila nodded just as the company stepped out of a side street and found themselves standing before the high, curving stone wall which separated the Keep and its courtyards from the rest of the city. To their left, about two stones' throws away, Geoffrey could see the servant's entrance, open and already busy with a steady stream of porters and cooks heading in and out with tables, chairs, and provisions for the evening feast. To his right, he knew, lay the main gate through which he would enter in only a few moments. He felt his adrenaline surge as Vincente gathered them all together for one last word.

"Alright," he whispered. "Here we are. Keep your minds clear, your eyes open, and the Way of Lucherium before and throughout you. If all goes well, we'll rejoice and rest with each other again very soon, and if it does not, may our cause for rejoicing and rest be even greater."

And bidding Geoffrey a brief farewell, Vincente, Carlos, Ayila, and Julius turned toward the servant's gate which led into the courtyard. Geoffrey watched them depart for a moment, feeling very much alone, before rousing himself and heading for the ornately carved central gate which he entered without any trouble after a quick work with a guardsman who had obviously been informed that Geoffrey would be arriving.

Upon entering, Geoffrey found himself at the far end of a large open space in the shape of a half oval which was butted up against the mightier outer wall of city. Rising out of the same outer wall, about two-thirds down the length of the clearing, was the keep: a hulking rectangular tower which stood nearly twice as tall as the wall around it and which seemed like it could easily house the chambers of a dozen nobles and their families. In front of it several rows of long wooden tables had been set up, and over to the side, in the shadow of the battlements of the outer wall, a makeshift stage had been erected, upon which Geoffrey knew he would be playing. The space was lavishly decorated with lanterns of all sorts of colors and ribbons and banners bearing the official crest of Trastaluche, all of which stood in sharp contrast to the sullen look of the keep which jutted into the sky like a naked, blocky mountain of its own. It was not a beautiful structure, but it was nonetheless quite imposing. On the other side of the wall Geoffrey could hear the deep thrums and thuds of the war machines of the Hazcalucherian soldiers;

they had overrun Trastivo's armies in the field and had begun their assault of the city itself. Their attack did nothing at the moment due to the Curtain; boulders launched against the wall bounced off harmlessly, and arrows arcing overtop it seemed to burst into flame or to shatter as if striking an invisible crystal dome. Still, by the force and frequency of the noises, even Geoffrey's untrained ear could tell that if the Curtain were to be torn, Astraia would soon be breached.

The next hour seemed like an eternity to the bard as he did his best to mingle calmly with the servants and soldiers who had been tasked with preparing the courtyard for the banquet, and as he tuned his mandolin and warmed up his voice and his mind for an evening of entertainment and festivities in a place and at a time when almost anything else seemed more acceptable. He saw the other four members of the company once or twice as they worked to roll in the barrels of rare wine and hard cider that would be served to the guests, and as they bedecked the tables with shimmering cloths of silver and gold and highly polished cutlery which gleamed so brightly in late afternoon sun that Geoffrey found it hard to look at. Finally, not quite an hour before the banquet was to start, the first guests began to arrive, and Geoffrey breathed a sigh of relief as he was able to cease his awkward socialization and begin to play and sing softly in the background. The music helped to occupy and sooth Geoffrey's frayed mind, and the next hour passed quickly as more and more guests filed in, talking and drinking and laughing in spite of what loomed just beyond the courtyard's walls.

Suddenly there was a fanfare of trumpets which drowned out Geoffrey's own music, and a brightly clad herald announced the beginning of the feast and the entrance of its hosts and guests of honor: Eligesh, Senior Member of the Central Committee of Progress of Spiraluche, and his wife Lucia of Trastaluche. The trumpets sounded again, and at the end of a procession which contained several rows of guards and half a dozen other important dignitaries, Geoffrey saw Lucia emerge, her arm looped around the waist of a man who Geoffrey realized must be Eligesh, her husband. He was young and dark-haired, dressed in a formal, ankle-length tunic of light grey and bright red with the golden crest of Trastaluche emblazoned in its center. He smiled graciously at his guests and, in a speech which was formal yet disarming, thanked them for their loyalty to Trastaluche and for the many ways in which they contributed to the Progress of all citizens. He seemed a bit pompous to Geoffrey, but not at all the shadowy sort of figure which he normally associated with the Committees, and hope grew within him that Eligesh might be swayed- or perhaps had already been swayed- after all.

As the guests of honor were seated, the banquet was officially begun, and Geoffrey began to play and sing in the background once again. Food was brought out and the talking and laughing swelled once more. After they had finished their own plates, Lucia and Eligesh worked their way from table to table, greeting certain guests and thanking them for coming. As they passed by the set of tables nearest to Geoffrey, Lucia caught his eye and gave him a slight shake of her head. "No," she meant, "he's not quite there yet." Geoffrey gave a nod almost as imperceptible in reply, and several minutes later when Ayila happened to be serving tankards of ale to the same set of tables, Geoffrey caught her eye and passed on the slight shake of the head. Ayila gave no outward indication of having seen the bard, but Geoffrey could see her eyes darken with concern. They were running out of time. Of course, they could never be sure, he knew. It was possible Eligesh was already sympathetic to their cause and had just not told his wife, but they had no reason to think that they knew any better than Lucia, and once they began to try to break through the Leaden Curtain, harnessing Lucherium to draw it out and illuminate its weaknesses, their blanket of secrecy would be destroyed, and all hell would break loose. He thought of the night in front of the house of the Family Xavier, and how the crackling, glowing tendrils of the Conexio had illuminated the streets around the house for half a league. Once they began to attack the Curtain, they were sure to be found out. The timing had to be perfect.

Meanwhile, the banquet moved steadily on as the guests ate more than their fill of the roasted beef and pheasant, the heaping loaves of bread, the plates of candied fruit and sweet dates, the mountains of boiled potatoes and exotic cheeses, and the freshly picked vegetables which seemed to come in every shape, size, variety, and color imaginable. Once the dinner platters had been exhausted, more ale and choice beer were procured and passed around, and along with it baskets of warm, sweet buns glazed in sticky, melted sugar. Toasts were made: to victory against the rebellious forces of the Lord of Oppression; to Progress Before All; to the Committees; to Trastivo, the glorious leader of Trastaluche; and to Eligesh and Lucia, who stood briefly to officially thank their guests once more and to offer toasts to them as well.

Then a song and more drinks were called for, and all eyes turned toward Geoffrey, who was the promised entertainment for the night. Putting aside the soft, soothing pieces which he had selected to waft throughout the background of the meal, Geoffrey started to play a more striking tune and, forgetting his fear, began to truly perform, his voice ringing clearly throughout the reaches of the courtyard. He sang of jesters and their kings, of feasts and drinks for all, of harvests gold and brimming, of lovers lost and found, of dragons fought and slain, and once again of wanderers in the high roads of an unknown place, searching for a home which they had no reason to believe existed but which they clung to nonetheless. As song built upon song, the audience swayed and cheered and danced and cried as if spellbound by the music which swirled around them and seemed to inundate their very beings, and even the guards on the high outer wall seemed to forget their posts and turned inward, listening as Geoffrey, harnessing all that he was and could be by the Light of Joaquin, gave them a night that would be spoken of for seasons after.

Not long after he began, he noticed Lucia lean over to whisper something to Eligesh, and the two got up and made their way quietly through the mesmerized throngs of officers, dignitaries, and Committee Members and into the central doorway of the Keep. The ultimate effort, the final part of the mission, had begun, Geoffrey realized, but he had no time to worry about it, so caught up was he in the music which seemed to him to be an expression of his very self and yet more than what he was. Still, he kept an eye out for their return, which Lucia had promised them would happen only once she was convinced that her husband was on their side.

Ten minutes passed. Then twenty. Then thirty. And then Geoffrey had been playing and singing for almost an hour, and there was no sign of Eligesh or Lucia. The crowd below was still captivated by the beauty of the music, but Geoffrey knew that it would not be long before the festivities would begin to wind down.

Then he saw it. A silent movement gliding through the shadows which lined the inner wall of the courtyard. A figure dressed in a cloak, moving as if they were one with the growing darkness which flickered around them as the sun began its final descent. Geoffrey couldn't see the person's face, but by the long, graceful gait he could tell it was Ayila. She crossed the length of the courtyard unseen and faded into the darkness cast by the Keep onto its far side. Several minutes passed, and then another figure followed- either Carlos or Vincente, Geoffrey could not tell- and then again, several minutes later, the third of his companions.

Geoffrey glanced around the courtyard, but he still could not see Eligesh and Lucia. "Perhaps she has sent word to Vincente secretly," he thought. He hoped that were the case. More likely, he knew, Vincente had decided that they could wait no longer to begin the Rite, and that they had no choice but to trust that Lucia's efforts had not been in vain, even if she herself did not know it. He also looked around for Julius, but he was nowhere to be seen, which was odd because Geoffrey had not noticed him depart with Lucia or Eligesh or enter the Keep after them. Geoffrey began another song, this time about a "Shepherdess fair and sweet/ whose true love she did meet/ on the banks of a mountain stream/ on a day more fair than a dream." He guessed it might be a favorite of the inhabitants of Astraia, who practically lived in the shadow of just such a fairytale, and the cheers and enthusiastic accompaniment from the crowd, many of whom held their loved ones close, tears in their eyes as they swayed from side to side and listened to the impossibly hopeful strains of the ballad, assured him that he had guessed correctly.

"It won't be long now," he thought as he played. Ayila, Carlos, and Vincente were highly trained warriors, and infiltrating a Keep which was so loosely guarded and so distracted by the goings-on both inside and outside of its walls would be child's play. Then the Rite would be invoked, and after, the three of them would attempt to penetrate the Curtain, an act which would surely promote mass confusion and not a small amount of panic from the banquet-goers below, as they saw the sky above them suddenly light up with the whirling, humming tendrils of their voided shield.

Geoffrey began a second song, hoping to give his companions as much time as they might need, when, in the ever-growing darkness, he realized there was another figure moving through the night. He sensed it first rather than seeing it; a tall, thin shadow dressed in black, lurking at the outer reaches of the banquet near the main gates. At first, he thought it might be Julius, but for some reason that didn't seem right at all to him.

Then he realized exactly what he was sensing. It was the same dark, cold presence which he had felt when he had passed some of the more senior Committee Members and captains of Astraia: the presence of someone who was less than he should be, who had harnessed the Void or consorted many times with those who did. A tingle of fear moving down his spine, Geoffrey strained his eyes in the direction of the hooded person who was moving toward the rear entrance of the Keep, and he suddenly noticed that the shadow was not alone. Behind him were several more hooded, wraith-like figures, and behind them... the crimson red and dull bronze of more than a dozen Trastalucherian soldiers; and not just any soldiers, but, from the looks of their embroidered insignias which flashed in the dying sunlight, they were members of the elite Guard of the Committee of Social Order. Worry now surging within him, Geoffrey glanced frantically around for Julius, seeking to alert him to this new, unplanned threat, but the red-haired man was once again nowhere to be found. The guards and the hooded figures were moving quickly, filing silently toward the place where Carlos, Ayila, and Vincente had made their entrance only minutes before. Their leader, however, stopped for a moment, and appeared to be taking in the sight of the banquet. Geoffrey was on the verge of panic, unsure of how to warn his friends of the nasty surprise which was rapidly approaching them, when the tall shadow stepped out of the darkness of the wall and removed his hood, the last rays of the dying sun catching his face as he stared directly at Geoffrey and smiled.

And the bard felt his heart turn to ice, as his words seemed to stick in his throat. For it was the face of Emore, and Geoffrey could tell from his smug, serpentine grin that he knew exactly what was happening. Emore's smile widened as he saw the fear in Geoffrey's eyes and, giving a sardonic bow to the bard, he turned and strode after his subordinates. Sheer force of habit moved Geoffrey to continue his song after only a heartbeat, so that unless someone was listening closely, they wouldn't know that only a moment ago his voice had nearly frozen in terror. He finished the ballad and shakily began another one, originally designed to be his last song of the night. He knew at that moment that the mission was doomed, that those inside the Keep would not be coming out, and that if he did not flee at that instant, he would not live to see the morning.

And in his fear and weakness, Geoffrey made a choice, one which he was almost certain he would regret for the rest of his life. As the final strains of his music floated into the deceptive calm of the newness of night, and the crowd roared their approval, chanting his name over and over, Geoffrey bowed deeply and, slipping off the stage, melted into the crowd and began to weave this way and that through the mass of bodies as fast as he possibly could. Within moments, he reached the heavy oak door, which lay open and unguarded before him, and reaching out for whatever Lucherium lay within his reach, Geoffrey breathed deeply and barreled straight through the arched entrance which led to the interior of the Keep.

Chapter XVI

The Destruction

The inside of the Keep was dark and deserted when, less than half an hour before, Ayila, Carlos, and Vincente had swiftly and silently disarmed the guards at its rear entrance and disposed of their unconscious bodies where they would not be found until morning. The final task had begun. Moving in single file, they ghosted from hallway to hallway and staircase to staircase, ascending ever further, their weapons at the ready and their way lit only by Lucherium. The Keep was as silent as a tomb, and the few sentries they did encounter never saw them coming. Or going. Outside, Geoffrey's music rang out, sweet and piercing, and Ayila felt as if it were the beating of their small band's heart, urging the three of them on through the darkness which seemed to grow ever more oppressive the closer they drew to the central chamber of the Committees of Astraia. As they reached the upper level of the Keep, they suddenly heard voices in one of the many richly furnished bedrooms and stopped, wondering who it might be.

Inching forward, Carlos peered through the keyhole of the door into the room from which the sounds emanated, and in the flickering candlelight within he could see that it was Lucia and Eligesh, deep in discussion, her face hopeful and pleading as she gestured in the direction of the burning fields, the columns of soldiers, and the piles of corpses which dotted the valley below them, his a bit stern but more surprised and confused than anything else, as if he wasn't quite sure what his wife was trying to tell him. Carlos motioned the "all's well" to Ayila and Vincente, and the three crept onward down the hall until they reached their objective: a large, rectangular room which occupied almost a third of the Keep's upper floor and which served as the meeting chambers for the seven Committee Chiefs of the city of Astraia. It was lavishly adorned with rugs and gilded chandeliers of brass and crystal, and in its center sat a massive oaken table and seven ornately carved matching chairs. The most striking feature, however, at least that night, was the row of windows which stretched across the entire length of its eastern wall, revealing a vista of sprawling valleys and towering mountains which normally would have been simply spectacular, but tonight, with the battle for Astraia raging, seemed to be something out of a nightmare.

There was no time for admiring or despising the view, however. As soon as Vincente was assured that they were alone in the room, he set about the task of preparing himself to invoke the Rite of Lucherium, a feat which required an especially strong connection with the Light and Life of Hazcaluche, and which would be particularly difficult in a place of such darkness, death, and void. Carlos set about helping him, while Ayila turned back toward the set of double doors they had entered to barricade it closed in case anyone was to reach them before the Curtain had been penetrated.

She never got the chance to do so.

As she reached out her hand to ensure that the bolts were properly set, the entire doorway seemed to vaporize, sucking her into the space where it had once stood and then just as suddenly throwing her across the room with ruthless force. Caught off guard, Vincente and Carlos spun around, raising their weapons and summoning shields barely in time to block the onslaught of crossbow bolts which hissed out of the black smoke billowing from the doorway, followed by the band of soldiers who had fired them, who now brandished their weapons as they sprinted across the room to engage the two Followers. Behind them strode two hooded figures, clad in dark robes, who held the crooked staves and long, pale swords of the Committee of Social Order's wielders of the Void.

Chanting in unison, their voices harsh and discordant, they raised their staves, hurling orbs of hissing black energy at Carlos and Vincente, who were each busy engaging half a dozen soldiers at once, the combined might of which were no match for the two warriors. His short sword a blur, Vincente cut through his attackers faster than they could fall upon him, his Lucherian shield glowing all the brighter as it absorbed the blasts being cast at it. Carlos, who looked as if he didn't have time for this nonsense, simply slammed his sword into the ground, shouting as he did so, and his own humming sphere of energy seemed to explode outward, striking his attackers as if with bolts of lightning and hurling them down, burnt and lifeless. The two then turned to face the now rather nervous-looking Void-wielders, whose efforts to break through the shields of Carlos and Vincente had been completely in vain. Seeing the Followers begin to advance in their direction and their companions destroyed in a matter of mere seconds, they turned to flee, only to be stopped by none other than Julius, who bounded out of the passage, red hair flaming and his long, two-handed sword sweeping through the air at impossible speed, first to his left, then to his right, as the last two enemies crumpled to the floor.

"See to Ayila," he called out. "I'll guard the door."

Grunting a quick thanks to Julius, who had appeared in the nick of time, Carlos and Vincente turned their attention to their companion, who was sprawled, stunned, on the floor on the far side of the room, and only just now regaining her senses. Opening her eyes, she looked up at the faces of Vincente and Carlos staring down at her, her face full of fear and a scream building in her throat.

"It's alright, love. You're in no danger now…"

Much too late did Carlos notice that her eyes were not focused on him, but behind him.

He turned to be blinded by a splatter of blood as Julius brought his sword downward in a devastating arc onto the back of Vincente's neck, and the son of Xavier collapsed, his head rolling to a stop several paces away from his body. Julius was swinging again before Vincente's body hit the ground, a morbid, triumphant grin on his face, and Carlos barely had time to begin to leap out of the way, shouting as he did so to summon his shield to protect him and Ayila.

It almost worked. Almost. Julius' massive broadsword shattered as it came into contact with Carlos' shoulder, bursting into a thousand shards which flew in every direction, ricocheting off of the hastily constructed shield which had formed around Carlos and Ayila and scattering throughout the room, including into the exposed torso of Julius. He screamed in pain and sank to the ground, blood seeping out of his stomach and chest in a dozen places.

But next to him Carlos did the same. For he had not been able to stop the sword in its deadly path, only to deflect and destroy it, and Ayila watched in horror as its remnants severed his remaining arm. Julius opened his mouth and a horrible, bubbling cackle came out, most likely meant to be a crow of triumph but now evidence of his own broken state.

"You... fools!" he gurgled. "There is no Light and Life that can save you... Not anymore... You and your backwards... twisted ways...."

Then there was a flash of darkness and Julius went ridged, his body convulsing even as the death-blow of the Void coursed through him and caused his corpse to half-crumble into dust.

"Julius always was such an imbecile. I told him to kill you, not disarm you."

Emore's voice, silky yet noxious, filled the room as he emerged out of the black, smoky entranceway, followed by several more of the hooded Void wielders and another dozen or so soldiers, the last set of which escorted between them- and none too gently- a bewildered Eligesh and his wife Lucia, a horrified look spreading across her face as she saw the carnage spread out before her. Ayila began to struggle to her feet, but Emore shouted, and it seemed as if a dark mist enveloped her and Carlos, sucking them to the floor and making Lucherium impossibly difficult to reach.

"Still," Emore grinned, "I suppose this way will be a lot more fun... for some of us at least...."

Geoffrey bounded down the hallway of the Keep, his heart pounding as his mind seemed to split in two, half of it screaming at him to get out of there while he still could, half of it insisting that he couldn't leave his friends. Unsure of where the stairs were, he yanked open the first door he came to... and yelped as one of the unconscious guards which

Vincente, Carlos, and Ayila had dispatched tumbled out of the storage closet where he had been hidden, crumpling on top of Geoffrey. The bard heaved the inert body off of him, and snatching the guard's spear from the ground where it had clattered, he continued on his way. After two or three more tries, he found the stairs which led up to the next level and began to leap up them two at a time before bursting into a similar hallway on the second floor.

It was there that he found the first set of soldiers.

There were four of them, left by Emore to secure the lower regions of the Keep and to ensure that no more Followers of Joaquin were lurking in the unoccupied rooms. They started as Geoffrey careened into the hallway not a dozen paces from them.

"Halt, you!"

The leader of the band, most likely a sergeant by his garb, reached for his sword and strode toward the bard.

Geoffrey's only response was to grip his weapon more tightly in both hands, as if it were the oaken staff he had spent so many hours training with, and to charge toward the guards. The other three soldiers began to draw their weapons as well, and Geoffrey saw the sergeant's lips begin to curl into a contemptuous sneer at the thought of a single, untrained bard thinking that he could engage even one soldier of Trastaluche. His sneer stopped and his eyes went blank as Geoffrey leaped off of the wall to his right, slamming the butt of the spear into the other man's head as he did so, before turning in midair to bring its metal end down with ferocious speed onto the shoulder of the second guard. He heard the bone crack even beneath the armor which the soldier wore as his shoulder was thrown out of its socket and his half-raised sword clattered to the floor. The last two soldiers turned to face him, but it was as if they were moving through water, so slow were their reactions to the superhuman energy of Geoffrey's Lucherium-infused attack. He lashed out with two quick strikes and both guards slumped to the floor, unconscious, leaving the way clear for him once more.

Geoffrey continued on. He found the stairs much more quickly this time as he learned the pattern of their location, and he traversed the next three floors in a heartbeat, dispatching any enemies he found with the same almost laughable ease as he had the first batch. Surging up his fifth flight of stairs, he emerged into a hallway which was filled with black, choking smoke and which felt cold and lifeless despite its richly carved panels and doorways. He had almost reached his destination. Knowing that there was no time to waste, he started down the hallway and, finally emerging from its dark interior, he burst into the chamber of meeting for the Committees of Astraia.

The sight which greeted him was one which would haunt him for a very long time.

The doors had been shattered, what was left of them spread across the room in a charred semi-circle. Half a dozen elite soldiers of Social Order stood in a similar pattern, guarding the doorway, and they turned in utter surprise as Geoffrey entered. Another half-dozen were congregated to the left of the massive wooden table which dominated the center of the room, and between them Geoffrey could see the figures of Eligesh and Lucia, the former protesting indignantly, the latter sobbing quietly. In the middle of the room stood Emore, flanked by three other similarly hooded figures. Next to him was a nearly disintegrated corpse, so badly burned that Geoffrey could not tell who it belonged to, and before Emore, their faces contorted with a nameless pain, were Ayila and Carlos, both held to the floor by some unseen force, the former stunned, the latter bleeding heavily from the mangled stump where his remaining arm had once been.

Behind them, in an ever-spreading pool of blood, lay the body of Vincente.

"Ah, Geoffrey!" Emore turned from his captives and began gliding toward the bard. "So nice of you to join us. Saves me the trouble of having to hunt you down later."

Before Geoffrey could recover from the shock of the sight in front of him or attempt to summon any sort of defense, Emore stretched out his hand, and Geoffrey felt an invisible force drag him to the ground, pinning him there as if he were being chained to it. He struggled against it, even attempting to form a shield, but it was as if the black mist which seemed to shroud the room had sucked away his ability to move or to harness Lucherium.

"Move him over next to the others!" Emore shouted to two of the guards, who handled Geoffrey as if he were made of paper, despite the fact that he couldn't lift a finger to move himself. "But where are my manners?" Emore continued. "You must be allowed to greet your friends. After all, you may not be able to do so later." His grin widened as he snapped his fingers, and Ayila and Carlos exhaled suddenly as their bonds were loosened just enough to allow speech, but not so much as to permit any real movement.

"Geoffrey, are you ok?" For all the wretchedness of the moment and his own miserable state, Carlos' first concern was for the bard.

"Yes… yes, I'm fine… But what happened here? What happened to you? And where's Julius?"

"Julius betrayed us." Ayila's voice was bitter. "He must have alerted the Committees. They burst in here and knocked me out, but Carlos and Vincente fought them off. Then Julius came and he… he…." Her eyes filled with horror, unable to finish the thought.

"He attacked myself and Vincente," broke in Carlos, his voice measured and his bearing composed despite his helpless state and the awful wound which he bore. "He took us by surprise, and he got to Vincente first. Then he turned on me, but I managed to disarm and wound him. Then this other one," he looked in the direction of Emore, "came in. He disabled us and killed Julius…."

"Once a traitor, always a traitor, Carlos," Emore interrupted. "My, my, you of all people ought to know that, seeing as how close you were to Vincente. If you can't trust them once, then there will come a time when you won't be able to trust them again. Julius was just a liability."

"But how is that possible?" Geoffrey looked from Carlos to Emore, seeking an answer from whoever would give it. "I mean, he drank from the Cup, did he not… or did he?"

And then he remembered that dawn in Spiraluche, and Julius excusing himself, saying that he had too much to do in preparation and that he would not be able to join them for the Rite. And it all made sense to Geoffrey: Julius' monologues about his own progress on the Committees, his mention that he was in too deep to be seen with the

Followers of Joaquin very often, and even the off-putting and overbearing manner with which he had treated the city guards.

"You turned him, didn't you?" He asked Emore. "You've probably been turning him for a very long time, but he only just recently rejected the Way of Lucherium completely, didn't he?"

"Very good, Geoffrey," Emore smiled evilly. "Your intelligence does you credit. I genuinely meant it when I told you before that we could use people like you. Not like that blundering upstart Julius. He saw the reality of things and the truth of the Way of Progress not a week before he was summoned to Spiraluche. He told us everything he knew the day before he left the city of Covern, and he was supposed to fix it so that each of you entered the city alone so that he would be able to make contact with the Committees as soon as he arrived, to tell us who *you*, madam," he suddenly turned savagely on Lucia, "were trying to turn."

"Now wait a minute, what the devil are you talking about, Emore?" Eligesh tried to step forward, his face still as confused as when Geoffrey had arrived. "My wife hasn't tried to talk to anyone out of the ordinary since she arrived; I can guarantee it. She isn't involved in any of this... are you?"

He turned to Lucia, who raised her chin bravely and, looking her husband directly in the eyes, spoke in a voice so calm and sweet that she might have been in bed with him on their wedding night.

"My love, you know you mean the world to me, but not... not *this* world," she said, gesturing at the carnage of the room and the burning fields and screams of the dying which arose from outside the Keep. "Look around you. Is this what you want to be remembered for, what you want our child to remember you for?"

She grasped her husband's hand and placed it on her belly, and Geoffrey suddenly realized that Eligesh's stunned look was not just due to the chaos around him. He had learned- and recently, too, by the looks of it- that he was to be a father, and such a realization had rocked the foundations of his own life.

"I've been trying to tell you," Lucia continued, her voice beginning to tremble, "and I haven't had the chance... but I chose a different life and a different world not too long ago, and...."

"Silence!" Emore shrieked, and one of the guards clamped a hand over Lucia's mouth, pulling her away from her husband's arms and preventing her from saying anymore. "You are a fool, Eligesh, a blundering fool! You didn't even know your wife was involved, and yet she... *she* has joined in their horrid blood rituals and who knows what else. She is in this as deeply as the rest of them, and had I not been the one to write the order that she be accompanied by two guards at all times, she might have been able to make contact with the traitorous scum she had been trying to reach and the whole city might have fallen. The two of you I'll deal with later. But as it is, it doesn't matter all that much, does it?" He turned back to Carlos, Ayila, and Geoffrey. "Because you just weren't quite fast enough. And now, my friends, the entertainment begins. For you see, Julius might not have told me who Lucia was going to contact, but I'm quite sure that all of you know, and much more besides…."

"You'll get nothing out of us, I'm afraid." Carlos' voice was as measured and firm as Lucia's, and Geoffrey was glad that he had spoken for all of them, for as much as he wanted to say the same, he wasn't sure if he would have ever been able to get the words out.

"Oh? Well, perhaps not from you… you don't seem to have much to live for." Emore smirked, glancing down at Carlos' crippled state. "But as for the other two, especially the bard… well now, they aren't near as strong as you, eh? But you're the example, now, aren't you? Well, we can't have you failing in your duties…."

And Ayila screamed as Emore drew his long, pale sword and sliced downward in a vicious arc, severing Carlos' right foot and ankle from the rest of his body. Carlos' eyes filled with pain and a small cry escaped his lips, but then he clamped them shut and faced the Minister of Social Order as calmly as before.

"Sever my limbs if you wish, snake," he spat, "but I shall never be as serpent-like as you."

Emore's eyes glittered with anger, the first emotion Geoffrey had ever seen them shine with, and raising his sword above the helpless, bleeding figure which lay before him, he stabbed downwards, the blade piercing Carlos' left calf and cutting so deep that it tore out the other side and embedded itself in the floor. Wrenching it out with monstrous strength, Emore stabbed again.

And again. And again, his face a mask of sheer rage, ignoring the horrified cries of Ayila and Eligesh's shocked outburst against the brutality of the Minister of Social Order. Up and down went the blade, and Carlos' whole body went rigid with pain. Yet he kept his mouth shut and his eyes clear in spite of it all, a fact that seemed to infuriate Emore all the more. The last thing Geoffrey saw was Carlos' face as he smiled encouragingly at the bard one last time. Then he turned to Ayila, and in a voice which was somehow still quiet and full of peaceful pain, he spoke the only words his tormentors would wrench out of him.

"I love you, my star, and I will always be near you. Walk in Light and Life with me until we meet again, until we live in love forever...."

And then Emore's sword came down in the final stroke, and Ayila screamed, and mangled, impaled, and almost dry of blood, Carlos of Hazcaluche breathed his last, unconquered to the end.

The room was suddenly silent, except for the broken sobs of Ayila as she saw the life of her promised one suddenly and horribly torn from his body. Geoffrey was too shocked to utter a sound, and he felt an all-too-familiar wave of uncontrollable fear begin to rise within him. Opposite him, on the other side of the room, Lucia's face was frozen in terror, and Eligesh, although still confused, looked both disgusted and outraged at what he had just seen. He appeared to be about to open his mouth to protest the proceedings in front of him, but Emore, still seething with rage, gave him no chance.

"Well now, who's next?" he hissed, as his gaze flicked back and forth between Ayila's miserable, tear-stained face and Geoffrey's fear-filled eyes. "It appears that the lady here," he gave Ayila a sharp kick, "needs some time to compose herself. So why not you, bard? After all, you've known what was coming to you since that day we met in Spiraluche, just after I finished… initiating Eldrige. Well, I'm sorry to say, he just wasn't up to the task we wanted him for. But I think you'll do quite nicely, eh? Bring him to the table!" he snapped at two of the guards, who dragged the bard roughly to his feet and shoved him into a lavishly carved chair, stretching his helpless arms out in front of him.

Geoffrey struggled to move but found that was still unable to do so. Fear began to surge over him, and it was all he could do to remain in control of his own faculties and to not succumb to the urge to scream for mercy, a tactic which he knew would not work, no matter how much he told Emore of the lives and doings of the Followers of Joaquin. The Minister of Social Order strode over to him, pulling out a long, curved knife, and the image of Eldrige tore its way into Geoffrey's tortured mind as his fingers and hands began to scream in anticipation of the pain they knew was inevitable.

"Let's start small, shall we? And then we'll see what you can remember. You'd be surprised how a little prick can help you focus…."

Emore grinned at Geoffrey's terror, and leaned toward him, knife gleaming, as he licked his lips in anticipation of what was to come.

Geoffrey was all but panicking now, his breath coming in short, rapid gasps, as he strained as hard as he could against the unseen bonds which held him in place.

The first cut was over in the space of a heartbeat, but for Geoffrey it seemed to last forever.

First there was a sharp flash of blinding pain, followed by an explosion of shock and terror as the metal of the blade, which seemed to be both boiling and freezing at the same time, sliced through the meat of the pinky of his right hand. Then a second, more jagged feeling as the finger separated from his body and his mind lashed out, seemingly trying to keep it in place by pure will. Then the gush of blood, and finally, as the full import hit his senses, a third type of pain: this one nauseating, overwhelming, and growing in intensity as wave after wave hit Geoffrey, and he screamed, drowning out the cries and protests of Ayila and the retching sounds made by Lucia.

"Now wait a minute, Emore! This has to stop!" The sharp words came from Eligesh, who had finally found his voice and was trying to push his way through the pair of guards detaining him. "If these men are guilty of the crimes you accuse them of, they must be brought before the Committee and tried. That is the way of Progress, and you of all people ought to know that."

"The way of Progress?!" Emore whipped suddenly around, a look of disdain on his face, his eyes black with bloodlust and the death of the moment. "What would you know of Progress, you insolent youth?! Look at you! Your wife is one of them, and you had no idea! If it were left to people such as you, Trastaluche would have already fallen. Have you ever tasted the power of Trastivo and harnessed it against Trastaluche's enemies?

That is true power, and true Progress, not this petty nonsense of courts and trials you blather on about. Now keep quiet and don't interfere further, lest you be considered a traitor as well. In fact, I think we've had more than enough meddling from you and your wife…"

He let out a harsh, guttural incantation, and suddenly Eligesh's protestations went silent, as if the sound accompanying the words he was trying indignantly to utter was cut off. Emore turned back to Geoffrey, but then stopped, and even in the midst of his agony, Geoffrey's blood froze as he realized Emore had been struck by a glint of gold shining out of the pouch of Vincente, which he had placed on the table only moments before he, Ayila, and Carlos had been ambushed. Stabbing his knife into the table, Emore reached for Vincente's bag and drew out the golden box which contained the finger of Joaquin. Geoffrey and Ayila both gasped as they saw him open it, a confused look on his face, and Geoffrey remembered the words of Xavier as to what might happen if it were to fall into the wrong hands. Emore noticed the new fear in the eyes of his two prisoners and opening the box he drew out the finger bones, which Geoffrey now saw were not in separate pieces but rather mounted on a dull, silvery dart which reminded him of the spears holding up the rest of Joaquin's corpse. Emore examined his new prize, holding it out in front of him, and his face suddenly lit up with an expression of gleeful malice as he realized what he was looking at.

"My, my, now this… *this* is not something I expected to see here. You really must be more careful with your things," he cackled, as he mocked Geoffrey and Ayila in a chiding tone. "But of course, you had no idea that I would be here. Rest assured, I know exactly what I hold here; Julius and our other members who have infiltrated your little group have told me that much about your treacherous activities. Trastivo will be most, *most* pleased when I bring him this."

"It is not yours to use, vermin; put it back before you destroy us all!"

Ayila spoke for the first time since Carlos had been killed, and her voice was hoarse and sore from crying. Emore's smile widened, and he began to toss the finger into the air over and over again, catching it as it came down.

"So it is not mine to use, eh? Well, perhaps I ought to return it to the two of you...."

Moving with unearthly speed, he brought his arm downward without warning in a deadly arc, plunging the Finger of Joaquin into the flesh of Geoffrey's hand, and Geoffrey screamed again as a new type of pain, more ragged and invasive than the first, coursed through him as the center of his hand was pinned to the table by the sheer force of Emore's blow, and his bones and nerves were crushed. Emore laughed once more at the bard's pain and picked up his knife.

"If you think I need the ungodly powers of your disgusting rituals or the corpse of a tyrant to get the truth out of the two of you, then I'm afraid you're quite mistaken. And as for you...," he spat in Ayila's direction, "I think we've heard quite enough from you for the moment as well." He uttered the same words he had used against Eligesh and Lucia, and Ayila found herself reduced to a stifling silence as well, despite her desperate efforts to speak. "What's that you said?" Emore asked, taunting her, before returning his attention to the bard stretched out before him. "Now then, Geoffrey, shall we begin with the location where these dirty rebels are located, or do you perhaps need more convincing?"

Fear surged within Geoffrey once more, and the pain radiating from his hand was almost unbearable. His eyes began to fill with tears, and his lips opened of their own accord, on the verge of beginning an incoherent babble to plead for mercy. His mind was a whirl as memories surged in and out of it: of Eldrige, of his first time witnessing the Rite of Lucherium, of Ayila telling him "Courage and Love," of swearing loyalty to Joaquin and drinking of the Cup with Lucia. In his terrified state, he tried to focus on anything but the knife, which was descending so slowly that it was agonizing, yet far too quickly at the same time, toward his bloodstained right hand and remaining four fingers. As he cast his gaze wildly around the room, his eyes fell on Eligesh, who had been restrained once again by the guards but was watching everything that went on through eyes filled with horror, confusion, and one other emotion which Geoffrey could not quite make out. And he marveled that he should be wondering about that, of all things, at this horrible moment. Then Eligesh shifted his focus from Geoffrey to Emore, and the bard suddenly realized what it was. It was the same look he himself had worn after witnessing the killing of Eldrige, and it was the same state he had felt when he saw the violence against the bard Lursio that night in the tavern and the cries of his two little girls.

It was repulsion: repulsion for Emore and his kind and all that he stood for.

And then suddenly a bolt of lightning flashed through Geoffrey's mind, and he realized three things, things which perhaps he should have noticed long ago but had been unable to focus on in the fear and confusion of the moment. The first was that Emore did not know that it was Eligesh whose loyalties Lucia had been trying to sway, at least not yet. The second was that Vincente had not had time to invoke the Rite of Lucherium. The third was that Eligesh had indeed, perhaps only at that very moment, perhaps before, turned in his loyalties. While he may not have yet embraced the Way of Lucherium, he had most certainly rejected the Way of Progress.

And his mind cleared, and Geoffrey knew in an instant what he needed to do.

"Well, Bard?" Emore hissed in his ear. "Are you going to give me the place, or do you need a little more… stimulation? We've got nine more tries and then after that, who knows? I'm known to be very… creative."

Geoffrey gulped and took a deep breath, gathering what little focus he could muster. Then, turning his head, which was the only part of his body Emore had left unchained so that Geoffrey could witness the carnage around him, he looked the Minister straight in the eyes, and in a voice which was so calm he hardly recognized it as his own, he spoke.

> "*By Author Life and Light were formed,*
> *in Guide were Light and Life infused,*
> *that both for glory might be used*
> *by man, and union not abused;*
> *that Story may be well performed.*

and man throughout might be transformed..."

"What's this? Poetry from our bard? Why, it's more sickening than that trash you were spouting down below at the banquet!" Emore's face showed confusion at first, and then anger, as if he thought that Geoffrey were mocking him. Geoffrey ignored his derision and continued, his voice growing stronger.

> *"...Yet now book burns and scroll is torn,*
> *and Guide is cast out from his throne.*
> *No Life is lived, no Light is shone,*
> *but man in darkness bleeds alone;*
> *for Darkness Life from Light has shorn,*
> *and Darkness rules o'ertop the morn..."*

"Enough!" snapped Emore. "Your nonsense won't save you from the pain, you blathering fool!"

The knife slashed downward again, its wicked edge severing skin, then flesh, then bone, then flesh and skin again, and Geoffrey felt the waves of needle-like pain explode for a second time as his finger fell away and the blood began to flow more thickly.

"Well?! I'm losing my patience, bard! Tell me what it is I need to know or next time it'll be two fingers from your left hand!"

Geoffrey swallowed his fear and agony and continued onward.

> *"...But still writes Author in the night,*

> *that Guide in wisdom shall foresee*
> *that Light and Life, though dimmed may be,*
> *yet in their falling, rise shall He*
> *and come victorious from the fight;*
> *that in Him, might rest Life and Light..."*

The knife flashed twice on Geoffrey's left, and the pain was so excruciating that the bard thought there was no way he could endure it and live. Summoning all that was in him and more, and relying on the strength of a Lord who dwelt within him and yet at that moment seemed so far away, his voice rose to a defiant shout as the final verses of the Rite of Lucherium rang out.

> *"...So come now man to fallen Guide,*
> *within whom Life and Light yet hide,*
> *that power new He might provide!"*

And suddenly there was Light, and there was Life.

It began in Geoffrey's hand. An almost unbearably warm feeling which caused him to cry again in pain as fresh blood spurted from the finger of the Lord Joaquin and mingled with his own. But this was no evil pain of icy metal severing flesh and nerve. This was the pain one's limbs feel when, after they have been asleep for a very long time, blood rushes back into them, reviving them with the shock of a thousand dancing sparks.

And then Geoffrey could move. And he could do much more than that.

His body began to shine by the Light and Life of Joaquin within it, and in a sudden burst of energy he rose and shouted in a clear, strong voice, and the air around him hummed to life with the joyous crackling of fire, a fire that expanded outward with incredible speed and force, blasting Emore, his soldiers, and the other Void-wielders off of their feet and hurling them into the walls and out of the windows which lined the meeting chamber.

Moving as if he were made of Light himself, Geoffrey flew over to a stunned Ayila and, yanking the finger of Joaquin from his mangled, bloody hand with his three remaining fingers, he held it to her lips where, unencumbered by the dark restrains of the now senseless Emore, she grabbed hold of it and drank, and drank deeply, her own body beginning to shine with the same tremendous life-force as Geoffrey's. Leaping to her feet, the finger of Joaquin tightly in her grasp, she embraced Geoffrey so tightly he thought she might squeeze the life out of him where Emore had failed. Then, striding to the room's eastern wall and tilting her head upwards, she began to chant in a strange, beautiful tone.

> *"Light illumine what is dark;*
> *pierce through forest, rock and bone.*
> *On hidden evils, shed your spark*
> *that severed, they shall die alone!"*

The smoky night air outside of the Keep of Astraia hissed as if it were a massive, black serpent being riled and uncoiled, and then it burst into a cascade of buzzing, angry tendrils of dark energy which glowed with a pale, haunting green, casting a ghoulish glare across the war-torn countryside as it spread outward, until it took the shape of a massive domed web which encircled the city and formed part of a long chain stretching along the border of Trastaluche in both directions for as far as Geoffrey could see. Ayila stretched her arms upward, repeating the same verses, and Geoffrey looked on in awe as the dome separated itself into seven separate half-spheres which towered above them, enveloping the night sky. A thunderous, triumphant roar arose from the countryside below as the forces of Dantius witnessed the Curtain made visible and surged forward, preparing for the final assault. Geoffrey could hear cries of panic and alarm within the city as well, and he realized that it would not be long before they were swarmed with additional soldiers securing the Keep and preparing for its defense. Then Ayila chanted once more, and in each of the seven spheres, a single tendril began to writhe and convulse, as if it were trying to break free from the others, its color changing to a deep red. As Ayila finished the verse and began it a fourth time, the first of the red strands broke free from its web and began to gather in a massive orb of pulsing energy directly above the Keep, growing brighter and brighter until, having been drawn entirely up into itself, it seemed to explode into a cascade of falling stars.

The first layer of the Curtain had been penetrated, and Geoffrey saw the remaining strands waver and fade in intensity, their integrity beginning to weaken.

Her eyes afire and her body alight with Lucherium, Ayila began her chant again, drawing out yet another foreign tendril and releasing it in a shower of pure, white flame which reigned harmlessly down over the city and the surrounding countryside. And then a third. And then a fourth. And Geoffrey, despite the fear and pain which still besieged his battered body, felt a surge of hope within him. The Curtain was being penetrated. He heard voices below him as the Trastalucherian guard, having sensed the source of the problem, poured into the Keep and began to ascend toward Geoffrey and Ayila, but he knew that by the time they gathered enough force to harm them, it would be too late.

Ayila had just drawn out the fifth weakened tendril of the Curtain and dispelled it when suddenly the room seemed to grow darker and colder, and she faltered slightly. For behind them, Emore stood once again, his senses regained and his eyes dark with murderous rage as he realized what was happening before him.

"No!" he shrieked. He strode toward them, a wave of black energy surging from him as he did so, only to be met with a shield of Lucherium, as Geoffrey summoned his own and expanded it to envelope both himself and Ayila in the nick of time.

The force of the blast nearly knocked Geoffrey off of his feet, and his shield wavered and flickered worryingly. At that moment, a squadron of guards from below burst into the room and charged toward the two Followers. Their attacks bounced off harmlessly, but Geoffrey could feel his control and his strength fading as the Void around him grew stronger, threatening to suck away the Light and Life which protected him.

Behind him, Ayila began her chant again, her feet rising from the floor as her body shone ever brighter. Her whole attention was focused on the mission at hand, and Geoffrey realized that it was his task to protect her for as long as he could. Summoning a second wave of his luminous safeguard, he shouted, *"Light within, your shield begin!"* once again just in time, as Emore gathered his hatred and his strength and unleashed a second, even stronger blast of dark energy against Geoffrey's meager defense.

The world flickered before Geoffrey's eyes as he and Ayila were enveloped in Emore's brutal assault, and the bard felt his strength dwindling and his courage fading as he struggled to keep the darkness and the cold out. His efforts were almost in vain. The flames of Emore's blast came so close that Geoffrey could have reached out and touched him. And then suddenly it was over, and he and Ayila were still alive. And Ayila had dispelled the sixth weakened tendril of the Leaden Curtain and was even now drawing out the seventh. And the forces of Dantius had begun their final assault, moving closer and closer to the city.

And Emore, seeing Geoffrey at the point of defeat, and he and Ayila all but exposed, grinned fiendishly and moved in for the kill, focusing his energy on the source of his anger: that pesky bard from Spiraluche who had already foiled him once tonight and whose feeble attempts at harnessing Lucherium threatened to do so again. He would not survive another attack, he knew. His shield was not strong enough.

And Geoffrey, faint from loss of blood, recognized the same thing. He had not been enough. There was no way he could protect himself and Ayila long enough for the mission to be completed.

And in weakness and fear, Geoffrey accepted defeat. And out of courage and love for a Lord in whose presence he was soon to stand, and by the power of that same Lord whose lifeblood coursed throughout the bard's broken frame, Geoffrey shouted as Emore and his forces released their final and most powerful attack. He drew his shield in tightly as he poured the last of his strength into it, shrinking it smaller and smaller until at last it stood, intact and impenetrable one last time, around the figure of Ayila, who at that moment spoke her final verse, drawing out the last remnants of the tendril belonging to Eligesh, the non-loyal weaver of the seventh layer of the Leaden Curtain.

And as the black flames of the Void surrounded Geoffrey; and as above him a luminous red orb exploded into glorious light and the Curtain of Trastaluche wavered and faded; and as the forces of Dantius surged forward, their war machines springing into action; and as the walls of the city crumbled and its gates were broken open; and as Ayila, the mission completed, turned to face her attackers with a power and a ferocity the likes of which they had never seen nor would ever see again, the world of Geoffrey of Hazcaluche went black.

Chapter XVII

The Awakening

It was light, and not the sort of light one finds in the flickering tongues of a fire that keeps the darkness and cold away, or even the brighter sort of light that courses over hills and into deep, shaded glens as the first rays of the dawn peek over the horizon. It was not even the fiercer type of light that leaps and dances in red-hot sparks from the blacksmith's forge. Rather, this was a different sort of light altogether. It was the kind of light that fills you with warmth and peace and joy, which penetrates your very being, bringing with it the promise of a new and glorious morning. It was a light that seems to enkindle all it touches with the spark of life itself.

It was into this sort of light that Geoffrey awoke.

He was lying in a bed covered with quilts so downy that they seemed to be made of lamb's wool, in a room smelling of spring and flowers and filled with a soft, warm sunlight that spilled in from the three windows adorning one of its walls. It was one of the many bedrooms that lined the middle floors of the Keep of Astraia. Opposite the windows was an open door, and out of it floated snatches of pleasant conversation. Somewhere, tossed aloft by the breeze of the morning, the elusive notes of a song, simple and sweet, reached the bard's ears, and he found himself humming along contentedly, his fingers plucking the strings of an imaginary mandolin.

"One, two, three; one, one, two; three, one, two; two, fou-…"

Yet there was no four, and Geoffrey looked down, confused.

And then he saw his hands, still swathed in bandages, the damage painfully apparent.

Suddenly, the memories surged back like a flood, and he saw the bodies of Vincente and Carlos, the knife of Emore dripping with blood, the faces of Eligesh and Lucia, the power of Ayila as she unwove the Leaden Curtain, and finally the cold, black flames of the death-blow that had enveloped his defenseless body, causing all to fade to darkness and nothing.

And yet, all was not darkness and nothing, but Life and Light. For Geoffrey lived. How, he was not sure, but the fact remained that here he was, in spite of it all.

He struggled to sit up, and a searing pain shot through his chest and up into his neck. Gasping in shock, he reached up gingerly, grimacing as his hands and wrists shrieked in protest, and touched the origin of the pain with his remaining fingers.

The skin under his hands felt rough and burned, as if it were fashioned from coal, and Geoffrey traced the scar downwards and outwards as it coiled around his neck and onto his torso. Pulling away the light linen shirt he wore, he examined himself and saw that he was adorned with the same, lightning-shaped mark which Xavier bore. It was the mark of the death-blow of the wielders of the Void. Yet for him, it was the mark of one who had overcome death when by all accounts he should not have.

"Ah, so our guest has been roused!"

The words, quiet and gentle like those of an angel, came from the open doorway, and Geoffrey lifted his gaze to see Lucia, clad in a simple white dress, her eyes sparkling with joy and relief and a perfect smile spreading across her face. She danced over to Geoffrey and helped him gently into a sitting position, pouring him a glass of cool, sweet water to drink, and then suddenly embracing him so fiercely that the bard grunted in pain again, causing Lucia to release him just as quickly.

> "I'm so sorry! I didn't mean to hurt you. It's just, we're so glad to see that you've awakened. We weren't even sure you were alive when we first brought you here, and even then Dantius' best healer said he didn't know if you were going to make it. But here you are and I'm so, so happy, Geoffrey! You and Ayila did it! The Curtain has been torn, and our troops have occupied Astraia!"
>
> "But not without a bit of help from Lucia here."

Ayila had entered the room as well, greeting Geoffrey as she did and taking his wounded hands gently in hers for a long moment. And Geoffrey thought that he had never seen in someone's eyes such a mixture of happiness and loneliness.

> "Yes, what... what happened, could someone please tell me? How did I survive? And are Carlos and Vincente... are they really...?"

Ayila's eyes filled with tears, and Geoffrey needed no answer to his second question. The memories overwhelmed him once more, and for the first time since he had departed on the mission, Geoffrey began to weep bitterly. He wept for Carlos and Vincente. He wept as he remembered the screams of Ayila when her beloved was taken from her. He wept as he imagined Vincente's parents receiving the news of their son's death, news which would fill them with pain and pride, with grief and joy for the rest of their lives, the triumph of the hour forever intertwined with the sacrifice of their child. He wept for his own mangled hands, for the evils Julius and Emore had caused, and for the horrors that he, Ayila, and everyone else had gone through. He wept, and Ayila and Lucia wept along with him, for a long, long time. Yet to his surprise it was Ayila who wiped her tears first and smiled bravely at him.

"But now is no time for you to be weeping," she said, "not after awakening from such darkness and pain. And to answer your first question, I am quite certain that you would not be here, and perhaps nor I, if it were not for Lucia. She is the reason that you are alive, Geoffrey. You see, when you invoked the Rite, one of the guards around her was knocked into her and pinned her to the floor, stunning her. She awoke not long after Emore did and managed to harness a Conexio just in time to summon her own shield which she used to protect you, just as you did for me. And for that last act, I owe you my life, and my deepest gratitude," Ayila added, taking Geoffrey's hands in hers once more.

"And mine to you, Lucia," Geoffrey added, smiling at her.

Lucia returned the smile, her cheeks reddening at the praise. "It was nothing, really, at least compared to what the two of you did. And anyway, Emore wasn't paying any attention to me, so I had no need of it for my own protection."

"Still, it was an act that can never be repaid, and I, for one, think it was quite a lot more than nothing," laughed Geoffrey. "I happen to quite like living."

The others laughed with him, and as they did so there was a soft knock at the door, and Eligesh poked his head in, accompanied by a tall, muscular man with skin as dark as Ayila's, a head full of long, curly hair, and a well-trimmed beard. Eligesh had changed from the extravagant clothing he had worn last time Geoffrey had seen him and was dressed now in a plain, dark blue tunic and trousers with a silver belt. The man behind him bore the full regalia of a battlefare commander, and emblazoned in gold on his silver breastplate Geoffrey saw a flaming sun above a flowering tree: the symbols of Light and Life and the crest of the armies of the Lord Joaquin.

"I heard voices; is it alright if we enter?" Eligesh asked, and Lucia flew over to her husband and, practically dragging him, led him to the bed where Geoffrey sat, while the other man followed close behind.

"Eligesh, he's awake, isn't it splendid? Geoffrey, this is my husband Eligesh, who you never got to officially meet. It's ok, he's seen the truth of things and is on our side now."

"Indeed I am," spoke Eligesh, "and I owe you many thanks for that, good sir. Might I introduce someone who has been wanting to meet you?" He turned to the warrior behind him and said, "Geoffrey, this is Dantius, commander of the forces of the Followers of Joaquin and now temporary regent of Astraia."

"And forever in the debt of you and the Lady Ayila for ensuring our advances were not in vain," Dantius added, extending his palms to Geoffrey and bowing deeply at the same time. "It is truly an honor to meet you, Geoffrey of Hazcaluche."

"And you as well," responded Geoffrey, returning the signs of greeting as best as he could. "Perhaps, now that you are all here, you could help shed some light on all that has happened since that night, and how I ended up where I am now."

"Gladly," answered Dantius in a voice which was gruff and weathered from his years as a soldier. "It has been three days since the forces of Trastivo were routed, and the city of Astraia fell into our hands. Since then, much work has been done in tending the wounded, such as yourself, and in burying and mourning for the dead. The mountains around the city were secured as well, and the main army is preparing to continue its advance within a week's time toward the city of Covern. The Northern Regions, as you know, have never looked kindly upon Trastivo and the Committees, and the armies of Trastaluche often make raids into their lands, killing and burning as they go. If the threat on their borders is removed, they might very well be convinced to join us in the war against Trastivo. However, as to what happened in the central chamber of Astraia three nights ago, you'll have to ask these other three young people. In fact, we have all been wanting to hear what happened from your view as well."

And so each took turns telling their part of the story. Lucia and Eligesh told of slipping away from the banquet, of Lucia's news of her recently discovered pregnancy, and of their deep conversation concerning the battle which raged outside the city walls and all the pain and carnage it was causing, a conversation that was quite suddenly interrupted when a group of Trastalucherian guards burst in and forced both of them to come along without telling them what was going on. Geoffrey told of his time in the courtyard below, of seeing Emore and knowing something dreadful was about to occur, of being unable to find Julius, of making the decision to enter the Keep, and of what he beheld when he burst into the upper chamber. Ayila told of their own infiltration of the Keep, of the attack of the guards, of the treachery of Julius, and of the felling of Vincente and the wounding of Carlos before Emore entered the room.

And then all four joined in to inform Dantius of the final hours of the mission, filling in gaps and blanks where the story was too clouded or too painful for one or the other to continue. They told of the bravery of Carlos and the horror of his death. The described the turning of Eligesh, who had only in the past few days, Geoffrey learned, after much time in conversation with Lucia and with Dantius, decided to swear allegiance to the Lord Joaquin and had, in fact, done so earlier that very morning, partaking in the Rite of Lucherium along with Lucia, Ayila, Dantius, and thousands of joyous, weary soldiers, many of whom had been awaiting this moment for decades. They recalled Geoffrey's resistance and his own invocation of the same Rite, and Ayila's success in unraveling the seven layers of the Leaden Curtain, all the while shielded by Geoffrey from the rage of Emore and his servants. Finally Lucia recounted once again the tale of her awakening and of her own harnessing of Lucherium to shield the battered and defeated Geoffrey as the final thread in the Curtain was undone.

"And then, Geoffrey, you should have seen her." Lucia spoke almost reverently, her eyes filled with awe as she gazed on Ayila. "As soon as the Curtain was ripped through, she turned to face Emore and his band, and let me tell you, she was so brilliant that she made his attacks look even punier than my own use of Lucherium. And then, in seconds, it was all over, and I was searching desperately for Eligesh, and I found him- he had been knocked out as well during all the fighting- and the Keep was under attack from the soldiers of Dantius and the room was ablaze from the battle between Emore and Ayila. Ayila scooped you up, even though we didn't know if you were alive or not, and we all ran out as fast as we could and took refuge in one of the lower rooms. The walls had been breached, and everyone was fleeing this way and that, and the Trastalucherian forces were in disarray, and then it was all over, and Dantius himself arrived, looking for you and Ayila. He had you taken straight to a healer. And the rest you know already."

Geoffrey closed his eyes as Lucia finished, the memories of three nights ago washing over him and threatening to sweep him away yet again, and it seemed to him that they alone were enough to fill up an entire lifetime. He heard music and laughter once again from outside the Keep, and rousing himself back to the present, he looked up at Eligesh.

"And the people of the city, what of them? How did they respond to it all?"

"With about as much of a mix as you would expect, I think," answered Eligesh. "Some, of course, especially the Committee members and the dignitaries, fled along with the remnants of the armies. Others accepted their defeat, although begrudgingly enough. But a great number of them, especially now that the city is almost put back into order, have found, oftentimes in spite of themselves, that life under Trastivo was much darker and much harder than they ever realized. Oh, rebuilding a city is no easy task, to be sure, but with the Curtain torn and at least partially lifted, it's as if a thick smoke were blown away that you didn't even know was there. You had been breathing it in and coughing and blindly struggling through it without realizing it, and suddenly it's gone, and the sun is shining and the air is clear, and people are starting to realize, even without knowing why, that life is much, much better this way. A few, in fact, have already asked about the Way of Lucherium. It helps, of course, that none of their loved ones have been eaten or mutilated by the forces of Dantius, despite what the Committees said would happen."

"Yes, I imagine that if we did something like that, they wouldn't appreciate it a whole lot," added Dantius dryly, "but speaking of eating, I would expect that our bard here might appreciate some provisions now that he has awoken."

With that, food and drink were called for and brought up for everyone, with a double portion allotted to Geoffrey, "so that he might start catching up from the three days that he missed," teased Ayila, while helping the injured bard with his plate, a lovely lunch of roast chicken, potatoes, and spring melon. More conversation followed, and Geoffrey learned that Xavier had sent word only yesterday on the state of affairs throughout the rest of Trastaluche in response to a letter Dantius and

Ayila had written to him regarding the fall of Astraia and all that had occurred there. Ayila produced a folded piece of parchment from her trouser pocket and read it aloud for Geoffrey's benefit.

My dear friends Geoffrey, Ayila, Lucia, Dantius, and now, I have been informed, Eligesh as well: Greetings to each one of you, and may Light and Life shine upon and throughout you. I was greatly saddened to hear of the deaths of Carlos and Vincente, but I rejoice that they were not in vain; as you and I both learned a few nights ago, our missions in each of the seven central cities of Trastaluche were successful, although not without cost. And even as I grieve that they have departed from us, I am comforted by the thought that they now enjoy a friendship with the Lord of Light and Life Himself of such depth and beauty that human words cannot describe it. Many fine men and women were lost, but the power of Trastivo and the Committees has been severely weakened, and the news of Dantius' advance brings us great hope.

I will dwell no longer on the pain and evil of the past, which I'm sure needs no help in to be remembered, and will speak only of plans for the future, and of my wish to see each of you as soon as possible. However, for the moment I am afraid that wish shall have to go unfulfilled. Trastivo is, understandably, quite furious at this sudden and most humiliating defeat within the strongholds of his own nation, and he has sent the Committees of Social Order and Progress out to hunt down those responsible with a vengeance. In every city except your own, we are facing pursuit, persecution, and death, but fear not, for we are quite confident that our sanctuaries shall not be discovered. Nonetheless, it would be suicide for you to try to return to Spiraluche now, with your names known and reviled by Trastivo himself. Therefore, I ask that Geoffrey and Ayila remain with the armies of Dantius, both to assist them in further campaigns and to act as guardians of the Finger of the Lord Joaquin and as those authorized to invoke the Rite of Lucherium and to distribute the Cup to the Followers. Eligesh and Lucia, I have been told, wish to stay in Astraia for the moment as its temporary guardians, a desire which I wholeheartedly support, for they are both truly loved by the people and will do wonders transforming the city into a place far more glorious than before. Dantius, of course, will leave the two of you with sufficient men and weaponry in case Trastivo should try to retake the city. However, with his forces in disarray, I doubt that will be the case, at least for the moment.

In the meantime, know of our love for all of you, and of our well-wishes for success in following the Way of Lucherium wherever it might take you. I myself shall try to meet you outside of Covern in the coming weeks, both to offer any assistance I can and to discuss the plans for the conquest of the interior of Trastaluche with you. You shall have help from the Company of Followers within the city, of course, but be wary of them until you have ascertained whether they, like Julius, have been turned away from us in their loyalties. However, I suspect you shall find that most of them have remained true to us and our cause.

I look forward to many meetings in the future, and I offer you again my gratitude for the Life and Light you have given in service and in love of the Lord Joaquin.

Very Wholly Yours,
Xavier of Hazcaluche

The next several days were happy ones for Geoffrey, and they were spent in a wonderful combination of resting, of healing, of deep conversation with old friends and new acquaintances, of long walks through Astraia and the countryside surrounding it, and of preparation for the main army's departure within the coming week. There were banquets of celebration and honor for Geoffrey, Ayila, Lucia, and many others whose bravery and heart had been instrumental in the victory of the forces of Hazcaluche. There were dances, songs, and all kinds of merriment, which often lasted far into the night, ending with a small group of friends seated around a warm fire sipping cider and speaking of memories old and new. Each morning Geoffrey and Ayila would invoke the Rite of Lucherium, standing on the raised dais that was located at the top of the steps leading to the main entrance of the Keep, and each morning Geoffrey would greet his fallen yet glorious Lord face to face and drink His blood in the Cup of Life and Light, immersing himself in that liquid, strange and sweet, in which could be found the source of the joyful rest that welled up within him, despite all he had lost. The courtyard below would be filled each day not only with soldiers and their families, but also with a rapidly growing number of the city's inhabitants who, struck by the beauty and the fullness of the lives of their conquerors, had embarked on a journey of discovery that had ended with their decisions to swear loyalty to Joaquin and to join his Followers in the Way of Lucherium.

But not every moment was a happy one. Especially in the times of quiet, Geoffrey would find himself immobile in the upper chamber of the Keep once again, the corpses of Vincente and Carlos bleeding next to him, and the knife of Emore creeping closer and closer as it descended toward his fingers. It was in one such moment of grief that he found himself on a bright, crisp morning one week after the fall of the city. He had just finished breakfast with Dantius, Eligesh, Lucia, and Ayila. Dantius and Eligesh had bidden them farewell to go see to the rebuilding of the city walls. Lucia had gone along to be close to her husband, and Ayila and Geoffrey were left alone in a room not at all unlike the one in which Geoffrey had awakened a few days before, staring out the window at the breathtaking vista which surrounded the city.

"It's funny, you know," Ayila said softly after a long period of silence. "One moment I think of Carlos and all that he was to me, and I can't bear to go on without him here by my side. And then I think about what has been accomplished, and I look outside, and I realize that I have gone on, and that going on means going towards him, towards a forevermore of love and joy with him and with the Lord Joaquin…. Yet at the same time, while I'm still on this earth, a part of me shall always be stuck, pinned to that dreadful floor upstairs, unable to move…."

She trailed off, her voice breaking and a single tear sliding down her face, and it was quiet again.

"I think I understand what you mean," said Geoffrey slowly, "at least a little bit. And it's strange, because it's as if life is so much fuller, so much more whole now, and yet with friends departed and all that has happened, you feel like you're so much less, as if a part of you is gone forever."

He gazed at his mangled hands, each one with two fingers missing, and he felt the twisted black scar which ran across his neck and chest, wincing at the memory of the pain which had torn through him as the knife of Emore had wrought its nefarious work. Then he remembered the power of Lucherium, the Life and Light of Joaquin Himself, surging through him, and the clearness of mind and fullness of heart which he had possessed in a moment when all else seemed to be death and darkness. And he felt so full, so peaceful inside, and yet at the same time fragmented and lost.

Then, as he looked back on everything which had taken place since that night outside of the house of the Family Xavier, he realized... wasn't that how it had always been?

"Perhaps," he found himself saying, "perhaps it was always that way, but it just never felt quite so real. I mean, that's the point of the Way of Lucherium, isn't it? That you alone are never enough, but in living by the Light and Life of Joaquin, you become more of yourself than you ever thought you could be. It's always been a heart-wrenching sort of happiness, a broken sort of wholeness, I guess. It's just especially so now, when you've lived it yourself and seen it firsthand; when you've seen your friends follow the Way of Lucherium so fully that their deaths end up being a lot like that of Joaquin. And you're happy... you're so, *so* happy, not just for the good that has been done here and throughout Hazcaluche, but even for Carlos and Vincente, who *really* lived the Way, even to the point of dying for it, and who have moved past this life to the even greater reality of Life and Light with Joaquin beyond death. And perhaps that's how moments like this are meant to feel. As awful as it is, it's noble and splendid and *true* at the same time, and I don't think for a moment that I'd want to feel anything else."

They stood in silence for a long while again, watching the sun cast its rays on the lush, green valleys, the flower-filled meadows, and the brilliant, snow-topped peaks high above them, until at last Ayila turned to him and smiled that warm, proud smile which Geoffrey had first seen in the training room beneath the streets of Spiraluche on a night which now seemed to be ages ago.

"Geoffrey of Hazcaluche;" she said, "such words of wisdom suit you, my friend."

And she embraced him for a long, long time before bidding him a brief farewell; then, she left to go attend to her own preparations for their departure with the forces of Dantius the next morning.

And Geoffrey the bard stood alone, gazing out over the vast, raw beauty which surrounded the city of Astraia. The music which he had heard the day he had awakened caught his ear once again, and looking down, he located its source in a small clearing just outside the city walls. A young, Hazcalucherian soldier with fair hair and deep, blue eyes had been posted on watch there, and to pass the time he had pulled out a small, stringed instrument from his pack and begun to sing a ballad whose tune and lyrics were unfamiliar to Geoffrey. Around him a group of children, dressed in the colors of spring, had gathered to listen and to sing along, and Geoffrey saw one small girl in a bright yellow dress, a crown of daises in her hair, begin to dance with the joy and freedom which only little children can manage to express, as the words of the young man carried her away to a place of comfort, beauty, and adventure.

In ages black and full of death,
in land besieged by endless night
arose four heroes filled with light,
and life was given by their breath.

Vincente, Carlos, two were named,
both warriors strong and ever true,
no evil could their souls subdue;
thus fighting, both their lives were claimed.

And darkness rose, its might unchained,
against the heroes that remained;
yet Life through Geoffrey was sustained
and Light through Ayila triumph gained.

So withers darkness; night is torn
by rays of glorious dawning morn.

Geoffrey closed his eyes as he nodded in time with the music, and
he thought that in a different time and a different place, this young soldier might have made a pretty talented bard. He smiled, reflecting on
how very odd it was that his experiences from only a week before had
already become the stuff of tales to be sung around the fire and told and
retold throughout the seasons. And he thought of how little the song of
the young man really told, and about the seemingly infinite seas of pain
and loss, of peace and fulfillment, which could never be expressed no
matter how many ballads were composed. And yet... there was a fullness to the simple piece as well, and although its verses could never
convey all that Geoffrey had seen and heard and lived within only this
past week, they were in some way fitting and more than fitting, as if
they, like Geoffrey himself and all that was part of the Way of

Lucherium, were both broken and whole at the same time; both positively insufficient in what they were, and yet conveying so much more through what they did.

And Geoffrey of Hazcaluche opened his eyes once again to the beauty and the brilliance of the morning and, wiping away his own tears, turned from the window and began his preparations for the journey that lay ahead.

The End

www.ingramcontent.com/pod-product-compliance
Lightning Source LLC
Chambersburg PA
CBHW012204030726
47494CB00022B/2257